You Are Enough

THE MORE THAN ENOUGH SERIES
Book 3

DONNA R. MADDEN

Also By Donna R. Madden

The *More Than Enough Series*

More Than Enough

Your Love is Enough

You Are Enough

Orlinda Valley Series

No One But You

No Love Like Yours

No Place Like Home

No Heart But Yours

Book Club Novellas

Sand, Sea, and Shenanigans

This book is dedicated to my mom.

I am glad I finally got you to read after all these years,

but please don't read this one around me.

Love ya, Mom.

{{Blushing face}}

You
Are
Enough

Chapter 1

If someone would have told him he'd be sitting at a wedding and pining for a relationship, while he watched so many couples spin dreamily arm in arm with their significant other on the dance floor, he would have scoffed and told them they needed to get their fucking head examined.

Adler Warfield was a typical handsome, charismatic, egotistical rich playboy, and the heir to the biggest meat company in the United States, Warfield Meats. He had never had a problem finding a girl to drape from his arm, or to warm his bed. Ever since he was sixteen and finally talked the beautiful captain of his college prep academy's volleyball team to accompany him to his formal and ended up "getting some" for the first time in the back seat of his jeep, girls had been easy, and sex had been prolific.

Last night was no different. He and Desiree, the woman he had been sort-of seeing, had a typical night of groundbreaking sex. That woman was creative, that's for sure. Now here he was, at the wedding of someone he hardly knew with Desiree. Unfortunately, she was off working, helping the caterer, and cutting the cake, and he was left sitting alone, like so many girls he had left in his wake.

Okay, so he sort of knew the bride. He'd met her at the end of last summer when he and his cousin Tristan were at a convention in Gatlinburg and spent the last weekend hiking and enjoying the area. Tristan had ended up with Stacey, his now girlfriend, and Adler met Elizabeth, today's bride, who was at the time on the outs with her fiancé, today's groom. Elizabeth was one of the few women who didn't fall for Adler's charms. There was a first time for everything.

But now, as he watched Elizabeth and Brady dance in each other's arms with their son cuddled between them, he couldn't deny she was happy. Any idiot could see that. Both her boys adored her, the tiny one with brown curls and his dad. Good for her.

It was a good thing they didn't start a relationship. Adler didn't do kids. Maybe one day, if they're his own, but someone else's baggage? Yeah. Not his thing.

Adler's gaze roamed the tent. It was a perfect May night for an outdoor wedding. The temperature was mild, with a little nip in the air, but ideal for those dressed in formal wear. His gaze stopped on Tristan and Stacey. They were holding each other tight and dancing to the slow song that played over the speakers. Adler's mom might get her lifelong dream of becoming a grandma after all.

Tristan and Stacey were perfect together. He was head over heels in love with her, and Adler was sure she felt the same way. Tristan deserved to be loved and happy. He'd had a hard enough life. His father died when Adler and Tristan were just babies. Tristan and his mom moved onto the grounds of Adler's house. Their moms were sisters, so Tristan and Adler, who were only one month apart in age, ended up growing up more like brothers than cousins. Then

Tristan's mother came down with cancer and passed away, forcing him to move into the main house when he was in sixth grade, and was raised like a son by Adler's parents, Don and Elisha.

Adler let out a sigh and emptied his beer. *I can either sit here like a creeper, watching everyone dance, wishing I had what they had—which is just fucked up—or go pull Des away from the cake table long enough to dance and get my mind back on the here and now. Being with a sexy, hot woman.*

Adler pushed himself up and sauntered to the other side of the tent. He admired Desiree the closer and closer he got. She was hot and trouble, two things that always got his attention.

She'd pinned her auburn hair on top of her head, and it looked elegant along with her spaghetti strap formfitting maroon dress. It clung perfectly to all her curves and accented her breasts—his favorite.

"Hey. I was studying you as I crossed the room. You look hot tonight," Adler said as he approached.

"You were studying me? What am I, a textbook?" She placed a slice of cake on a plate.

"Maybe. Sometimes you're as hard to crack." He smiled his sexy crooked smile that met his eyes.

Desiree shook her head. "We'll get some studying done later."

"Sounds like a plan." He picked up a plate with cake on it.

Desiree looked up. "So, you're finally ready to try my cake? I figured you'd be one of the first in line."

"I've heard cake is an excellent substitute for sex, and with what you're doing to me in that dress, I need something to take the edge off."

Desiree laughed and stared at him, her eyes hot and focused.

"Excuse me." The young woman Adler had noticed helping Desiree earlier was at the table with a large empty tray. He stepped out of the way as she filled it with more cake slices.

Her downplayed attractiveness caught his eye. It wasn't the first time he'd seen her. He'd seen her around, knew she worked at the boutique in town and sometimes helped Desiree, but this time, her being there, this close to him, sent a strange sensation into the pit of his stomach.

Up close, Adler could tell she wasn't drop-dead gorgeous like Desiree, but she was cute and very attractive. Her brown hair reflected the light and fell in soft waves over her shoulders. She wore very little makeup and had a spattering of freckles across her nose. They were adorable and made her even more attractive. His gaze lingered there.

When she looked up, their gazes locked, and he noticed her eyes were a unique hazel color that drew him in. A smile ticked up at the edges of his lips. Yeah, she was hot, but in a different way than Desiree. She seemed almost innocent.

She gave him a small smile as she picked up the now full tray and continued her job.

Adler admired her from behind as she walked away. She wore a red dress that fell just below her knees. The sleeves were ruffled and short, barely covering her shoulders, and the bodice was cut in a scooped neckline which showed some tantalizing, yet tasteful, cleavage.

He studied her as he ate his cake. See, he did a lot of studying. Her hips swayed enticingly as she walked. A tighter dress, fitting snugly around those hidden curves, would be interesting. *I bet she's got some curvy hips and a nice ass. Too bad she's hiding it.*

"Why are you zoning out?" Desiree followed Adler's eyes and raised her brow.

He tore his thoughts from across the room and turned his attention back to his date. He shoved the last bite of cake in his mouth. "This is delicious. Do you think there'll be any left?"

Using the cake knife, Desiree slid another piece onto his plate. "Shouldn't be much. It doesn't matter. You won't be needing cake."

He raised his brows.

Desiree laughed and bumped him playfully. "Anyway, Leila's doing a great job of making sure everyone eats. Usually there's so much cake left because no one takes it."

"Leila?" Adler asked as he scooped up a bit of icing from the cake onto his finger and offered it to Desiree, who licked it from his skin. That small movement sent blood straight to his cock and put it at attention.

He placed the finger she'd licked into his own mouth and winked.

"You're too much." She shook her head. "Leila, the girl I've introduced you to at the bakery. The one you were just ogling as she delivered cake across the room."

What? Adler turned all his attention to Desiree. "What are you talking about? I wasn't ogling anyone. I don't ogle. If I want to watch, I watch. I stare. I've even been known, as presented before, to study. But ogle?" He shook his head, wrapping her in his arms. "Now you, I stare at and watch. I study. I've been studying you all night as you've been working. Okay, I might have ogled you a little, trying to picture you skinny dipping in my pool later. I like what I see. I like what I'm imagining, and now I'm wondering if there is anything creative we can do with this extra icing. It's good. I like it."

"I'm glad. It's my secret recipe."

"Hmm, I like secrets. And since it's that amazing, it really would be a shame to waste it."

"I think we can figure out something to do with it."

Damn. This was one of the many things that made Desiree so intriguing to him. She had a dirty mind that rivaled his own and was up for anything.

"Save it, then." He winked. "Now, do you think you can pull yourself away to dance with me? We haven't danced all night."

"I know. I'm almost done here." Just then, Leila came back with an empty tray. "Here, Leila, I'll take that from you. I need to clean up anyway. Could you do me a huge favor and occupy my date? He needs to dance."

Leila looked like she had seen a ghost. Her eyes were wide.

He searched her face as she talked with Desiree. She looked endearing and sweet. Innocent even. He usually liked them tattooed, loud-mouthed, and wild—like Desiree. But endearing and sweet, something about those qualities suddenly grabbed his attention.

Change may not be a bad thing.

"Come on." He offered Leila his arm. "Let's dance and let Des finish cleaning up."

"You want to dance with me?" Leila's gaze traveled down his body, then back up without a bit of interest.

Okay, this might be a challenge. Her face sure didn't light up like a woman's usually did when admiring his body. "Yeah, why wouldn't I?" Adler placed her hand on the crook of his arm.

Again, Leila eyed him, then shrugged. Adler led her to the dance floor.

A new slow song started when they got onto the floor. Adler held her at a safe distance to help her feel more comfortable. "So, Leila,

I know we've sort of met before, but never officially. Nice to meet you."

Leila smiled. "You too. I've always thought Adler was a unique name."

"It is. My parents are unique people. They knew what kind of son they were going to have and named me accordingly."

"What kind of son is that?" Her voice was short and static.

Her body stiffened under his touch.

He backed up and scrutinized her features. Her hair blew slightly in the night breeze as they danced in and out of the crowd. He had an overwhelming desire to touch it and see if it was really as soft as it looked. Her eyes, an enticing hazel, glimmered under the lights and held him in their grip. His pulse picked up its tempo, and his suit jacket became constricting. Suddenly it was as if there were only the two of them on the dance floor. He tightened his hand around her waist, and her back straightened under his grip. Time to lay on the Adler charm and get her to relax.

"Well," he cleared his voice and regained his composure, "Adler means eagle, and it just so happens I'm laser focused and can see what I want from miles away. When I go for what I want, like the eagle, I hardly miss." He shot her what he considered his "melt their panties off" smile. It usually had girls falling at his feet, but all he got from Leila was more space between them and a raised brow. His mouth became dry. A drink would be great right now.

"Here's what I know about you," she started. "I know you're from a rich family. You enjoy women—lots of women—and you think very highly of yourself."

A smile ticked at the edge of his mouth. Maybe she was a little interested. "You've been asking questions about me?"

A soft laugh came from her chest, and her face lit up, causing her expression to relax. She was even more beautiful when she laughed and let herself go a little.

"Don't put your ego into overdrive, Casanova. I haven't asked any questions about you. Desiree talks, and so do some of my friends. You are quite the conversation piece. The girls you dated before Desiree were a bit. . .how can I describe them. . .brainless? Fake? Easy?"

Damn, that made him sound shallow. He tried to swallow, but his mouth was dry. He really needed that drink. "Hey, be nice. They all had their own special qualities and talents, but did Desiree say we were dating?"

Leila's brows raised, and she put a little more space between them. "No, I just figured with as much time as you two were spending together, it had to be called something."

"So, is that maybe a bit of jealousy I'm detecting from you?" Adler wiggled his brows. Maybe she did think of him, even a little.

Again, she laughed, but this time her head tipped back, exposing her neck. His heart stopped. Her skin was smooth ivory, and he longed to caress her neck with his lips. To feel the vibration from her throat against his lips as she moaned his name. *Adler, what the hell is going on with you?*

Her smile lit up her face, and her gaze met his. "Not a chance, Adler."

His dark eyes held hers, and he shook his head slightly to clear the thoughts that were taking over. Thoughts of his lips on her skin and the erotic sounds he could imagine coming from her throat. He pulled her closer and tightened his grip, adding in some fancy two-step footwork as he led her around the dance floor.

His mother had forced Tristan and him to take a ballroom dance class in high school. She said it would help them with the company dinner parties they had to attend. At the time, he'd hated it. As an adult, it helped to impress women.

Well, usually. Again, not so much today.

But he enjoyed dancing with Leila. They fit together well. She was the perfect height. He'd guess five-foot-seven, which fit his six-foot frame perfectly. He slid his hand down over the arch in her lower back as he continued his trek around the dance floor.

A smile lit up her face. He winked, and his hand slipped lower on her waist. He could feel a soft panty line under the light fabric of her dress. He slowed to a more comfortable speed and gave her a chance to catch her breath. "Why don't you tell me something about yourself, Leila? What brings you here to the wedding?"

Leila tilted her head, holding his gaze as she reached around and raised his hand up a bit and stepped back to put more space between them. "I work with Elizabeth at Main Street Boutique in town. She's my boss." Her eyes traveled around the tent.

Adler smirked. Again, his advances were being ignored, and now he got the feeling that he annoyed her. "Got somewhere to go?" He followed her gaze.

She stopped dancing. "Honestly, yes. I need to get home, so I figured I'd go tell Elizabeth and Brady goodbye. I'll be working for her while they go on their honeymoon." She pulled out of his arms. "Thanks for the dance and the conversation. It was surprising. I'll talk to you later."

She gave him a small smile and walked away, leaving Adler alone on the dance floor. That was a first. He watched her retreating form and knew he needed to see her again.

"All single women need to meet on the dance floor immediately. All single women." The DJ's voice thundered through the speakers. "Single guys don't go far. You're next."

Adler found himself surrounded by Tristan and his friends, Chad and Jacob. Tristan handed him a beer. Thank God. He was spitting feathers.

"Thanks, man." He raised the beer to his lips and downed half the cold liquid immediately. God, that tasted good. He was thirstier than he'd thought. "Where's the girls?" He wasn't used to seeing Tristan alone. Stacey was usually glued to his side. What had happened to them being single guys enjoying all the girls? Oh well. He'll need to get in touch with some of their friends from college.

Tristan pointed with his beer. "Out there. It always amazes me how excited women are about catching the bouquet."

Jacob and Chad started talking with Tristan, but Adler wasn't listening. His attention was on the dance floor. He spotted Leila between Jessica, Stacey, and Stacey's best friend, Kristen, and they were surrounded by women of all ages. Even in a crowd, Leila stood out to him like she was the only woman at the wedding. He couldn't tear his gaze from her.

As quickly as the women gathered, the music started. Elizabeth entered the floor and turned her back on them. Then she tossed the bouquet over her head, and it was like she threw gold. The women jumped toward it, hands flailing in the air. Some of them fell to the ground as they tripped over each other. Limbs sprawled everywhere, screams were heard over the roar of the music, but then Jessica whooped and hollered congratulations.

The mob of women stepped away from a wildly blushing Leila, who was left in the center of the floor holding the white and pink bouquet of roses. The blush put some extra color on her already pretty features, and Adler's heart missed a beat.

"What?" he asked as the guys were being pulled onto the floor. He found himself in the center, joined by Tristan, Jacob, Chad, and other men. None of them were as excited as the women, as they stood there with their hands in their pockets or clasping their beer with both hands, and there was a fight—which no one wanted to win—over who would stand in the front.

Before he knew what happened, Adler was pushed to the front of the mob just as Brady let the garter fly, and it landed right in his hands. There was no fight, no screaming, no one falling on the floor. Just a bunch of men acting like getting touched by the garter would give them cooties—if they still believed in those childhood creatures.

"Well, Adler, have fun." Tristan gave him a hard pat on the arm as Adler was drug over to Leila by the DJ. *What the hell is going on?* It was like he were in a dream. First, he was alone on the dance floor, now he was with Leila again, but everyone's eyes were on them. He tried to catch her gaze, but she was looking anywhere but at him.

"Okay, everyone," announced the DJ, "It's time for the bachelor to put the garter on the bachelorette." He leaned in close to Adler as if he was going to tell him a secret but whispered into his microphone. "Okay. Now, you're a good-looking guy. She's a pretty lady. We want a show. Don't we?" He yelled the last two words, getting the crowd riled up.

And yes, they got involved. Everyone cheered, and there were a lot of catcalls. Adler was certain he should be embarrassed, but luckily embarrassment wasn't within his range of emotions. Leila, on the other hand, had a blush on her face that matched the pink of the roses in the bouquet, and it was getting redder by the minute.

When he looked over at Tristan and the guys, they were laughing and jeering.

"Go ahead and kneel in front of her," instructed the DJ. "When the music starts, put that garter on her leg and put it up as far as you can. Keep going until the music stops."

Here he was on the floor, kneeling in front of Leila. Her blush now matched the red of her dress, making her even more endearing. This wouldn't be bad at all as long as his heart slowed down a bit. He gave her a large, toothy smile. "Well, so much for getting out of here." He brushed his knuckles against her shin, sending a chill up his arm. He cleared his throat. "Want to give them a show?"

She huffed out a breath and stared at the ceiling. "Just get it over with."

He held up his hands. "I can't do anything until the music starts." The music started. He wiggled his brow and turned to the crowd, putting up his hands and letting out a holler. He was going to enjoy this.

"Good grief, get on with it," said Leila as she shot daggers at him with her eyes.

The music was sexy with a hard beat. He touched her shin again and brushed his hands up her leg, causing his heart to skip. *Damn. It's not the first time you've touched a woman, Warfield.* He took a deep breath, then slipped the garter around her foot and slid it up slowly.

Yeah, this is nice. Her skin was soft and smooth. He dragged his hand slowly up her calf to her knee and felt her shiver. His pulse picked up speed even more. He was tempted to kiss her knee and finally taste her soft skin that had been tempting him all through their dance, but instead he placed his palm on her inner thigh as the garter traveled past her knee. He breathed in, and his eyes caught hers.

She looked shocked. And something else. Maybe she was enjoying this more than she let on. He sure was.

He swallowed hard, and his eyes slowly trailed up her leg. God, he was wrong before. She was sexy and hot.

He brushed her thigh with his knuckles and continued creeping the garter up higher until his hands finally dipped beneath her dress. His heart thumped quickly, pumping blood to all parts of his body and causing the crotch of his pants to become a little snug. He gripped her thigh as he moved to adjust the tightness.

Leila took in a sharp breath, and his focus snapped to her face. Her hazel-green eyes sucked him in like they were an endless hole.

His breath caught, and she bit her lower lip, causing his attention to go straight there. He had an immediate need to place his mouth on hers. To finally taste what he had been desiring all night.

The voices and catcalls all around increased.

He cleared his throat. "It's all a show, beauty," he said, his voice thick. This shouldn't be turning him on, but it totally was. Touching her soft skin sent electricity running through him, not a feeling he was used to. He suddenly realized he was caressing her skin when her legs closed hard on his hand.

"Party's over, Casanova." Leila's eyes were smoldering as if they could burn him up from the inside out. "You've put on your show. Now it's time to remove your hands."

Yeah, she might be over it, but she had to have felt something. There was no denying the unmistakable connection between them. *Pull yourself together.* He winked. "You've got it. I'll remove my hands—for now." He threw his hands in the air, surrendering to her.

She wrenched her leg from his touch, breaking their connection. "Whatever," she said.

He winked before he stood, raising his hands over his head in victory.

He pulled her up and held her hands in the air while the hoots and hollers continued until the dance music started and everyone filled the floor. The electricity that was unmistakable between them was gone, but his heart was still going mad.

Adler held on to her hand, not ready to fully let her free. "Come on. Stay and dance." Their faces were close. He could smell her perfume, flowers and something he couldn't pinpoint but wouldn't soon forget.

"Like I said, I've gotta go." She pulled away from his grasp.

His hand was suddenly empty and cold. He made a fist, willing the warmth of her touch to remain. *What the hell are you doing? Pull yourself together.* "Well, thanks for letting me put my hands up your dress. I hope it was as good for you as it was for me." Adler chuckled uncomfortably, trying to make light of the situation, but his pulse was still racing, and the heat that had seeped through his fingers when he touched her skin had traveled throughout his body. *Yeah, this was so good for him.*

"Oh, you have no idea." She tipped her head, and for the second time that night, she left him standing alone on the dance floor.

He raised a brow while he watched her retreat and had to resist running after her and begging her to stay. He'd relished the feeling of holding her in his arms and feeling her skin against his fingertips. Soft and right. She was beautiful, but when she smiled and relaxed, that beauty tripled and took his breath away. What was going on with him?

She had a different kind of spunk. She didn't give in to his flirting. Usually when he said that about his name, with that smile, the girls fell at his feet. Leila didn't. He liked that, and he liked her, but she might just be a challenge.

His smile filled his face. Oh yeah, she might be, and he never backed away from a challenge.

Chapter 2

"I'm exhausted." Desiree kicked off her shoes as she fell hard on the plush couch in Adler's spacious living room.

Adler stood at the kitchen bar watching her. There was no doubt the woman was gorgeous. Any other night, he'd be by her side, waiting impatiently for Tristan and Stacey to get to bed so he could have fun with Desiree, but ever since Leila left him on the dance floor, he had a heaviness in his chest and an ache in his heart which wouldn't go away, and he didn't understand.

Stacey sat across from Desiree. "I know. I'm exhausted too, and I didn't do any of the work you did. I just danced." She accepted the glass of wine Tristan gave her as he sat next to her, and she snuggled close to his side. "The wedding was perfect. I know y'all didn't know Elizabeth's father, but he was the sweetest man and absolutely adored her. Elizabeth and her mom really struggled for a while emotionally after his heart attack last year. The dedication they did at the end was so sweet."

Tristan placed his hand on the back of Stacey's neck and gave her a massage. "It was. It's hard when you have important moments in your life and someone you love isn't around anymore to witness it with you."

The look that passed between Stacey and Tristan wasn't missed by Adler, and his heart went out to them. They'd both lost their parents earlier than anyone should. Stacey's was more recent, Tristan's much longer, but from what Tristan had always said, the pain never really goes away. It just gets easier to deal with. Adler finally sat next to Desiree. She had a glazed expression in her eyes also, like she was lost in thought as well.

Damn. There were too many deep feelings in this room. It was getting dreary. "Okay, enough of this. Y'all are killing the party vibes. Who wants to continue the fun and take a midnight swim? Suits optional?" Adler stood and offered his hand to Desiree. Maybe if he did what usually interested him, he'd start feeling a little better.

She pulled herself up. "I'm game. Grab another bottle of wine. The bakery's closed tomorrow. I need to unwind."

"Sorry." Tristan pulled Stacey to her feet. "We only swim clothed with other people around." He held Stacey at arm's length, eyeing her from head to toe. "This body is only for my eyes. I don't share."

"Me neither," answered Stacey.

Tristan closed the space between them and closed his lips on hers. "I think we're going to call it a night. Keep the noise down."

"See you in the morning." Stacey waved and pulled Tristan behind her.

Adler watched them go, and his heart tumbled and turned in his chest, a feeling he hadn't experienced before. Like it longed for what they had. That's ridiculous. *Get your mind back on the activity at hand. Skinny dipping and a beautiful woman.* As soon as they closed the bedroom door, he turned to Desiree. "Well, with just you and me, bathing suits are no longer optional. They're banned."

"Really?" Desiree winked as she walked toward the large sliding doors, which exited onto the pool patio. "I guess this isn't needed then." She stepped through the door and onto the patio as she pulled her arms from the spaghetti straps of her dress and let it fall to the ground. She stepped out of it, and Adler's eyes went wide.

Her bare back was muscular and curved down to her sexy hips. Those hips had the elastic of a tiny thong wrapped around them. The thong showed off a very shapely ass. He loved her ass.

Or he used to.

Now he looked at her naked body and hesitated. She was offering herself to him, and his body didn't react. There was nothing. *God, Adler, it's just sex. Stop overthinking it.*

"Adler," Desiree breathlessly said his name. "What's wrong?" She wiggled her finger, and he closed the space between them as her gaze bore into his.

She touched his cheek and brushed her hand along his face. He closed his eyes and leaned into her touch, trying to empty his mind of the memory of brown hair and hazel eyes. He focused on his breathing and the warmth of Desiree's hand on his skin.

"Let me help you with this." She unbuttoned his shirt and caressed his chest.

He felt nothing but her touch on his skin. No tingling, no quickness of his breath, no hardness growing in his groin.

That was new. A hot woman was caressing him, and he felt nothing.

He concentrated on his body, and his emotions, then slowly opened his eyes. *Maybe seeing the desire in her eyes will help him want more, to want her.* He held her gaze for a bit, then glanced at her lips. Those sensual pink lips, which were warm and soft and just last night did some amazing things to him.

Before he could react, she leaned toward him and closed her mouth over his. Their kiss was deep. He wrapped his arms around her and cradled her head in his hands as her tongue danced with his.

He broke the kiss and let out a heavy breath as he took a small step back. He bit his bottom lip. *Dammit. What the hell?* His gaze traveled over her. She was a work of art. His hands glided down her side, brushing along all her curves, and his gaze followed. Her curves were flawless, with enough muscle that her shape was pure perfection. "Girl, you are hot. Very hot."

"Then come here and warm yourself up." Her chest rose and fell quickly as she breathed.

He was a guy. He'd be crazy if he wasn't turned on by her, and he was, but he couldn't do this. He let out a heavy sigh and walked away.

"What the hell, Adler!" Irritation clipped onto every word.

He picked her dress up. "Here. Put this on. I'm sorry, Des. This isn't right."

She yanked the dress from his grasp and stepped into it. Anger blazed from her eyes. "What do you mean it isn't right? It was right last night and the night before that. What's changed in the past twenty-four hours?"

"Des, I don't know." *What had changed?* He filtered through his thoughts. *What had changed? Could meeting Leila really have done* this to him? His heart was heavy. Guilt maybe? He couldn't figure it out. "Des. I'm sorry. This is just not enough."

"What. Sex? All of a sudden you want more?" Her words were loud and sharp.

He closed his hands on her arms. "Des. Shh. Please. Again, I'm sorry."

She nodded. "Yeah, okay." She grabbed her purse from the chair and slipped on her shoes. "Call me if you get your head on straight. I'll always be up for a good time."

He watched her leave and stared at the door. A picture of her naked body flashed through his mind. God. Was he crazy? She was fun and creative. Hot. Sexy. Really sexy.

He wanted more, but not with Desiree. "Adler, seriously?" He stalked to his room, undressed, and climbed into bed.

He grabbed the extra pillow and placed it over his head. When he woke up, maybe this craziness would be gone and he could go on like normal, having amazing, meaningless sex with Desiree and not caring about what happened next. Not expecting anything to come from it. Better yet, not *wanting* anything.

What the hell was going on? What was wrong with him? Needing more? Not fully satisfied? Feeling things?

He never wanted more. He never needed anything more than a hot woman and sexual satisfaction. He never put the word feeling in his thoughts. Damn. He sounded like a lovesick child—he sounded like. . .Tristan.

He let out a yell and tossed a pillow across his room. It smacked into his dresser and toppled the frame he had sitting there.

"Shit!" He flung himself out of bed and picked up the picture. Good, it wasn't broken.

This was one of his favorite pictures. It was a picture of his mom and dad, him and Tristan, and Tristan's mom. It was the last Christmas before Tristan's mother passed away.

His family. A smile filled his face as the memory of that day came to his mind. His father had his arm around his mother. There were smiles on everyone's faces. Adler had never doubted how much his parents loved each other; how much family meant to them. How much they wanted and deserved grandchildren.

He froze as Leila filled his mind—her long brown hair and large hazel eyes, smiling as he led her around the dance floor. The blush on her cheeks as his hands traveled up her leg. The heat between them when their gazes met was impossible to ignore.

Shit. Now he needed a shower.

Chapter 3

Leila walked toward the nursery to pick up Skylar, her little girl, after the church service let out. She had had a difficult time focusing on the service this morning because her mind was on the phone call she had earlier with her mother. Talking with her mom never led to anything positive, so she wondered why she continued to call her to inform her about Skylar's latest milestones. Things between them would never change. Her mother didn't care at all about Skylar, or Leila for that matter.

It had always been this way. When Leila was ten, her parents had gotten divorced, and her mother had run off with her to Florida as soon as the divorce was final. Leila hardly saw her father after that and spent years making up for her daddy issues by dating anyone who gave her the time of day, and if her mother didn't approve, well that made it even better.

To top it all off, Leila's mom had kicked her out as soon as she found out Leila was pregnant by that "useless thing" Leila called a boyfriend. Luckily, her father and his wife, Diane, took them in six months ago with open arms.

"Hey, Leila."

Leila turned and saw Jessica and her fiancé Chad walking toward her. Jessica worked at the Crisis Pregnancy Center, the place that saved Leila when she found herself single, pregnant, and in a new state, and gave her the much-needed support to face becoming a young, single mom.

"Hi, Jessica. Sorry, I was lost in my mind."

The girls hugged.

"Not a problem. We're picking up Grant and keeping him for a while today to give Mrs. Parks time to decompress after the wedding. We'll walk with you."

"How was your dance with Adler last night?" Chad asked as they took the short walk to the nursery. "That show with the garter you two put on looked pretty hot."

"Chad!" Jessica hissed under her breath as she elbowed him hard in the ribs.

He rubbed his side. "What? It looked as if they were enjoying themselves. First dancing, then the garter thing. It was just an observation."

A knot grew in Leila's stomach as she remembered the trail of fire Adler's touch left behind on her skin. "Honestly, I was just doing Desiree a favor, which was taken a bit too far. He's not my type. Too much like Skylar's father—conceited and stuck on himself." Thankfully, the conversation ended as they approached the nursery. Last night was not something she wanted to talk about.

"Hi, Mrs. Parks." Jessica hugged Charlotte as they reached the nursery door.

"Good morning, Jessica. Hi, Chad."

"Good morning." Chad gave her a quick hug.

"I'm surprised to see you both here. You were at the house late last night. Thank you so much for helping clean up."

Chad swiped his hand through the air. "Don't mention it. It wasn't a big deal. Please let us know if you need any more help with anything today."

"Yeah. We can help with anything you need," Jessica said. "But honestly, it wasn't easy getting here this morning. Staying home was tempting, but we needed to pick up Grant, so it seemed like the best choice."

"Well, I'll be finished here in a bit. Let me say goodbye before you take him. Hi, Leila. Skylar was a perfect angel." Charlotte let Leila enter and helped her gather up Skylar's bottle and place everything in her bag.

Leila picked up Skylar, who was still napping, kissed the top of her head, and bounced her to keep her asleep. "I'm so glad. Thank you for texting me during the service. It helped me relax knowing she was doing well. This was the first time I'd left her with anyone besides Dad or Diane."

"I know it's been quite a while for me, but I remember how it feels to leave your baby. Trust me, it doesn't get much easier even when they get married." A cloud crossed Charlotte's face, but it only lasted a short while before her face lit up due to the sound of tiny stomping feet.

Grant entered the room like a miniature tornado, his brown curls bouncing, and jumped into his grandmother's arms.

Leila smiled as Grant wrapped his arms around Charlotte's neck, planting a kiss on her cheek. *Oh, my goodness. He's so adorable.*

Charlotte laughed and placed kisses all over his face. "There's my boy."

He squealed with pure joy.

"Shh, buddy. The baby's sleeping," Charlotte reminded him.

Grant cocked his head to the side as Leila hooked Skylar into the car seat.

He pointed his tiny finger. "Baby." Then put his finger to his grandmom's lips. "Shh."

Charlotte grabbed his finger and kissed it. "That's right," she whispered and kissed his cheek. Her face glowed.

Grant didn't realize how lucky he was. He had the love of an amazing grandmother to grow up with, and his parents were in love and married. Leila watched her daughter sleep. *You may never have the love of your real grandmother, but Diane loves you anyway, and family doesn't have to be blood. No matter what, I'll try my best to make sure you know you're loved every day.*

Jessica appeared at Leila's side. "I know you have your hands full, but we're heading to the Pizza Place. We always meet there after church. Would you like to go?"

Leila looked at her sleeping baby. Hanging out for a bit would be great, but she really needed to get home before Skylar woke up and needed to eat again.

Leila's forehead wrinkled as she fought through her decision. It was just too hard to go out with such a young baby. Maybe next time. "I'd love to, but I really can't."

Charlotte took the diaper bag from her. "Nonsense. You go. I'll take both Skylar and Grant home. I'll feed them both, and Grant and I will babysit. You still have one more bottle I can heat up in case she wakes up. When you're done, just come by the house and pick them both up."

"Are you sure?" Jessica and Leila said in unison.

"Absolutely." She asked Grant. "Buddy, would you like to babysit with Grandma?"

"Uh huh." Grant nodded his head hard.

"Anyway, Jessica, I was running late this morning and forgot to bring his clothes, so it'll give me time to pack him up for your house."

Jessica shrugged. "Sounds good, Mrs. Parks. We'll stop by as soon as we're done eating."

Leila chewed on her lips. Eating without a crying baby would be a treat. Eating a hot meal would be heaven. "As long as you're sure?"

Charlotte shooed them away. "Go. Get."

In the short time Leila had been in town, she'd found the Pizza Place to be not only her favorite place to eat but popular for the locals to go any time of day. After church seemed to be the same. The restaurant was busy. Even the patio was full.

Leila followed Jessica and Chad to a table with a few empty seats. She smiled at Stacey, the nurse who'd taken care of her when Skylar was born. They'd talked last night. She was a very sweet person. Tristan, her boyfriend, was sitting next to her. She recognized everyone else from Elizabeth and Brady's wedding. Jessica and Chad took the seats next to Jacob—Stacey's brother—and his wife, Kristen, leaving only one seat for Leila next to a guy whose back was to her.

Great. She never did well talking to guys. Her words came out wrong, and she always felt like an idiot.

She sighed as she pulled out her chair, then the guy in the seat next to her turned his head and her heart stopped. Literally stopped.

Really? It had to be him?

Adler looked a little different from how he had last night. Ruggedly handsome—like he just pulled himself out of bed. His dark hair was sticking up in an organized I-meant-to-do-this kind of way. He wore a faded and well-worn gray T-shirt and faded jeans. She rolled her eyes and took her seat.

When their eyes met, his face lit up. "Well, hey Leila. How ya doing?"

His features were flawless, as if an artist's hand had chiseled him out of marble. It should be illegal to be that perfect. He was exactly the kind of man that made her toes curl, and not in a good way.

"Hey, everyone," Jessica said. "Y'all remember Leila. She was in church, so we invited her along." Jessica introduced everyone at the table.

"Hi." Leila smiled and accepted the water the server placed in front of her.

"It's good to see you, Leila." Tristan smirked. "So, did you have fun last night?"

"Tristan." Stacey shot him a look and turned to Leila. "Ignore him."

"Well, I don't know about her, but I know I had a good time." Adler gave her that smile again, the one she was sure turned all the girls to mush. Not her. She was immune to the self-centered male ego—now, anyway.

She turned slowly toward him, and her stomach clenched tightly. She wasn't wrong about him. He was crazy good looking with conceit to match. Typical. "Yeah, for one song it wasn't bad." Leila took a breadstick and dipped it in marinara. "Desiree pawned you off on me so she could get work done. I'm sorry if touching a girl's leg was the most excitement you've had in a while." She held his gaze. "I thought you were overly experienced with women and touching a woman's leg wouldn't be that exciting to you, but I guess I was wrong."

The corner of Adler's mouth ticked up. "Don't let her fool you. My dance moves impressed her, and she shivered when my fingers brushed her thigh."

"He wishes." She mumbled and dipped her breadstick back in the marinara. *Jerk.*

Tristan laughed. "I'm not going there, but I saw you pulling her around the dance floor, taking advantage of those dance classes we were forced to take. So, Leila, I'm guessing his dance moves didn't impress you as much as he always thinks they do."

"I don't think it did." Jacob said with a smirk. "I saw her ditch him on the dance floor in the middle of the song."

"Actions speak louder than words sometimes," Leila answered. "I do have to say though, I didn't just leave him. I thanked him for the dance first." She shot him a crooked grin and didn't miss the shake of his head. "I would've been long gone if I wasn't forced back for the garter nightmare."

"Saved by food." Chad changed the subject as the pizza was placed in front of them. The conversation and laughter blended together into a harmonious sound as they ate.

Leila enjoyed herself and couldn't remember the last time she'd had such a good time with others. They were all friendly and bantered back and forth. Even Adler seemed to get over the pounding his ego took and had a good time.

Soon the food was gone, the tab was paid, and everyone left the restaurant.

"Leila, would you mind if I jumped in with you?" asked Jessica. "Chad has some errands to run first and will pick me and Grant up when he's done."

"Of course not. We're going to the same place."

Jessica sat in the passenger seat of Leila's compact car as she drove the short distance to Charlotte's house.

"So, how're things going at home with your dad and stepmom?" Jessica asked once they were on the road.

Leila shrugged. "Things are good." She gave her a quick glance. "I don't know how much you know, but my mom kicked me out when I was six months pregnant. She didn't like that I did everything she told me *not* to, and that I was choosing to be a single mom. I came here because I had nowhere else to go."

"I'm sorry. That must've been so hard."

"At first it was, but now it's not so bad. My dad and I haven't spent much time together throughout the years, so we hardly know each other, but he took me in any way. Diane and I are getting along well. They never had kids of their own, so it's just us." She pulled into Charlotte's driveway. "I'm just thankful to be here. With my dad and Diane, the pregnancy center, and all of y'all, I have so much more than I ever dreamed possible." She smiled at Jessica as she turned off the car. "I just hope things continue going well. I want better for Sky."

"I hope so too. Don't hesitate to ask for help, or better yet, if you need anything, just give me a call."

"Thanks. And thank you for inviting me today and for listening. I needed that."

"Anytime. That's what friends are for."

After being away from Skylar for so long today, Leila rocked and cuddled her in her small bedroom in the basement of her father and Diane's house. She'd enjoyed church this morning. Being around people and hearing the sermon was a good change of pace. Next week, she might try Sunday school for her and Skylar. Jessica had told her she and Chad were in a thirty-something Bible class with Jacob, Kristen, Elizabeth, and Brady plus others. It would do her good to get to know more people. Outside of her not having a significant other and being the odd one out, it sounded amazing.

"Sky, so far everything's been great for us here." Pastor John's sermon, *Seeing the Good After the Bad*, came back to her. That was the story of her life this past year.

This time last year, she and her mom were not getting along and started fighting constantly, not that they were ever best friends. Leila started to spend a lot of time at the community college's library and began talking to a guy who was in her Intro to Chemistry class. Ben was good looking. Okay, more than good looking. Hot was more like it, with a crooked grin which showed off his white teeth and an understanding of Chemistry—both in the class and the bedroom—which left her knees weak. She fell fast and fell hard.

Once her mother found out they were talking, she made sure to let Leila know she wasn't good enough for him and he was way out of her league. That made Leila determined to prove her mother wrong.

Ben was everything Leila never wanted and always swore she would avoid. Egotistical, wild, bad news, but damn. He was sexy. His smile finally bore right into her soul, and before she knew it, she was head over heels in love—or so she thought—in his bed—and pregnant.

Her mom, upset that she hadn't listened, was finished with her. She kicked Leila out with nothing but what she could fit in a duffel bag and the small amount of money in her bank account. Scared and homeless, yet fed up with her mother's attitude, she held her head high and called Ben.

He took her in, and everything seemed to be going well. They got along, or so it seemed at the time. Looking back, she could see that he wasn't home much and expected her to take care of the home "duties" while she also kept up with her schoolwork. She was there for a week before she told him about the baby. They didn't have a discussion. He didn't hold her and tell her it would all work out. He gave her money for an abortion and told her not to call him again until she "dealt with the problem." She wasn't sure what she'd expected. He was all about himself and his future. She should have realized a baby wasn't in his well-established plans.

She left his apartment heartbroken and scared, yet knew there was no way she could end the life growing inside her.

Instead, she ended up in an Uber at the airport. With his money and what she had in her account, she had just enough to buy a one-way ticket to Nashville International Airport and hope her dad, whom she hadn't talked to in a while and hardly knew, would take her in. Luckily for her and Skylar, he and Diane had, with open arms. They were so welcoming and loving. It was like she and her dad had never been apart. That was probably how family was supposed to be. When you really loved someone, you wanted to be with them and hoped they were safe and happy. At least that's what her father told her.

Leila brushed her hand over the soft hair on Skylar's head. Her heart always fluttered when she held her close and relaxed with her in her arms. This feeling of contentment was God's doing. She was in a great place, had a beautiful girl, a job she loved, and an amazing group of friends.

And determination.

Determination to never let a guy take advantage of her again. Especially not a ridiculously good-looking, egotistical, cocky, bad idea.

Adler's handsome face flashed in her mind.

Chapter 4

Adler stepped outside the Pizza Place and glanced up and down the street. He'd tried getting out quicker, but Tristan mentioned having a pool party at the house, and he got stuck planning food with the guys.

Fuck. He'd hoped to catch Leila and invite her over, but he'd missed her. He deflated a little, but his eyes fell on the sidewalk and road in front of the bakery. *Focus on Desiree and get your mind off Leila.* Desiree's car wasn't parked in front. It was probably in the back. That would make sense. *Go there, see her, and get your mind off Leila.*

"Hey," Tristan slapped Adler on the shoulder causing him to jump, "we're heading to Stacey's for a bit, then everyone's coming to the house. We'll see you there."

"Sounds like a plan." Adler lifted a brow but kept his gaze down the street. He let out a heavy breath as he realized he didn't care if Desiree would show up at his house. She wasn't the one he wanted to see.

"Hey, Warfield." Tristan nudged Adler hard, causing him to lose his balance.

He grabbed Tristan's arm to keep from falling over. "What the hell." He pushed Tristan hard, causing Tristan to laugh and bump into Stacey.

"I finally got your attention. You were zoning out." Tristan put his arm around Stacey's waist. "Don't worry about Desiree, bro. Kristen already told her we were heading to the house to swim. She said she'd meet us there later."

Adler shrugged. "Not worried at all about Desiree. I told her last night we should stop seeing each other."

"Seriously? Was that before or after the skinny dipping?"

He shook his head. Not that this was any of Tristan and Stacey's business, but he knew Tristan wouldn't back off until he knew everything, or as much as he needed to know. Adler swung his leg around his motorcycle and unhooked the strap of his helmet. "Not that it's any of your business, but we didn't get to skinny dipping." He hooked his helmet under his chin. "I asked her to leave soon after you two went to bed."

A look passed between Stacey and Tristan.

Heat grew inside him. They were stunned that he had turned her away. He lifted his face to the sky. "What?" he asked between gritted teeth.

Tristan put his free hand in the air in surrender. "Nothing. Nothing at all."

"Good." Adler kicked the bike to life, lifted his hand in salute, and squealed away from the curb.

Cars were already in the driveway when Adler pulled in and cautiously entered the garage. He went into his room to slip on his swim trunks.

"Hey." Stacey was grabbing some chips off the counter when he entered the kitchen.

"You act like you live here, rooting through things like it's your house." He pulled a beer out of the refrigerator. Stacey wore a thin white throw over a sexy black bikini. She had a nice body and was beautiful. Perfect for his cousin.

"I think I do belong here. Does that bother you, your cousin being off the market?" Stacey asked, her arms full of bags of chips.

He shook his head and took a pull from his beer. "Surprisingly, no. You two are perfect together. I'm glad he has you."

"Thank you, Adler." Her smile lit up her face. "Can I be honest?"

He lifted his beer in an "of course" gesture.

"I didn't know how much I'd like you at first. You're a pretty snotty and arrogant person."

He nodded in agreement. He could be.

"But you've grown on me. I just wish you'd settle down. You deserve someone who really loves you."

Her gaze held his in a friendly way but made him uncomfortable. It was like she could see into his thoughts and his soul. Suddenly his stomach felt heavy, and his hands were clammy. He closed them both around his cold beer and shrugged. "Yeah, maybe one day I'll find the right person." He drowned the heaviness in his stomach with a large gulp of beer. This conversation needed to be over. He had a party to get to. "See you outside."

He held her gaze for a second more until she walked past him with a smile, then followed her through the sliding doors onto the patio.

The conversation he had just had with Stacey didn't leave his mind. It was weird and the most uncomfortable he'd been with a woman in a while—well, not really. Turning Desiree down last night was pretty damn uncomfortable.

He cleared his throat and took a sip of his beer and breathed in deep. The smell of hamburgers and hot dogs grilling hung in the air. It was a perfect afternoon for a barbecue, drinking, and swimming. Time to have fun and get relationships off his mind.

"Let's turn up the music and get this party started," he hollered, raising his beer to Tristan and Chad over at the outdoor kitchen. There was another guy with them. He met him last night at the wedding. He racked his brain to remember his name. Finally, it came to him. His name was Don. He was married to Charity, Desiree's best friend.

They raised theirs with smiles and hollers of, "Hell, yeah!"

He chugged the rest of his beer, glanced around the pool area, and froze as a little boy jumped into Jacob's arms into the pool. On closer inspection, it was Grant. Why was he there? His heart sank. A baby was at their pool at a party. Why?

Adler trudged heavily over to Tristan, who was flipping the burgers in the outdoor kitchen, plopped onto one of the stools at the bar, and chucked his empty beer bottle into the trash.

Tristan slid him another. "Hey, bro."

"Hey." Adler's voice was flat, and he tipped his head toward the pool. "Who brought Grant? It's not every day there's a kid at our parties."

"Jessica and Chad are watching him, so they brought him along." Tristan raised a brow. "Is that a problem?"

Adler shook his head slowly and laid his arms on the bar, clutching his beer in his fist. Not much of a party could be had with a baby around. Talk about a buzz kill.

Like Tristan could read his mind, he consoled him. "Don't worry. They won't be here long. They'll be eating and leaving. They're babysitting. Giving Elizabeth's mom a break."

"Yeah man," Chad cut in. "We won't be staying long. Promise."

"Guess it's a good thing I left my boy at home," said Don.

"You have a kid too?" Adler asked.

Don chuckled heartily. "Yeah, and I promise they're not as bad as you think." Chad and Tristan joined Don in hearty laughter.

Adler raised a brow. Did these guys lose their minds? "Did I miss something?" He gestured with his hands.

Tristan breathed deeply to get his laughter under control. "If you could see your face. It's like we were talking about eating babies or something."

"Adler," said Chad, leaning on the bar. "You'll need to get a better handle on children if you ever want a relationship. Good thing that doesn't interest you."

Adler shook his head and noticed that feeling in his stomach again. He laughed off the rest of their jokes, turned his back to them, and leaned against the bar. His attention snapped immediately to the group of girls across the pool. Jessica, Stacey, Kristen, Charity—and Leila.

His throat went dry as his gaze swept over Leila, and he took a deep sip of his beer. Her wavy brown hair was pulled up on top of her head in a messy bun. Stray pieces blew around her face in the gentle breeze, causing her to have a laid-back look, which was beautiful on her. She held a drink in her hand, though not a beer, and her smile lit up her face.

Suddenly, she tipped her head back as her laugh rang out. Adler's lungs constricted. Yeah, she was breathtaking, and he was hooked.

She looked up, and their eyes met. Adler's heart stopped for a quick beat, like he was caught peeking at something he shouldn't be looking at. He smiled a small smile. She stared back. No emotion. No smile.

She pivoted her attention back to the girls in their circle as they were joined by another. Auburn hair and a skimpy white swimsuit filled his view. Desiree caught his gaze and followed it, stopping at Leila. Her eyebrows shot up.

Fuck. Adler did the only thing he could do. He winked, lifted his beer, and turned back to the guys.

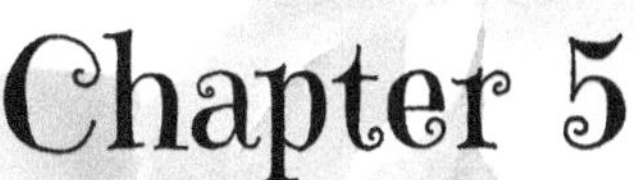

Chapter 5

*R**eally, I know this is his house and all, but I was hoping he'd be gone for the afternoon.* Leila had heard Adler's bike way before he walked out of the house.

She was only there because Jessica had talked her into asking her father to watch Skylar. She always hated to impose on them, but her dad and Diane were quick to jump in and help. Diane said she wished Leila would ask them more often. They really wanted to spend more time getting to know their granddaughter. So here she was.

"Leila?" Snapping fingers caught her attention. "Want a drink? I'm going to the bar," Desiree asked.

"I'm sorry. I didn't hear you. What was that?" asked Leila.

The woman smirked. "Your mind seemed to be somewhere else."

Kristen laughed. "Or on someone else."

Leila shook her head. "What are y'all talking about? The only one on my mind is Skylar. I'm glad my dad and stepmom asked to watch her."

"They seemed eager, from what I could tell," said Jessica. "They all but pushed you out the door when we got there."

"Yeah, that's great." Desiree gestured with her hand for Leila to hurry up. "So, do you want a drink? I'll find you something good. One drink will be fine."

"Sure. A glass of wine would be great. Moscato if they have it," replied Leila.

"One glass of Moscato coming up." Desiree and Charity left together.

Leila sipped her water, watching Desiree out of the corner of her eye as she stopped next to Adler, yet he didn't seem to acknowledge her. You wouldn't know they were a thing. They didn't hug, didn't act any differently than Adler would with anyone, outside of a quick wink she caught him give her.

"Adler's cute. Could even be considered hot. Don't you agree, Leila?" Kristen broke into her thoughts.

Leila glanced toward the bar. Adler was leaning with his back toward her, and what a nice back it was. He was tan, broad-shouldered with perfectly sculpted muscles, and his black swim shorts sat low on his hips, showing off each detailed contour. Her mouth was suddenly dry, and she took a quick sip of her water. Luckily, she was always quick on her feet and able to regain her composure. "He could be, but that enormous ego gets in the way" She glanced at Kristen. "You must never have talked to him. Don't let him hear you say anything that positive about him. It instantly goes to his head."

Stacey jumped into the conversation. "Yes, he's a lot to get used to, and has had at least three girls with him since I've been with Tristan, but he grows on you. Tristan says he's really a softy and all that ego stuff is just for show. I'm starting to agree."

Desiree and Charity came back, their hands filled with drinks, which they quickly passed around.

"Let's join Jacob and Grant in the pool. It's getting a little warm." Desiree peeled off her thin wrap and threw it over the chair, exposing everyone to her very small string bikini. There wasn't much to it, and Leila couldn't help but notice the perfection of the girl's body. How could she work in a bakery and still look that fit?

Jessica must have been thinking the same thing, but she asked instead of keeping it in her head. "Okay, Des. How do you keep looking that hot when you work in a bakery? If I were around all those baked goods every day, I'd be the size of a house."

"Simple. I work out religiously. Y'all go to church to worship. I go to the gym. It's the only way I can eat like I do."

"Oh, please," Charity chimed in. "That's such bullshit. You looked like that, maybe with a little less muscle, in high school. You've been blessed with perfect genes. Just wait. One day you'll have a baby, and that body won't be looking like that."

"That's the truth." Leila agreed before she realized what she was doing. This was why her swimsuit went above her stomach and was more of a tankini than a bikini.

"And that's why babies are not in my future." Desiree handed Leila her wine and dove into the deep end. A beautiful and elegant dive.

Leila glanced over. Yes. All the guys noticed. It figured.

The rest of them weren't as elegant. They just walked into the pool at the shallow end. There were seats around the edge of the pool. Nice. Leila took a seat next to Jessica. She enjoyed watching everyone as they interacted. Kristen sat on the other side of Jessica, and Charity was next to Kristen. Jacob and Don were playing with

Grant. He kept climbing out of the pool and jumping in for one of the guys to catch him.

"Charity, where's the little squirt?" Desiree asked as she joined the girls and sat down next to her best friend. "You should have brought him."

"He's with my parents. They have him until Wednesday. We have nothing but quiet. So, if you come over, make sure you knock. We aren't being very decent."

Desiree nudged Charity's arm. "Oh, yeah? Trying for baby number two?"

She shrugged. "If it happens, it happens. You know we don't want much space between our babies. Tom-Tom's already two."

"See. I don't need to have any babies. I just live through my friends. They have the babies. I get the love."

"You also don't get stretch marks," Charity added. "They'd do a number on that body of yours."

"I hope my beautiful wife isn't talking about stretch marks," said Don as the guys joined them.

"Oh, she's just talking about stretch marks and how her body might be getting more if you two succeed with all the fun you're having in the bedroom," Desiree filled them in.

"Really, another baby?" Jacob sat behind Kristen, wrapping his arms around her.

"If things work out," said Don. "So, when are you two going to start a family?" he asked Jacob and Kristen.

The look on Kristen's face was priceless. Her eyes became the size of saucers, causing Leila to snort-laugh.

"Did you just snort?" Jessica squealed as she shouldered Leila.

Leila sucked in a deep breath. "Yes." She laughed as she looked at everyone. "I do that sometimes when a laugh sneaks up on me."

"A laugh snuck up on you?" replied Chad, who had just joined them.

Leila made room for him next to Jessica. "Yes. It was because of the fear on Kristen's face. She looked like she had seen a ghost coming after her with a sword, ready to do her in or something."

Don laughed. "Kristen, your look was priceless. It's only a baby."

"Yeah. Just a baby. I've told Jacob he can hang out with Grant anytime he wants to, and y'all can have him babysit as well. I'm so not ready for that. We just got married."

"Yeah, but you can't hold Jacob back for too long. Y'all aren't getting any younger," replied Don.

Jacob lifted Kristen onto his lap. "Hey, it's all right, babe. No babies. Not yet, anyway." He kissed her, and she seemed to relax.

Those two were sweet, and newly married. Only about a month. Leila hadn't gone to their wedding. They were married at a justice of the peace, then celebrated with a party in Stacey's backyard. She had just had Skylar and was up to her neck with breastfeeding and dealing with dirty diapers. No time for fun.

"Do you need another drink?"

Leila hadn't noticed that someone had sat down next to her. She jerked her head toward the new, yet familiar, voice. Adler. She looked around and noticed Desiree still next to Charity, with a seat next to her. Why didn't he go over there instead of sitting by her? She studied Desiree. She didn't look concerned. *I guess when you look that good, you aren't concerned with needing to be jealous. Must be nice.*

She was saved the need of answering him when Tristan called them from the pool. Time to eat. She quickly exited, glad to put some space between herself and Adler.

Leila filled a plate and sat with Jessica and Chad at a stone picnic table overlooking the pasture, as Grant was trying his best to climb over the fence that separated them from the horse pasture.

"Hey, you, don't climb through that fence," Jacob said to Grant. "Horses have been known to eat little boys."

Jessica and Leila's mouths dropped as Jacob joined them at the table.

"That's awful," Leila said.

"Yeah, you're gonna scare him," Jessica agreed. "Grant, don't listen to Jacob. Horses don't eat people."

Grant spun around toward the group, scrunched his face tight, placed his finger in front of his face, and pointed it at Jacob, making everyone laugh. He really was a cute little boy.

"Maybe one day your mom and dad can bring you here and I'll give you a riding lesson on a pony," Adler said to Grant.

Leila watched the fake mean expression on Grant's face melt away and turn to surprise while, at the same time, her stomach curdled, and Adler took the only empty seat. Next to her.

Jacob chuckled. "That's something I'm sure Brady will jump at. His wife bringing their two-year-old here to get riding lessons from you—the guy who hit on her."

Leila had talked with Elizabeth about what had happened between her and Adler, which wasn't anything. She was someone else who hadn't given in to the Adler charm. She joined in the laughter and turned toward Adler to make a smart comment but stopped herself.

Adler looked away from the group, and she could see the muscle in his jaw clench. Their ragging was irritating him. She quirked a brow. She hadn't taken him for the sensitive type.

"Nah, Brady's good," said Chad. "Though I think it'll take him a bit more time to leave Adler alone with Elizabeth. Heck, from what I hear about you, we all need to be watching our women around you." Chad put his arm around Jessica's shoulder and held up her hand. "Engagement ring. She's mine. Hands off."

Adler shot eye daggers at Chad, and the muscle in his jaw pulsed.

"Problem, Casanova?" Leila asked as she bumped her shoulder into him. "Is the fact that someone didn't fall for your charms hurting your ego?"

He looked at her, and his gaze held hers. He had large, deep dark brown—almost black—eyes. Right now, they were smoldering, and her stomach lurched. He reached over and moved a strand of hair from her face. Her heart did a weird flip when his finger touched her skin. What was that about?

"She wasn't the only one able to resist the Adler charm, but luckily I seem to be getting used to it." His eyes never left hers.

She squinted. What was his deal? He moved his hand, and she looked away. Suddenly her throat was dry, and she took a quick drink of water to quench her thirst and try to calm her churning stomach.

Chad broke into the conversation and stood up from the table. "Look, I hate to be the bearer of bad news, but I think we need to be going. Grant needs a bath and needs to get to bed."

Thank God. Leila stood quickly. She needed to get some space between herself and Adler.

Jacob joined Chad. "I'll get him ready for you. Grant, come here, bud."

Grant ran across the yard and jumped into Jacob's arms.

Jessica turned to Leila. "You ready?"

"Of course." Leila started to clean up, and Adler was right behind her. They walked into the kitchen, their arms loaded with food.

"It was good to see you again." Adler stood unnecessarily close.

Leila placed the food on the counter and turned to him, her arms crossed across her chest. "What's your deal?" She couldn't help it. Why was he wasting his time talking with her when he was going to be in bed with Desiree tonight? Yeah, they might not have talked much, but you could see it when they looked at each other. And she'd worked enough catering events with Desiree to know that the two of them had been together more than once.

"What do you mean? I'm just being nice," Adler answered, placing chips in the pantry.

"Yeah, maybe, but why? It's weird."

Adler looked at her and shook his head. "Someone really did a number on you, didn't they? You don't trust anyone."

She held his gaze. *He needs to mind his own business.* Her stomach churned as heat rose into her cheeks.

She was saved from answering when Jacob emerged from one of the bedrooms with Grant in his arms.

It was time to go. Leila turned and walked away.

⁂

Adler sat at the bar on the patio. Everyone had left, and everything was cleaned up. He leaned on the bar and absentmindedly picked at the label on his beer bottle. He suddenly had no energy, like it was all zapped from his body, leaving him limp and lifeless. This wasn't a feeling he was used to, and he needed to figure his shit out. What was he going to do about Leila? She despised him, yet he couldn't get her out of his mind. He'd tried to show her a different side of him tonight, but she kept throwing his past in his face and gave him the cold shoulder. And that name, Casanova. God, it irritated him.

"No, no, no, no, no!" Stacey ran out of the house screaming and ran around the pool.

What the hell was going on? He sat up and glared at Stacey.

Tristan chased after her and stopped, his hands on his knees. He looked across the pool at her, his eyes shining. "You better run, woman. Things aren't going to be good for you if I catch you."

"I'm not scared," she screeched.

They stared long and hard at each other until Stacey finally took off one way and Tristan darted in that direction.

She ran toward Adler. "Help!" she screamed as she ran around behind him and wrapped her arms around him.

Dammit. Couldn't a guy be left alone? "What the hell are you two doing?" he asked as he stood in front of Stacey.

"Really? You're guarding her?" Tristan stood with his hands on his hips and a smirk on his face.

Stacey tried to catch her breath, and Adler could feel it on his neck. He put his arms up. "Look, I'm not one to let a guy bully a beautiful woman."

"Thank you, Adler. See? You're a good guy. Some girl will be lucky to have you." Stacey stuck her tongue out at Tristan as she hunkered down behind her protector.

Tristan stood and pushed his shoulders back as he glared hard at his cousin. "Oh, please. Adler, I was in my room. She had gone to get a drink. When she came back, she put her arms around me. I thought she was going to be sweet and show me some lovin', but she wasn't sweet at all. She put a handful of ice down my shorts and froze my fucking dick! When I catch her, I'm throwing her in the pool."

Adler held up his arms. This was ridiculous. "Look. I'm not in the mood. You want to throw her in the pool? Fine, whatever. I'm out of here." He pushed past Tristan and stalked into the house, went straight into his room, and slammed the door.

Chapter 6

The week was going by like any other. Between being a mom and working, Leila didn't have any time for herself. On Thursday morning, she dropped Skylar off at the Mother's Day Out program at the pregnancy center—a free service the center provided. Volunteers and center workers staffed it on Tuesdays and Thursdays. Leila was thankful for this, and at the center and on Wednesdays and Fridays, Skylar went to work with her. Thankfully, Mrs. Stanzel, the owner of Main Street Boutique, understood the restrictions of being a single parent and supported her wholeheartedly. The fact that Elizabeth had sometimes had Grant there when he was a baby helped.

This morning, she found herself with extra time, so after parking in the boutique's lot, she walked across the street to Desiree's bakery. She didn't know why, but today was going to be a great day. She could feel it deep in her bones. Skylar woke up happy, and it was easy getting out the door this morning. Diane told her she'd be happy to watch Sky Saturday when Leila went to work, then to the pregnancy center to help prep for the yearly fundraiser. Things were going well.

The smell of fresh-baked cinnamon rolls and coffee wrapped her like a warm hug as soon as she opened the door to the bakery. An older couple waited at the counter as Desiree filled their order.

"Thank you," she told the customers as they left, then turned to her with a smile. "Good morning, Leila."

"Hi, Desiree. It always smells so amazing in here."

"Thank you. What can I help you with?"

Leila ordered half a dozen donuts, a cinnamon roll, and coffee.

"How's your week been?" Desiree asked as she boxed up her order. The door chimed, announcing another customer.

"Surprisingly, it's been great. Sky's even been really cooperative. Not her usual fussy self."

"Sky? Who's Sky?"

Leila jerked toward the unexpected addition to their conversation and shook her head. Well, the day *was* going well. Then there was this.

Adler stood next to her, leaning against the counter. His hair looked like he'd just climbed out of bed and gone to sleep with it wet, yet there was an organized look to the chaos. He wore black pants and a green polo with *Warfield Meats* embroidered on the breast pocket—relaxed, yet business casual, and he carried it with his typical air of egocentric conceit, which boiled her blood.

"It's none of your business who Skylar is." She turned to Desiree. "How much?" She reached up and took her coffee, sipping it carefully, suddenly needing the caffeine.

"Add hers to my tab," Adler interjected.

Her gaze shot to him. "No, thank you." Venom dripped from her voice. "I don't need a handout from you, and I sure don't *want* one either." Raising an eyebrow, she took a step back from the counter. She hadn't known she could sound that hateful. But also decisive. She shrugged inwardly. She should sound that decisive more often. She liked it.

He pushed off the counter and turned his full attention to her. "It's not a handout. It's a friend giving to another friend."

Leila took money from her purse. "Well then, save it for a friend. That's not us."

"Come on, we've danced, we've talked," he raised his brow and smirked, "we've touched, and we've had dinner." His hands were out, palms up, and he gave her that smile.

She lifted her eyes toward the ceiling. "I'm sure that smile works on other women, but I know better. Put it back in your pants. You're wasting your time." She faced him, square on. "We were forced to dance, which made us talk, and the touching was not something we both enjoyed, and we had burgers at your house with everyone else. Don't make it sound like a date." She slapped her money on the counter.

He brushed it away.

She breathed deeply and drummed her fingers on the glass. "Take my money, Des." She slid the cash across the counter.

"You know what I think?" Desiree asked, looking at Leila while ignoring Adler. "I think if someone is this determined to pay for you, you should just let him. Your refusal has already hurt his ego, but we both know it takes a guy with brains to know when to give up. Trust me. That's not Adler. There's only one brain he thinks with, and it's not the one in his head. Well, the head that sits on his shoulders." Desiree winked.

Leila bit her lips, holding back a laugh. "You're right." She grabbed her money from the counter and turned her attention to Adler. "Thanks, but don't think this means anything." She grabbed her box of baked goods. "Elizabeth and Mrs. Stanzel say thank you, also." She tilted her head at him, said bye to Desiree, and grabbed her coffee before walking out the door and crossing the street.

Adler watched Leila as she left the bakery, then turned to Desiree. "I'll take two dozen glazed donuts."

Desiree chuckled. "I can't believe it." She shook her head and started boxing up the donuts.

"What?"

"You like her." The first box was filled, and she started on the second one. "I thought you were acting weird yesterday. I couldn't quite put my finger on it, but I see it now."

Adler leaned on the counter and shook his head. "No, it's not like that" He really hoped he sounded more convincing.

"Yeah, well fine, but promise me two things."

What could he possibly promise her? "What?" He turned and faced her.

She held up one finger. "One. Let's not be weird when we see each other. We need to be friends always."

"Of course. It won't be weird, and friends sounds great," he promised.

"I'm not done. That was all in number one. Two. Leila is a sweet, innocent girl. Don't hurt her. She has her daughter and will always choose her."

Adler took a step back. Daughter? Did he hear that right? His heart plummeted in his chest, and his hands became clammy. He rubbed them on the back of his pants, shaking his head as he dug through what he knew about Leila but came up blank. He'd never heard that she had a daughter. She hadn't said a thing.

A laugh escaped from Desiree. "You look like you just found out she's a serial murderer. I'm guessing you didn't know she's a mom."

He stared and hoped his heart would start up again. "Why didn't she ever say anything? She never mentioned it."

Desiree shrugged. "Don't know. But Skylar's only about four months old, and she's adorable."

Leila's face swam across his mind. He didn't know why, and he sure as hell couldn't explain it, but it was like she was the North Pole, and he was a compass. He was constantly being pulled in her direction and couldn't help himself. But a baby? Wow. That was something he didn't expect.

Leila was almost to the door of the boutique when she heard footsteps on the concrete behind her.

"Leila, wait!"

She glanced over her shoulder. Adler. Really? What did he want? She stopped abruptly and tapped her foot on the pavement. There was no way he found her interesting, and even if he did, the feeling sure wasn't reciprocated.

He caught up and walked next to her.

She raised a brow, glanced at him, and stopped steps from the boutique door. "What do you want?" She stood firm, and her gaze did the same.

"Look, I don't know what I did to make you dislike me, but I'm sorry."

He was sorry?

Before she could formulate a response, Elizabeth got out of her car and walked toward them. "Morning, Leila." She turned to Adler. "Adler. What brings you by?"

"Hi, Elizabeth. I stopped in to pick up some pastries for the office and happened to run into Leila while I was in the bakery."

God, some people. She gritted her teeth and turned her attention to him. Frustration fueled her. "Man, Adler. Your ego's ridiculous. I told you at her wedding that I wasn't interested. I tried my best to ignore you at your house. I was rude to you just now at the bakery. You can't be this desperate. When will you get the hint that your type doesn't interest me?" Her hands went up even though they were filled with pastry boxes.

Elizabeth grabbed them out of her grasp.

"Thank you, Liz. They're for us. Adler bought them."

Elizabeth puckered her lips. "Thanks, I guess?" She looked between Leila and Adler.

Leila shrugged. "Look, thank him if you want. I don't know what his deal is. He's with Desiree, but he's flirting with me. It doesn't make any sense, and anyway, I'm not interested in guys like him."

"First of all, Desiree and I aren't together, and second, please stop talking about me like I'm not even here." Adler's words were short and clipped.

She was getting to him. Probably not something he was used to. Good.

"Anyway, if you're not interested in guys like me, what type of guy are you interested in?" he asked, the clipped words replaced by amusement.

God, this man. "Not someone who's egotistical, self-centered, and thinks all girls will fall at his feet."

Adler looked between Elizabeth and Leila. "Yeah, well I promise you, not all girls fall at my feet. I know of at least two who are really good at ignoring my advances."

Elizabeth gave a small laugh and touched Adler's arm. "I'm sorry. But if it makes you feel any better, you were a complete gentleman when we met. You knew my situation and didn't try anything that I might not have been okay with." She turned to Leila. "When we met last summer, Adler was nothing but a gentleman, if that helps your impression of him any." She shot him a smile. "Come on, Leila, we've got to get to work." She pulled Leila away. "Bye, Adler."

Leila gave him a small smile.

"Goodbye, ladies." He answered.

Leila gave an exaggerated eye roll and let Elizabeth pull her toward the store.

"So, what's all that about?" Elizabeth jerked Leila's arm gently.

"If I only knew." Leila glanced over her shoulder. Adler stood there and shot her his sexy, toothy grin, then turned and strutted away.

Leila spun around quickly. *Don't think it. Don't think it.* She didn't think it but instead pictured his ass and how satisfying it looked in those pants.

She closed her eyes tight and tried to shake the image from her mind by answering Elizabeth's question. "I have no clue what that's about. As you and everyone else knows, we met at your wedding. It all started when Desiree asked me to dance with him so she could get things cleaned up. Then the garter fiasco." Her palm met her face, causing her to talk through her hand. "I've seen him a couple of times since then and . . ." And what? He boiled her blood with his condescending remarks? He set her heart skipping with a touch of his hand? She didn't have an answer, so she just shrugged.

"Well, I think he likes you." Elizabeth wiggled her brows.

Leila stopped walking, and her stomach fell. "He doesn't like me. There's nothing about me that someone like him would be remotely interested in." *Elizabeth is crazy. Almost as crazy as Adler.*

"I don't know. He's sure noticed you, so he must see something interesting. Anyway, why do you say he wouldn't be?" Elizabeth used her key to unlock the door.

"His type is like Desiree. Hot, amazing, tattooed, and a little bit bad. You know?"

The girls walked into the store and flipped on the lights as they went. "I don't know. He was interested in me, and I'm not any of those things. I understand why you wouldn't trust him, since you don't have a good track record with guys like him, but I think you might be misjudging him and throwing him in with Skylar's dad." Elizabeth held up the box of pastries. "Think about it. I'll go put this in the office. Hand me your purse. I'll put that away too, and you can start opening the front."

"Thanks." Leila handed Elizabeth her purse and turned on the radio, buzzed around flipping on lights, unlocked cabinets, and completed all the other small tasks they had to do before they turned the sign to open. But her mind kept going back to Adler.

Chapter 7

Elizabeth and Leila met Jessica at the Crisis Pregnancy Center after work for the volunteer meeting with the board about the yearly fundraiser, which was going to consist of a festival on Main Street, with vendor booths and a silent auction. The main event of the night would be a live auction. They'd already received a donation of a motorcycle from a supporter who no longer rode it, a zero-turn lawnmower from the local landscaping business, and a freezer full of beef from Warfield Meats.

Deloris Green, the director of the center, stood in front of the small group. "This is a wonderful start. We already have many vendors who've paid for booth space, and once we get donations from the town for the silent auction and a few more live auction pieces, I think this will be a very successful fundraiser for the center." She paused and looked around. "Anyone else have ideas for the live auction?"

"Why don't we auction off services?" Charlotte Parks spoke up.

Melanie Harper, next to her, clapped her hands. "Yes. I've seen live auctions like that before. People come up on stage, and if they are a girl or two who want to offer babysitting services, everyone would bid, and the highest bid gets their services for whatever it is they're offering." She looked around. "There could be babysitters, house cleaning, outside work, lawn care, landscaping, you name it."

"That sounds great. You can count the youth group in," said Tom Baggett, the youth pastor of the Christian church. "I'll place them in groups, and they'll go around helping lots of people."

Everyone started talking and speaking up with great ideas.

Deloris raised her hands to get everyone's attention. "This is great. Charlotte, can you make the flyer to get out around town and on the website? We'll make sure everyone's signed up by the end of the month. We'll have plenty of time to get everything together by the first of August." She glanced around the room. "Don Warfield, the owner of Warfield Meats, has offered to donate the food. One hundred percent of the proceeds from his food truck will be donated. He's also donating the tent and tables for the food area. So," she dusted her hands together. "It looks like the main food is taken care of. We also have an ice cream truck, and the coffee shop will be setting up their coffee bistro, not to mention vendors with food and drinks."

"This is going to be the biggest fundraiser we've ever had," said Melanie to Charlotte. "How exciting."

They said a prayer, and the girls got up to leave. Elizabeth, Leila, and Jessica talked together as they stood in the parking lot.

"I say we volunteer the guys to do some manual labor. Brady, Chad, Jacob, and maybe even Tristan would do something, I'm sure," said Elizabeth.

"Oh, I agree," answered Jessica. "What could we do, though? We need to do something."

They all got thoughtful for a moment. What could they do? Leila chewed on her bottom lip, then shrugged. "I'm sure we'll think of something, but I've got to go home. We can talk about this Sunday after church."

Elizabeth's face lit up. "Good, so you'll be going to lunch with us again?"

"Yep," agreed Leila. "I'm going to take Sky back to my house first and feed her, then my dad and Diane said they'd be happy to watch her."

"Good to hear. And how are you doing with that?" Jessica said as she placed her arm around Leila's shoulders.

Leila chuckled. "Diane is adamant that I leave Skylar with them more, but I still have such a hard time. I told her I don't want to be a burden."

"A burden?" replied Jessica. "What do they say about that?"

"Diane told me to get over it. Skylar's their granddaughter, and it's what grandparents do." She put her fingers up and did air quotes.

Elizabeth smiled. "That's the truth. My mom and Brady's parents can't get enough of Grant. Take advantage of the help and free babysitting. It's good for everyone," Elizabeth said.

"I know," Leila agreed. "And I'm going to try my best to do just that."

Jessica gave Leila a squeeze. "Good to know."

Elizabeth wrapped her arms around them. "I'm glad everything's working out so well for you."

"Thanks." Leila returned the hug. "Now I really have to go. I want to put Sky to bed, and I've got work in the morning."

Skylar screamed her head off the entire drive to the downtown square the next morning. Thankfully, it was less than five minutes, because by the time Leila parked and got her out of the car seat, Skylar was hiccupping from the amount of screaming she'd done.

"Skylar, come on, baby. It's okay. What's all this fuss about?" Leila cooed as she swept her daughter up and swung the diaper bag over her other arm. She bounced Skylar as she walked into the store.

Skylar was still red-faced and gasping as Leila entered the boutique and walked toward the back.

"Oh, my goodness." Elizabeth rushed around her desk and took the diaper bag from Leila. "What's wrong with her?"

Leila sighed. "I don't know. It was just one of those mornings where the car seat was seen as an evil monster, and she wanted no part of it." She got comfortable in the glider and prepared to nurse. "I just hope she's hungry, then she should go to sleep and maybe sleep for a few hours."

Elizabeth gathered her laptop from her desk. "Well, you relax. I'll open up, and as soon as she's set, come on out." She walked to the door. "No rush."

Thirty minutes later, Leila walked to the front of the store with the monitor hooked to her waist. "Thank you so much, Liz."

Elizabeth swiped her hand through the air. "Not a big deal. Remember, I've been there." She worked on her laptop at the front desk while Leila assisted the customers.

About noon, Leila was walking with a customer to the checkout, her arms loaded with clothing, when the bell over the door rang.

Elizabeth raised a brow, and a smirk grew on her face. She bent her head quickly to her computer.

Leila quirked the corner of her lip. *What was that look for?* She placed the customer's selections on the counter and had started to ring her items up when she noticed Adler. He stood at a rack of bracelets, looking interested in the inventory. Leila froze for a split second. *What's he doing here?* She glanced at Elizabeth with a raised eyebrow.

Elizabeth shrugged one shoulder.

Ignore him. Leila made small talk with the customer in front of her, trying to stay focused and not be rude. Soon the lady's purchases were paid for and bagged up. Leila gave her a sweet smile. "Thank you for shopping with us. Have a wonderful day."

"Oh, honey, I will. You were so helpful. Tell Barbara, Iris stopped by."

"I will," Leila promised.

Iris gathered her bags and caught Adler's eye as she walked past. Adler was walking toward the counter and nodded his hello at the older lady, then his eyes caught Leila's and a smile filled his face. "Hey."

Iris stopped, turned around, and gave her a thumbs up while she fanned her face in the universal gesture of "he's hot." Elizabeth sniggered next to her.

Leila closed her eyes briefly and breathed. *I have no clue why he's here. This is getting ridiculous.* She pinched her lips together before speaking. "What's up, Adler? What brings you in?"

He placed two bracelets on the counter. One had silver beads with a dolphin charm, and the other had light pink beads the shape of roses with a sterling silver plaque that said, "You are enough!"

Leila met his eyes. She had noticed this bracelet when she put it out. She loved the colors of the roses. Pink and white roses were her favorite. They represented royalty, friendship, and her favorite—first love. The saying on the silver plaque spoke to her, even though sometimes she didn't know if she believed it. She turned it over to read the back. Engraved there was a bible verse that had kept rearing its head since she found out she was pregnant with Sky—Psalms 139:13-14. It was her favorite.

She cleared her throat before she spoke and noticed suddenly that she desperately needed some water. "These are both so pretty. Are you getting them for someone special?"

Adler shrugged. "Haven't decided yet. Which one would you choose?"

She narrowed her eyes at him while she rubbed the bracelet mindlessly.

Elizabeth jumped in. "I know you didn't ask me, but we put those out yesterday. The one Leila's holding caught both our eyes. The rose beads are beautiful, and the saying is perfect, not to mention the verse on the back. It's something we all have to remember."

"That's good to know." He took the bracelet from her and flipped it over. "For it was you who formed my inward parts; you knit me together in my mother's womb. I praise you, for I am fearfully and wonderfully made."

Leila's mouth dropped open, and her eyes went wide. What? Did he just quote the scripture verse from memory?

Elizabeth turned toward her, brows raised.

A smirk crossed Adler's face. "You don't think I know the Bible? My mother and father go to church regularly. This is my mom's favorite verse, and she made sure I knew it."

"Interesting." Leila watched him through narrowed eyes. She still didn't totally trust his intentions, but there was something about him. Something more than his chiseled good looks, or his large brown eyes, which melted into her soul.

"Do you like the pink roses?" he asked, looking at Leila.

Her eyes popped wide. "What?" Her voice cracked, so she cleared it. *Get yourself together.* She breathed deeply.

The corner of his mouth curved up. "Pink roses, do you like them?"

"Honestly, pink roses are my favorite." She smiled. "They symbolize sweetness and elegance. And they're the rose of royalty. I think red roses are so overrated. These are perfect."

Adler placed the bracelet on the counter. "Well then you sold me. I'll take them both."

Leila raised her eyes to meet his. "Really?"

He smirked and nodded. "Yeah, really." He pushed them toward her and slid her a card for his payment. "So, I see you close at five-thirty. Would you be able to grab a quick bite to eat before you head home?"

Leila stopped mid-receipt tear and pointed to her chest. "Me?"

He chuckled. "Yeah, you. There's no one else around."

Leila turned to say something to Elizabeth, but at some point, her co-worker must have left. She hadn't even noticed. How long had she been here alone with him?

A soft cry reached her ears, and Elizabeth came up front with Skylar in her arms. Leila's smile reached her ears as she reached for her daughter. "I can't. I have Skylar." She laughed a deep chest laugh. Adler's eyes were huge and frozen on Skylar. She talked through her laughter. "Adler, meet my baby girl, Skylar. Sky, meet Adler."

Adler's eyes traveled over Skylar, and he slowly raked his hands through his hair. "She's cute. How old is she?"

"Almost four months." Leila bounced her gently. "So, I won't be able to go to dinner." *I doubt you still want to eat together*, anyway.

Adler grabbed his bags from the counter. "Sure, you can. I'll meet you back here at five-thirty. I'll have sandwiches from the deli, and we can eat quickly out at the picnic table by the parking lot. You can have her in her stroller. It's going to be a nice night."

Skylar wasn't a deal breaker? She snapped her mouth shut. "No, I can't have you do that."

"Yeah, you can. It's not a big deal. It's just a sandwich and a drink. Then, you can go home. I'll see you at five-thirty." He winked and left.

Leila was dumbstruck. She passed her eyes over Skylar. Her heart thumped hard against her chest. Why was he so persistent? What did he want? She shook herself as Elizabeth's laugh made her focus. "I figured once he met Skylar he'd run for the hills, and this weird interest in me would evaporate." She shrugged. "I guess not. How can I get out of that dinner? He doesn't take a hint."

"Seems as if Mr. Cassanova has taken a real interest in you."

"Yeah, I see that, but why? I'm not his type. He has a thing with Desiree. How can a guy go from her—tattooed, hot, sexy, and loud—to me?" She held her free arm out wide. "I'm a single mom who has zero tattoos, doesn't party, has never been drunk, doesn't have one-night stands, and hot isn't a word anyone would ever use to describe me. I'm just plain and normal." She sat hard on the stool behind the counter. "All I want to do is be a mom, go to work, go home, and lead a happy life."

Elizabeth just smiled and shrugged. "Sometimes you'd be surprised who could give you a happy life."

"Yeah, well, I'm sure he and I have different definitions of fun."

"Maybe, but give him thirty minutes of your time tonight. You never know. He might surprise you." Elizabeth reached over to wipe slobber from Skylar's mouth. "Either way, you'll get a free meal out of it."

"I guess, but he's really wasting his time. I am *so* not interested." Leila shook her head and huffed out a breath as she bounced Skylar on her hip. *A free dinner, and thirty minutes of my time. That's all he'll get from me, ever.*

Chapter 8

When Adler left the boutique, he ran home to clean up and change out of his Warfield Meats polo. He pulled on jeans and a T-shirt before combing his fingers through his hair and brushing his teeth. He leaned on the bathroom sink and looked at his reflection in the mirror. "I can't believe she really has a baby. Do you really want to go there, Warfield?"

When Desiree told him about Skylar, he wasn't sure how he would take it, but there was something about Leila that surprisingly overshadowed the fact that she was a mom. She was beautiful in an everyday way. She had a natural beauty that needed no makeup, and her hair lay in waves around her shoulders, which made him want to run his fingers through it and see if it was as soft as it looked. And those sun-kissed freckles across her nose. . .

Adler shook his head at his reflection, and his stomach made a weird move. "I don't know who you are. You're acting all weird over a woman—with a baby." He closed his eyes and focused on his breathing. He needed to get his thoughts straight before he left. His feelings were on fire. She was different. She was special, and he had to make sure she knew it.

Tristan and Stacey were sitting at the kitchen table with a pizza between them when he walked out of his room. "Hey, Ad, want some?" Tristan offered.

Adler grabbed a Coke from the fridge and popped open the can. "No thanks. I'm heading back to town."

"Going out with Desiree?" Stacey asked.

"Nope. I haven't been seeing her, remember?" Adler picked up his leather coat from the chair, ignoring them, but he could feel two pairs of eyes following him as he threw on his coat, then sat down to slip on his boots.

"So, where are you going?" Tristan asked.

Could he be any nosier? Adler slapped his hands on his thighs, and a Cheshire grin covered his face. "I've got a dinner date with a sweet and beautiful woman. Not that it's any of your business."

Tristan raised a brow toward Stacey and then turned to Adler. "Sweet woman? Not Desiree? Who are you going out with?"

"Leila."

"What!" Stacey's voice was shrill. "Why are you going out with Leila? I saw you flirting with her at the party, but I figured when Des told you she had a baby. . ."

How does she know what Desiree told me? He cast a searing look in her direction.

She stopped and glared right back. "Yes, she's my friend, and I talked to her. Anyway, I figured once you knew about Skylar, you wouldn't be interested anymore. A mom, especially one like Leila, isn't your type."

His gut heated, and his pulse raced. He was getting tired of people thinking Leila was too good for him. "Whatever. Maybe she isn't my typical type, but there's something about her that gets to me. I even met Skylar today, and she'll be with us tonight. We're going to have sandwiches at the picnic tables on the green way outside the boutique. Not a big deal."

He watched as Tristan and Stacey passed a look between them, and waited for the objection from his cousin. *Come on already and tell me how stupid I am. I've got to go.*

Tristan slapped his hands on the table. "Okay. Well, have fun. Don't let us keep you."

Adler raised his brow. He could tell something else was bothering Tristan because he wasn't meeting his gaze. Dammit. Tristan, his cousin, his best friend, didn't even believe in him.

A frustrated laugh escaped him, and he held his arms out wide. "Look, she's not a fan of the Adler charm, so don't worry about a thing. She can hold her own." He combed his hands through his hair again, getting the organized messed up look he was going for. "Tris."

Tristan's gaze finally met his.

He let out a breath. "I really can't tell you why, but I'm interested in her. I think she's beautiful, and I need to get to know her more." He shot them a grin. "It's all good, I promise. Anyway, if anyone gets hurt, I guarantee it won't be her. I gotta go." He walked into the garage, hopped on his bike, and headed back to town.

Leila locked the boutique's door behind her and noticed Adler as he placed the bags of food on the table. It was not hard to notice him.

His dark hair always had a disheveled yet sexy look to it. He wore his typical T-shirt which suctioned tightly against his skin and showed off his broad shoulders and ripped abs. The sleeves were always short enough so his eagle tattoo peered out.

She took a deep breath and ignored the slight flutter that started in the pit of her stomach. "Come on, Sky. Let's get this over with. It's not like he's going to stick around long. He isn't dad material." She pushed the stroller to the table.

His face lit up when she got closer, and he gave her that lopsided, toothy grin she was sure dropped many girls to their knees. She would not be one of those girls. Not again. Not ever again.

"Here we go, Sky," she whispered as she took a deep breath to calm the thumping against her chest and the fluttering in her stomach, then settled down on the bench opposite Adler. She gave him a small smile with a little attitude. "You actually showed up. I didn't expect you to."

"Ouch. That hurts. I invited you. I certainly wasn't going to stand you up. That would not get you to talk to me." Adler placed four sub sandwiches wrapped in deli paper on the table. He opened each one. "I wasn't sure what you liked, so I got a little bit of my favorites. There's turkey with vegies; an Italian with vegies, mayo, and vinegar and oil; a roast beef; and ham and turkey. You choose."

She chose half of the Italian and grabbed a bag of plain chips and a bottled water. "Thanks."

They were quiet as they ate. Leila kept her eyes down on her sandwich, or on Skylar. His eyes burned a hole through her as she fidgeted on the bench. Finally, she could not take the pressure of his gaze any longer and met it. "What?" It came out soft, yet short and irritated.

He slowly shook his head as took another large bite of his sandwich, a smile playing on the lips of his full mouth. "Nothing," he said after he swallowed, "I'm just glad you joined me." His gaze—dark and sultry—held hers.

Leila narrowed her eyes as she put a chip in her mouth. The corners of his mouth ticked up, and her stomach did a hard flop. She closed her eyes briefly. *Get it together. You don't have time for another egotistical ass. Nothing good can come of this.* She took another bite of her sandwich and gazed quickly at him. She couldn't figure him out. What did he want with her? Why was he here?

Honesty was always her policy, so she might as well just ask. "What's your deal? I've heard about the girls you've been with, and I know all about your relationship with Desiree. I won't be another notch on your belt. That won't happen here." She gestured between them. "Your playboy attitude does nothing to impress me, and honestly, I think you're a conceited, arrogant asshole."

Adler put his sandwich down and wiped his hands on his napkin as a laugh came from the depths of his stomach. A deep and slightly sexy laugh, not that Leila noticed. "Aren't you a single mom? Shouldn't you be sweet and nice—for the baby?"

She smirked and nodded as she took a swig of her water. "I used to be sweet and nice, and this is where it got me." She gestured toward Skylar, asleep in the stroller, making sure he noticed her. How could he miss her? "Now you need to earn sweet and nice from me. And not very many people will succeed, especially not self-absorbed, egotistical, rich assholes."

"Ouch." He placed his hands over his heart and backed up like he was sucker punched. "Well deserved." He raked his fingers through his hair, and a light sigh escaped from his throat.

Leila tilted her head to the side and narrowed her gaze as Adler's joking manner fizzled out in front of her. His shoulders slumped forward, and he chewed on his lower lip. Did her words really bother him? She sat up taller as her gut became all jumbled.

"Okay, the self-absorbed, rich asshole you're talking about surrenders to you and gives you nothing but apologies." He pushed away from the table and knelt in front of her.

Her brows lifted, and a flush crawled up her neck and onto her cheeks. "Adler, what . . ."

He held up one hand and reached for hers with his other. "I apologize for every self-absorbed, rich asshole who hurt you in the past." He bowed his head and brought her knuckles to his lips and kissed her as if she were royalty.

A tingle ran from the spot he kissed throughout her body, causing her to suck in a quick breath. His lips were soft and warm, and a weird stirring started in the pit of her stomach. But she'd learned to ignore those sensations. They never lead to anything good, ever.

She yanked her hand from his grip. "Stand up. You're not helping your asshole status."

He tilted his head. "Interesting choice of words. But you didn't say anything about the self-absorbed part. Maybe you realized I'm not."

"Oh, no. You are totally self-absorbed. There's just nothing you can do about that." She made sure to inject some attitude into her words and tapped into the bitchy side she kept hidden most of the time. "What you consider sweet and endearing I'm sure has worked to get into many girls' pants over the years, but this girl will not be one of them."

Again, that deep throaty laugh rumbled from Adler's chest as he rose to his feet, and heat rose from her groin. She grabbed a napkin and pretended to wipe her mouth to hide the flush, which had now spread to her cheeks. By the time he sat back across from her, she had control of herself and shot daggers from her eyes toward him.

He smiled as he picked up another half of a sandwich. "I promise I'm not here to get into anything of yours but your heart. Right now, though, you're a challenge, and I'm looking forward to getting you to see that not all rich guys are egotistical assholes."

Her heart skipped a beat. *He wants to get into my heart? What?* "Seriously?" She was finished with this conversation and this dinner date. She crumpled up her paper. "How can you go from. . ." She waved her hands in the air, flustered. "Lots of girls, Desiree...to me? It doesn't make any sense."

He took a bite of his sandwich. She watched him chew his food, and her heart beat wildly.

Finally, he smiled, a damn sexy smile, which started a swarm of butterflies to take up residence in her stomach. She really hated butterflies.

"Leila, I can't explain it, but I like you. When we were dancing, something clicked and . . ." He shrugged. "That night, I told Desiree I wasn't interested in her, and that was that."

She sat drinking her water and watching the town come to life as the white lights hanging in the trees turned on and cast a soft glow on the paths. His words hung in the space between them. She didn't know how to respond, so she stood and started picking up their trash and placed the sandwiches they had left back in the brown bag. "Look, this has been nice, but I really need to go."

"Fine." Adler wiped his hands on a napkin and stood also, taking a quick drink of his water. "I'm glad you took the time to have dinner with me. I hope you realize I'm not the jerk you think I am."

This is crazy. She walked the few steps to the trashcan, then came back to the table and stood behind Skylar's stroller. "Look, I appreciate dinner and everything you said, but I'm not interested in a relationship. I only have time for Skylar and work." She released the brakes, and they walked toward her car. It was then that she noticed his motorcycle parked next to her.

"I understand. Thank you for being so honest." He waited as she put Skylar in her car seat and folded the stroller. He then opened her car door.

She shot him a look.

"Sorry. My dad taught me to be a gentleman."

This made her laugh. "A gentleman? Really?"

He gave her one of his winning smiles. "Think what you want. I'll get you to go out with me again. I promise."

"Don't get your hopes up," she answered as she got into her car. "I wouldn't want to destroy that ego any more than I already have."

"Challenge accepted." He winked as he closed her door and hopped on his bike.

Chapter 9

"Okay, we need to form committees to focus on different aspects of the fundraiser." Deloris Green stood in front of the small group of twenty who were assembled at the pregnancy center. "Elizabeth is going to be the emcee for the night, with Jessica organizing the silent auction. Jessica?"

Jessica stood and smiled. "I'd love some volunteers to help me go around to the different businesses asking for donations. The more items we have, the better. I already have a donation of a cruise for two from Planning Vacations. We will use that in our auction. But if businesses can donate baskets, items, and gift certificates, that would work great for the silent auction. So, when we're done, anyone who wants to be on my list to meet Saturday, please let me know."

"Thanks, Jess," said Elizabeth as she stood. "Leila, would you be willing to work with the food trucks and setting up the eating area? The experience you have setting up venues with Desiree will come in handy. We'll need a large tent for the silent auction and the live auction. If we have it under a tent, it will be the focus of the night."

Leila shrugged. "Sure. I'd love to help."

"Great. I'll get you the address and phone number so you can go talk with the tent company."

Leila nodded.

More jobs were given out, and the meeting came to an end with groups splitting off to discuss various aspects of the night.

"Leila."

Leila looked up as Stacey came over to her. "Hi, Stacey. Were you here the entire time?"

"No." Stacey fell into the chair next to the one Leila had got out of. "I just got off work and rushed over. Elizabeth told me she was going to ask you to help with the caterer and setup."

"Yeah, she did. Why?"

"If it's okay with you, I'll help. Tristan's family is in charge of the main food truck and have donated the tents, and since I know them, I thought I could lend you a hand. I can't promise a lot of time, with my work schedule and all, but I do have an inside connection, and I've already taken off the day of the fundraiser."

That made sense and would make things a little easier. "That would be great. I'd appreciate it." Leila was excited to get things started. "Do you think you'd be able to arrange a meeting with them this Saturday? I'd love to see the different size tents they have so I can take notes and decide where everything can take place. I know it's early, but there's a lot to do, and it'll take a while."

Stacey took out her phone. "I work on Saturday, but I can see if Elisha would be available for you." She sent a text. "There, now we wait and see what she says. I'm sure Saturday will work. She doesn't usually work on the weekends. If she does, it's out of her home office."

"Great, thanks." Leila stood and put her purse over her arm. She needed to get home.

"Elisha answered," said Stacey as she glanced at her phone. "She would love to meet you Saturday. Would eight-thirty work?"

"Sounds good. Tell her thanks. I've gotta run."

Saturday morning, Leila was on her way to meet with Elisha Hensley. It was mid-June, and the weather was sweltering. It was going to be a long, hot summer. This was her first summer away from Florida, and she found herself longing for the blue water of the coast. At least when it was this hot in Florida, the breeze off the gulf cooled things off if you were at the beach enjoying the water.

She pulled up to the large wrought-iron gates with the W on the front and pushed the button to announce her arrival. The gates swung open, and she drove through. The sprawling grounds in front of her took her breath away, again. When she'd driven here with Chad and Jessica, it seemed odd that she knew someone who lived within these gates. Now she couldn't ignore the churning of her stomach. Not only did she know someone, but he was showing interest. Their dinner discussion came back to her. He certainly wasn't one to hide his feelings, and he'd said he liked her. She willed her stomach to relax as she pictured him on his knees with his lips on the back of her hand. Heat churned in her gut. *Get a hold of yourself. You don't have time for him.*

The long blacktop driveway, with the perfectly manicured lawn lined with trees and rose bushes, went on for what seemed like forever. Finally, as she turned a sharp curve, the massive turn-of-the-century house appeared. She parked by the first set of garages and stared at the monster house in front of her and laid her wrists on the steering wheel. "What could it have been like to grow up in this type of environment?"

She tried to picture Adler and Tristan running around the yard, playing tag and throwing a ball down the hall of this immense structure. She struggled to imagine Tristan. He was a sweet, laid-back guy with no evidence of overindulgence. On the other hand, she could see Adler perfectly within these walls.

This explains exactly why he acts like he does—or did. She couldn't deny that the guy she'd gotten to know lately was not as stuck on himself as she'd thought he was. Oh well. She had work to do. She climbed out of her car just as a woman was walking through the arched pathway toward her. Her long, straight black hair fell elegantly to her shoulders, and her tan skin looked lovely against her white top and black skirt.

"Good morning. You must be Leila."

Leila shook her hand. "Good morning, Dr. Hensley. Thank you for meeting with me."

"Please, call me Elisha. This isn't work, so we can relax."

"Thank you, Elisha." Leila liked her immediately, and her shoulders became lighter. She trailed behind Elisha as they walked through the stone archway and nearly tripped over her feet as she entered the expansive yard that stretched endlessly in every direction. During the swim party, she had only been at the rear of the property, at Tristan and Adler's residence. The existence of this entire area was a revelation to her.

The lawn was flat and backed up to an endless line of trees. To the left was pastureland with horses dotting the landscape as far as she could see. It looked much more immense than from the view of the guys' pool and grill. There were men standing around talking, and she froze when she identified one of them. His dark hair and broad shoulders made him easy to pick out of a crowd. Adler.

"I'm sorry," started Elisha. "But it seems as if I have something I need to attend to, but I'm going to leave you in the very capable hands of my son, Adler."

Adler turned from the group of men he was in discussion with, and his face lit up when he saw her. Seriously, it lit up. She gave her head a slow, disbelieving shake.

"Leila, hi." He reached out and squeezed her hand in greeting.

Leila needed to get herself together. She wasn't sure why she was surprised to see him here. It was his house, and his family's company was the main sponsor of the fundraiser. She was bound to run into him, eventually. She pushed her shoulders back, held her head high, and pulled her hand from his grasp.

"Hi," she said, making sure her voice was flat and held no emotion.

"So, as I was saying, Leila. Adler will be your go-to for the fundraiser." Elisha placed her hand on his shoulder. "He's been a part of many fundraisers we've held here over the years and knows what his father and I expect. Whatever you need, just ask him. He's to be at your beck and call and is to make sure everything is to your satisfaction and all your needs are met. No request is out of the question."

Adler's brows raised, and he cocked his head to the side.

Oh. My. Gosh. Seriously? She wanted to take back her need to work this part of the fundraiser—and her thoughts that he wasn't as bad as she first thought—but refused to let his ego get to her. She pasted on a smile and hoped her words came out more confident than she felt. "Thank you, Elisha. I'm sure everything will be just fine."

Adler shot his mom a confident grin. "Mom, don't worry about a thing. Leila and I know each other. She's a friend of Stacey's, so I'll make sure she gets whatever she needs and is fully satisfied with my services. We don't want her to get a negative impression of the Warfield name."

Leila glared at Adler. *What's up with him?*

Elisha's eyes closed slightly as they held on to Adler's a second longer. "No, son, we don't." She turned to Leila. "Leila, if there is anything else you need, or Adler isn't helping you, please let me know."

"I will. Thank you."

Elisha smiled and left them alone.

Leila's shoulders drooped forward a little, and her face fell into a frown. "Really?" She walked away from him across the lawn. She had no clue where she was going, but it didn't matter. She had to move.

He quickly caught up with her after excusing himself from the other man he'd been talking with. "What's up with you?"

She shot him a look she hoped might make him drop dead. But of course, she didn't get what she wished for. Did she ever? "You're going to make sure I'm fully satisfied with your services?" She stopped. "You were meaning satisfied with your help with the fundraiser, right?"

His smile ticked up. "What else would I mean?" His eyes held hers, and after a beat he winked.

Her stomach did that flopping thing it really needed to quit doing. "You're despicable." She shook her head and continued toward the pasture. There were horses in the fields. She went to the fence and leaned on it, watching the horses graze. The hills went on forever and seemed to meet the blue sky. She felt Adler's presence beside her. "It's really beautiful. How much land does your family own?"

"A hundred acres or so. This front part is for the horses. The back's for a small herd of cattle."

She glanced at him, and her butterflies came alive again. He looked natural with his boot on the bottom rung of the fence and his arms draped over the top. He was in a Warfield Meat T-shirt and a pair of jeans, and she had to admit, everything about him looked good.

He turned quickly. "What?" That crooked, toothy grin appeared.

She shook her head as a tingle grew in her groin, and her heart fluttered. Dammit, that smile finally got to her. She turned to the fields again, hoping her face didn't give away her feelings.

The summer sun was high in the sky, and the humidity was already thick, causing sweat to pop up on her shoulders. She was glad she'd chosen a tank top to wear with this skirt. It hung loosely around her and didn't stick to her skin. Her hair, though, was stuck like glue to her back. She should have worn it up. She reached behind her and gathered her hair into a ponytail, twisting it around her fingers into a loose bun. Hopefully, it would hold long enough to keep her from looking as hot as she felt.

Adler clutched her elbow and led her over to a large oak tree. The leaves and branches did a decent job of providing relief from the oppressive heat and humidity. There was a wooden bench under the tree. "We can talk about what you need here, or we could go to the main house and sit in the air conditioning. Your choice." He sat on the bench.

Main house? Who uses those words? Even though she was so out of her comfort zone with someone who had so many houses on their property, one was deemed the "main house", air conditioning and a glass of cold water sounded amazing. Being by herself with Adler in the main house was not going to happen. Here was just fine for her.

She sat next to him and took her notebook and a pen out of her purse. "Okay, I need to know how many people you can fit under the tents. We'll need one for food with tables and another with just chairs. A stage will need to be up front, and long tables taking up a side, depending on how many items we have for the silent auction. Once I see how large the tents are, I'll be able to come up with specifics on how we should set up."

He stared out into the fields. "We've had small get-togethers with just over a hundred, to really large gatherings with more than four hundred." He faced her and gestured around him. "We've done so many fundraisers. Most of them have been here, but some have been other places. We can accommodate almost anything you need." His eyes caught hers. "Dream big, and we'll make it happen."

Their gazes locked, and she found herself immersed in the deep pools of his chocolate-brown eyes. It was as if time stopped as they sat there looking at each other. Leila began feeling flush. She blinked and looked away. *Get a grip.*

"Come on. Let's go to the main house and get out of this heat." He stood and pulled her up. As they started walking, he placed his hand on the middle of her back. "Our cook makes amazing sweet tea, and I'm sure he has some cookies fresh from the oven. My dad insists on them almost daily."

Wow. He just said they had a cook. She probably shouldn't be surprised, looking around. Anyway, sweet tea would be perfect. She was slowly melting in this heat. "That sounds great. I'm from Florida, and I'm used to heat, but this humidity is crazy. I guess I was spoiled with the beach not far and the pool we had in our apartment complex. If it was hot, we were either inside or swimming either in the pool or at the beach. This is sweltering."

"Yeah, but hopefully August will be a little better. August nights are nicer. Not as much humidity. That way you'll get a good turnout for the auction."

She followed him up sprawling steps and through a large set of French doors, which led into a bright room with floor-to-ceiling windows. She was in awe of the beauty of the space. The windows brought the light from outside in, and the light gray walls with white cabinets made a clean and airy space out of what was the largest kitchen Leila had ever been in.

The chef, complete with a chef's jacket, was cutting vegetables at the counter. An amazing, sugary-sweet smell filled the air. He looked up from his work as she settled at a large circular table with chairs enough for six.

"Hello, Mr. Adler. How are you?"

"Doing great, Nico. Thanks for asking. This is Leila. We're working on a fundraiser together and came in for some tea and whatever you made that smells amazing." Adler reached into a cabinet and grabbed two glasses, filled each with ice, took a large glass pitcher from the biggest refrigerator Leila had ever seen, and placed them on the table.

"Working on a fundraiser, eh?" Nico glanced from Adler to Leila.

Suddenly, the short skirt and tank top Leila had chosen made her feel oddly uncovered. The knowing look in Nico's eyes sent shock waves through her. She tugged on her skirt as she cleared her throat. How many girls had he seen Adler with throughout the years? Did he think she was just that—another of his one-night stands?

Adler laughed deep and loud as he placed a plate of cookies on the table. "Yeah, funny Nico. My mother handed off the planning and organizing of the Crisis Pregnancy Center's fundraiser to me, and Leila's from the center. You'd better be nice, or you won't be asked to work extra hours for it. I'll get my dad to bring in another chef."

"Oh, you're funny, Mr. Adler. You know your dad won't do that." Nico placed a plate of vegetables and meats on the table in front of them also.

Leila was surprised, as she hadn't even seen him fix it. Oh well. It looked delicious, and she was suddenly famished. "Thank you. So much. This all looks delicious." She reached for a slice of meat and a green pepper.

"Oh, no problem. If you've spent time with Mr. Adler, I'm sure he didn't think of feeding you." He wagged his eyebrows.

Oh, my gosh! Seriously? Leila looked out the window as she took a drink of her sweet tea, and finally Nico left them alone with a deep chuckle.

"Hey."

A slice of green pepper bounced off her head. She shot Adler a death stare. "Seriously? You're throwing food at me?" She picked it up from the floor and placed it on the table. "What are you, a child?"

Adler shrugged. "Sometimes, yeah." He flashed her that smile.

She rolled her eyes, ignoring the stirring in her belly. "What exactly did he think was going on here?" She gestured between them.

"Nothing," Adler mumbled, his mouth full.

She shot him a glare.

He swallowed and took a sip of tea. "Okay, yes. He probably thinks you and I were. . .you know."

"Oh, my, gosh! How embarrassing. How many girls has he seen you with?"

Adler's brows shot up.

"Don't answer that!" She put her hand up to stop him. "I don't think that's something I need to know. Anyway, we have things to discuss. Are you sure you're up for this? You've never planned a fundraiser by yourself."

"You're right. I haven't, but I need to prove to my parents that I can do this. Believe it or not, even though I'm thirty, they have a difficult time giving me any responsibility with the company."

"I knew I liked your mother." Leila pointed a green pepper at him.

"Ha ha. Funny." Adler poured more sweet tea for them. "Let's get back to business. Tell me what you want and let's start planning what you'll be needing."

Chapter 10

Adler walked into Broadway Saloon, a new honkey-tonk in downtown Nashville, with his old college buddies, Daniel and William. It was jam-packed with bodies, typical for a Saturday.

William found them a high-top table and motioned for the server. "It's too bad Tristan couldn't join us. I guess that girlfriend of his has him tied around her finger."

Daniel, his eyes focused across the bar, added, "Yeah. It's been a while since we've hung out. You'd think he'd be here, anyway."

Adler followed Daniel's glance. Three women, two brunettes and a blond, all with long hair and tight dresses, were dancing together in a circle. He shook his head and accepted the beers the server placed on the table. "He said he'd talk to Stacey and see if she wanted to come down. You'll need to get used to her. They're getting serious, and they're really great together."

"Well, I'm glad for him," Daniel replied. "He was never into one-night stands." He gestured toward the three women on the dance floors. "Now there's some hotties—one for each of us."

William smiled wide and raised his beer. "There's fun to be had."

"Hell, yeah, there is," agreed Daniel with his beer in the air and enthusiasm in his voice.

Adler didn't feel the excitement that he usually did. He was here for the guys, but only Leila held his interest, and her brown hair and hazel eyes filled his thoughts. Even though their meeting today had its rocky moments, it ended up on a high note, at least for him. When she left the house, he had her number and a promise that they would talk soon.

"Ad." Daniel gestured to his beer.

Adler blinked rapidly, held his beer high, and took a deep and long drink.

The beer and whiskey shots William ordered helped Adler relax, and soon Daniel pulled another table up to theirs and invited the women to join them. Adler found himself next to the tall blond. She was beautiful, and her black dress left little to the imagination. She had moves, that's for sure, and dancing was simple and fun with her as his partner. The way she moved her hips left him speechless. By the end of the third song, he led her off the floor with his hand on her back. He was warm and needed a drink.

"Hey, there's more people at the table. Do you know them?" Adler followed her gaze and hesitated.

Tristan and Stacy had arrived, but with them were Elizabeth, Brady, and Leila. His heart fell and flipped at the same time. He dropped his arm. "Yeah. It's my cousin and some friends," he yelled in her ear.

His dance partner caught his eyes and flashed a sexy smile, settling in closer to him. He stepped away, trying to put space between them.

"Well, you finally decided to get off the floor and join us." Tristan smacked him on the back in greeting as Adler separated from the python-like grip of his dance partner. "And who is this? You two seemed to be getting along well."

Tristan was being obnoxiously loud. Adler raised his brows. "It's good to see y'all here. This is. . ." He hesitated. What was her name? She'd told him once or twice, but he had no recollection at all of what it could possibly be. He wasn't interested. Luckily, she wasn't shy.

She wrapped her arm around Adler's waist and leaned in closer to the table. "I'm Tabitha, but you can call me Tabby."

That was right. Tabby, like a tabby cat. Adler remembered now.

Adler again tried to move away from her grasp, but room was tight around the tables, and he had no choice but to wrap his arm around Tabby. In answer, she laid her palm on his chest. "Adler is a great dancer. We're having an amazing time together but need a drink."

Daniel handed them each a cold beer and a shot. Tabby handed Adler a shot glass, clinked hers against his, and smiled as she tipped hers up.

Adler's gaze roamed around the table, and as his eyes caught Leila's.

She held his gaze, and her brows lifted in question.

His heart skipped a beat. That wasn't a friendly look. He placed his full shot glass on the table and separated himself from Tabby.

"Drink up, Adler." Tabby patted his stomach.

He pulled his attention away from Leila and smiled down at the girl next to him before tossing the shot down. Maybe the alcohol would calm his heart and make him numb. He didn't like the look Leila gave him. It was as if she was scrutinizing him. Proving all the negative thoughts she had about him were correct. He put as much space as he could between Tabitha and him, but it wasn't much.

The talk around the table increased as the band went on a break, and the bar was quieter with music playing from the speakers. Adler was only halfway paying attention. His gaze kept settling on Leila. No matter how long he kept his gaze on her, she didn't look at him. She seemed to be in deep conversation with Elizabeth and sometimes William. His stomach clenched. That should be him next to her. Finally, Tabby and her two friends left the group and headed for the bathrooms. Adler stretched, enjoying the extra room. Maybe they wouldn't come back, and he could focus on Leila.

Adler grabbed his beer and walked around the table, but William took Leila by the arm and led her to the dance floor. Adler's gaze followed them, and a pit formed in his gut. He sat on the stool just vacated by William, so he could keep an eye on them both.

An arm flopped onto his shoulder, causing Adler to look away from the dance floor.

"What has all your attention?" Daniel's words were slurred. He always was a lightweight. "I think William has the hots for that little cutie. He's been ignoring the brunette ever since your friends showed up." Daniel looked around. "And I think the girls aren't coming back. Their trip to the bathroom was a one-way ticket to leave."

Thank God. His eyes caught Leila and William slow dancing, talking, and laughing on the dance floor. Leila's head tipped back as she laughed. The pit that was in his stomach became a boulder. He swallowed a large mouthful of beer, and his eyes narrowed as they focused on William's hand low on Leila's waist. Memories of dancing with her at the wedding flashed in his mind. That hand on her lower back should be his. Anger and something else that he couldn't identify formed deep in his gut.

Daniel whacked his shoulder. "Hey Ad. You aren't into that little hottie, are you? She doesn't seem like your type."

Adler's heart rate picked up, and it suddenly grew sweltering in the club. He pulled away from Daniel and squared up to him. "First of all, stop calling her a little hottie. Her name's Leila. And some of us tend to grow up at some point. We can't see women as pieces to fuck forever."

He could feel all eyes on him as the table got quiet. It was just Tristan and Stacey with them as Elizabeth and Brady were on the dance floor.

"Hey. Everything's cool." Tristan broke in between them as Leila and William came back to the table.

Adler's gaze fixed on William's arm sitting low around Leila's waist. He had a need and desire to tear that arm off her and replace it with his. Jealousy was a new emotion, and he didn't like it at all.

"I'm getting us some water. Anyone else want anything?" William asked. When no one said anything, just shook their heads, he turned to Leila. Adler watched as his arm squeezed her tight. "I'll be right back."

She gave him a crooked smile.

God, that was sexy. Adler had never seen that smile before and desperately wished it was given to him instead of William. He moved next to her, and the smile faded from her face, making his heart stop. He could feel his temper flaring. Yeah, jealousy, if that's what this feeling was, was something he didn't need to experience. "Looks like you're having fun." His voice was clipped and cold.

Up close, he could see that her cheeks were flushed, probably from the heat of dancing. He didn't want to think it could have been from anything else.

"Yeah, I am. William's a good guy. And he's funny." Leila scrutinized him. "And he knows how to treat a woman. He certainly wasn't gyrating with a stranger on the dance floor."

Ouch. "You saw that?" His voice was soft, and he looked at the table.

"It was sort of hard not to see." A smile returned to her face, causing Adler's heart to skip until he noticed she was smiling at William, who was on his way back with a pitcher of water and plastic cups.

"Hey, I know no one said anything, but I got us a pitcher of water, anyway." He placed it on the table. "And here's some clean cups." He poured water into some cups and handed one to Leila.

She moved a little closer to him. "How thoughtful." He smiled down at her.

Vomit rose in Adler's throat. He grabbed some water to wash it back down. *Yeah, how thoughtful. The jerk wasn't always so thoughtful. He held the record for the most girls in his dorm room. And he was damn proud of it too.* Though Adler wanted to say that, he was more mature now. "Yeah, it's amazing how we can all change when we grow up." He narrowed his gaze at William.

"Problem, Adler?" William asked as he pulled his shoulders back.

Adler shook his head. "No." He took a large swig of water. He needed to calm down. He knew that. But he couldn't help but let Leila know that William's reputation made Adler look like a saint. "I was just pointing out the obvious. We can all change as we mature. Don't you agree, William?"

"Yeah?" He drew out the short word and ended it in a question.

"Adler." Tristan's voice came out like a warning.

Adler ignored it. He was fine. He had everything under control.

"I'm dying. Could I have some water?" Elizabeth asked as she and Brady came back to the table.

Brady took a long swig of water and took in the group. "Is everything okay?"

William wrapped his arm around Leila again. "It would be if Adler would settle down. He's all worked up, and I'm sure it's because his piece of nightly meat left him high and dry. Rejection isn't a feeling he's used to."

Something clicked inside Adler. This would not end well. He squared his shoulders. "I seem to remember when your goal every night was to place more notches on your belt than I ever had." His eyes reverted to William. "And as I remember, you won by a landslide. Last year, when we came here, you were bragging about how many women you had bedded just the weekend before." He was getting worked up, so he took a deep breath and pushed away from the table. He turned toward Leila. "Careful, Leila. He's probably already planned for you to be next."

A spark flared in her hazel eyes, and she stood taller. He'd taken it too far.

William jumped in like he was her knight in shining armor. "Really, being a dick now, Adler?" He squared his shoulders and pushed away from the table.

Suddenly everyone seemed to be ready to separate the two men, but Leila was quicker. "Enough. Adler. Shut up. Just. Shut. Up!" She moved next to William and grabbed his hand. "Come on. Let's step outside. It's getting a little too warm in here." She pulled William away, and they walked toward the door.

Adler stepped away from the table. He needed to follow, but Tristan got in his way. "Let her go. She's not yours, man."

Adler's nostrils flared, and his blood pressure rose. *What the hell!* His breaths came in deep puffs. This was a totally new feeling, and he just wanted to pulverize something.

A smirk grew on Tristan's face. "Well, look at that. Adler can feel jealousy. Seems as if you really like someone. Welcome to adulthood." He whacked him on the shoulder.

"I need to go after her. He's not right for her. I need to make her see that."

"See what? That you can be a dick? Don't worry. I think she already knows that." Tristan turned him back to the table and placed a cold beer in his hand. "I think you need to calm down. Elizabeth and Stacey are checking on her. You're the last person she'd want to see right now."

He couldn't stand it when Tristan was right. He looked up, and his eyes met Leila's across the bar. She was standing with Elizabeth and Stacey, with William close by.

She was next to William but watching him.

His heart skipped, then she looked away.

Chapter 11

"It's so hot." Leila turned the air conditioner of her car on full blast as she got ready to leave the boutique Wednesday night. July had shown itself. It seemed like the entire town had been targeted by a fierce dragon, and its fire scorched everything in its path. Florida never felt quite like this. Maybe it was the slight breeze that always seemed to be blowing off the Gulf. Whatever it was made the never-ending summer of Florida seem bearable compared to the three months of pure hell here in Tennessee.

The car finally cooled off just in time for her to pull into her dad's driveway. She chuckled. Would she ever see this as her house? Whenever she thought of home, she thought of Florida and her mom's house. The one she was kicked out of. Meanwhile, the one she had been welcomed into with open arms was always her dad's or Diane's. Never hers or Skylar's. "You need to start seeing this as your home. You're here for good, or at least for a while until you can figure out how to afford a place of your own."

She walked to the back of the house. It was a simple one-story brick ranch with a small basement. She and Skylar had just moved into the basement now that it was finally finished. There were two small bedrooms, a living area with a small efficiency kitchen, and a tiny bathroom. It wasn't much, but it was a place of their own. As soon as she could afford it, she would start paying her dad rent, then see about saving up to move out. But for now, this was home. She unlocked the door and stepped into her living area. She laid her purse on the tiny table in the corner and walked up the steps to find Skylar.

She could easily enter the house through the garage or front door, but being able to enter through her own little apartment made it seem more like her own place. She found Skylar on her back on the living room floor playing with all the dangling toys on her baby gym. Diane was folding laundry close by.

"Hi there, my little princess." Leila sat on the ground and was greeted with the biggest smile from her adorable little girl. Her heart melted. She loved how excited Skylar became when she saw her. It made her feel like the most important person in the world.

Skylar rolled over and got a little closer, then pushed up on her arms. She was getting so big. Time was going by too fast. Leila picked her up and planted kisses all over her little face. "I missed you so much today. It looks like you and MawMaw had a great time."

"We did. She was such an angel today." Diane gathered her laundry and went to put it away.

"I'm glad to hear that." Leila sat on the couch. "Dinner smells amazing. I smell garlic."

"You have a good nose," replied Diane. "Lasagna, Italian bread, and Caesar salad. It'll be ready in about an hour."

Once dinner was over, and the kitchen was clean, Leila took Skylar downstairs to give her a bath and put her to bed. Then relaxed on her couch with her planning binder on her lap. She needed to finalize what they needed for the auction, and she'd have to get together with Adler again soon.

Adler. She absentmindedly put her pen to her mouth and started chewing on the end. She hadn't seen him since the incident at the bar. She shook her head at the memory. When she'd walked in and saw him dancing with that girl, she had to admit her heart fell. After their so-called dinner date, her feelings for him had softened a little, and they softened a little more after their meeting at his house. She went to the club that night looking forward to talking with him, maybe even getting another dance. But seeing him with Tabby changed those thoughts, and when William started showing interest, she'd jumped on it.

She went out with William a couple of times after that. He was really nice, and they got along well, but there was no spark for her, so that was that.

Her phone rang, pulling her from her thoughts. "Hello." Irritation oozed from her voice.

"Hey. Something wrong?"

She sat up straighter. "Umm. No." She glanced at her phone, but just a number appeared. "Who is this?"

"Sorry. It's Adler."

Her breath caught in her chest. She was speechless. What did he want? Her hands started sweating.

"I haven't seen you in a while. . .anyway, we need to discuss the setup for the fundraiser."

She finally breathed. That's all this was about. "I was just planning things and working through everything."

His deep laughter filled the line. "Look at that. Great minds think alike."

She put her phone on speaker, and they spent the next thirty minutes talking about the tents, one for food and one for the auction. They decided on the size of the stage they needed for the auction, and an area for the silent auction items.

"This sounds great," Adler said, paper rustling through the phone. "I know this sounds strange, but I'd like to draw up some blueprints of each tent and show them to you, then do a dry run with the tents and tables. Make sure you'll like them. There's just over a month, so now's the time to get it down, and small changes can take place the week before. What do you say I work on this and meet you for dinner. . .say. . .Tomorrow?"

Dinner tomorrow. Seriously? She stared at the phone and shook her head. "Is dinner necessary? We can just meet to look at the blueprints. We don't need to have dinner."

"It was just a suggestion. Fine. Where do you want to meet?"

She paused for a moment and thought about what he'd looked like at the club—his tight jeans and T-shirt fitting perfectly—then she remembered the sweet side she saw when they ate at the picnic tables outside the boutique and knew that spending time alone with him at the ranch wouldn't be a good idea. She was becoming interested. Her jealousy at the club was proof.

One thing she realized from her dates with William was that she needed to be picky about who she went out with. Everyone was possible daddy material, and she needed to make sure that her choices in men would be the right ones for Skylar. She breathed a heavy sigh. She'd need to go to the ranch for the dry run, but this meeting could be anywhere, and she would have Skylar tomorrow since the boutique was closed for the Fourth of July holiday. "I don't work tomorrow. We're closed for the fourth. Why don't you come here? My stepmother will be in and out, but we can be comfortable and spread out on the kitchen table." Did she just invite him to her house, knowing they would probably be here alone most of the time? Of course, there was Skylar, so they wouldn't be totally alone.

She heard him clear his throat and shook her head.

"I forgot what the date was," he answered. "Would nine-thirty in the morning work?"

She chuckled. First it was dinner. Now it was morning. He was hoping for a date. "Perfect. Sky should be napping."

"Great. See you then." There was a click, and the line went dead.

Leila puffed out a breath and tossed her phone onto the cushion. "Adler, Adler." She shook her head as she pictured him.

Her phone rang again, making her jump. She answered it.

"Hey. It's not too late, is it?" asked Elizabeth.

"Oh, no. I just got off the phone with Adler."

"Adler, huh? What did the two of you talk about?"

Leila laughed at the questioning tone in Elizabeth's voice. "Nothing exciting. We were working on the tents for the fundraiser, and he's going to get some floor plans together, and we're going to go over them tomorrow morning."

"Good. I wanted to invite you to go to the parade and carnival with all of us. It starts around two-thirty. It's a lot of fun. The parade goes through downtown, and then we'll head to the carnival after, eat a lot of junk food, ride a lot of rides, spend too much money, and watch the fireworks at dark."

A parade, carnival, and fireworks sounded awesome. "Sounds great. I guess I'll just meet you at the parade."

"Yep, I'll let you know exactly where in the morning. See you tomorrow."

Chapter 12

Adler was on his way to Leila's early the next morning. He had her address in his GPS and realized he would be going near the square, so he decided to stop at the bakery and pick up some cinnamon rolls. As usual, it smelled amazing when he walked in. Desiree was busy this morning, as was the square. It was the 4th of July. Adler had thought most stores would be closed, but it seemed that there were a lot of people still going to work.

"Well, look who stopped in." Desiree wiped the counter of crumbs as the last customers left. It was now just Adler and Desiree. "What brings you by? It's been a while." She looked amazing with her hair up in a loose bun and a T-shirt with Main Street Bakery on the front, tied on the side, showing off a little of her fit and tight abs.

"On my way to Leila's for a meeting about the fundraiser and thought I'd pick us up some cinnamon rolls." There were three left. "I might as well take all three." The bell chimed as more people came in. "Why is it so crowded this morning? I figured everything would be closed."

Desiree boxed up the cinnamon rolls. "Most stores are. The 4th of July parade starts around two thirty, and then there's a carnival with vendor booths at the park all day. Tonight, there's fireworks. Most people are setting up at the park." She swiped his card. "As soon as I'm sold out, I'm getting out of here, also. It's always a fun day."

A parade, a carnival, and fireworks. Maybe he'd have to find a reason to stay in town. "Thanks, Des. See you around." He walked out and continued on his way to Leila's.

Leila's house was a simple single-story brick ranch that sat on a slightly sloping lot with a double garage in the front. The lawn was well manicured and had lots of colorful flowers that Adler could tell someone took pride in. Before he could knock, the door swung open and there stood Leila.

A smile filled Adler's face, and his heart sped up. He hadn't seen her since the night at the bar a couple of weeks ago, and she looked—wow! "Good morning. I come bearing food." He held out the white box and willed his blood to flow through his veins and not pool in one area.

The joy on Leila's face matched his. "Come on in." He stepped inside, and she closed the door behind him. "Cinnamon rolls?"

"Yep. I remembered you liked them."

Leila led him into the kitchen and grabbed two plates and forks. "Desiree makes the best." She took the box from him and placed one on each plate. "Want yours heated with a cup of coffee?"

"Sure." He took a seat at the table as a squeal filled the room. Man, that was a high note. He didn't realize humans could squeal like that. He watched as Skylar pawed at a mobile while sitting in a bouncy seat. "Um, is she safe in that thing?" She was bouncing hard and looked like she might take off.

Leila put the rolls in the microwave, then placed some oat cereal on the tray of Skylar's saucer. "She's fine. She has some strong legs. You remember Skylar."

"Of course." Adler did not feel comfortable around babies, but there was something cute about Skylar, and he found himself smiling at her. "Honestly, I've not been around many babies. We have a cousin who lives in Texas. He's older than Tristan and me. I think he's. . ." Adler's eyes rested on the cabinets as he thought. ". . .thirty-six, or around there. He and his wife have two kids, but we hardly see them."

The microwave beeped, and Leila grabbed the cinnamon rolls along with two mugs of coffee and half-and-half. "Sugar's there if you want some." She pointed to the ceramic container on the table. They sat in silence as they ate and sipped coffee.

Adler spent the time looking around the kitchen. It was a nice space. Half was the kitchen, then a small kitchen island separated the kitchen area from the sitting area. The table was surrounded by windows, with the main color being white, allowing the small space to look larger.

"So, do you have the layout of the tables with you?"

Leila brought his thoughts back to the company in front of him, and what cute company she was. She wore leggings and a T-shirt which said I'd rather be at the beach, St. Petersburg, Florida, with a picture of the beach. The nape of her neck, exposed with her hair casually gathered in a loose bun on top of her head, revealed a slender and graceful curvature. The delicate line of her neck was accentuated, creating an alluring and elegant profile. He adjusted himself under the table and reminded himself to focus on his purpose for being there, not on Leila.

Leaning over, he grabbed his briefcase from the floor. "Yep, sure did."

He took out the papers and laid them on the table and moved to the chair next to her so they could both see them better. He glanced stealthily at Leila as she bent over the sketches he'd placed in front of her. She smelled nice, like strawberries and cream. This close, he could make out the beginning of a small red birthmark at the back of her left ear. *I wonder how that* birthmark *would taste.* He imagined kissing her there and again had to adjust his growing hard-on. *Focus Adler.*

"So, what do you think?" he asked.

They spent the next thirty minutes discussing needs and wants—Leila's and the pregnancy center's, not Adler's, though his wants were becoming clearer by the moment. He wanted to touch her ivory skin and trace the path of her freckles across her face. He wanted to brush his fingers through the strands of her hair falling over her shoulders. He wanted to kiss her soft lips.

As a cry from Skylar pierced the air, he took a deep breath, and Leila moved away from him to pick her up and sat in a chair, cuddling Skylar in her arms.

He watched her with Skylar, and something stirred in his stomach. Wow. "Coffee refill?" He got up from the table to put some space between them. He had to slow down his feelings. They were having a great time together. His goal was to keep this going.

"No thanks. I've had my two-cup limit." She smiled that small, crooked smile he saw at the bar.

This time it was for him. *Yes.*

"I'll be right back. I'm going to lay her down. Help yourself to more coffee."

He did just that and leaned comfortably on the counter with his ankles crossed and his mug of coffee in his hand. He thought of her lists of wants for the fundraiser. Nothing would be difficult. He'd make sure they had things set up Saturday morning, and he'd invite her to the cookout he and Tristan were having. Spending an entire day together would be great. He wanted—no, needed—to get to know her more.

"I think we have everything we need." Leila entered the kitchen and leaned over the table, looking at the sketches once again. "Does everything look okay to you?"

His eyes were glued to her ass. Those leggings hugged all her curves perfectly. Yeah, it looked nice. Really nice. "Oh, yeah. Everything looks perfect." He cleared his throat and pushed off the counter.

She sent him a glare that burned into him and threw guilt throughout his body. How could a look make him feel guilty? She didn't know his double meaning. Did she? *Change the subject.* "Desiree told me about the parade and the carnival this afternoon. Are you planning on watching the parade and going to the carnival?"

She shrugged. "I thought about the parade since I can walk just a couple of blocks. I think Sky might enjoy it. The carnival, though. . .I don't think so."

"Aren't there fireworks?"

Leila placed their plates in the sink. "You seem to know an awful lot about what's going on in this small town."

"I talked to Desiree. She told me."

Her brows ticked up. "Really? Still *talking* with Des?"

He didn't miss the stress of the word talking. He caught her meaning. "Honestly, no. I just talked with her today when I got the cinnamon rolls." Adler packed the notebook and papers back into his case. He caught her gaze and held on.

"Be honest with me." Leila didn't move her gaze.

"Of course."

"What really happened with you two?"

He just said he'd be honest, but how could he tell her his heart was taken and not with Desiree? "A relationship wasn't going to work."

"Oh, so Cassanova didn't want to be tied down." Leila rinsed their coffee cups in the sink, then leaned against it.

"Nope." Adler answered. "Not with her anyway." Their gazes locked for a moment, and the need to kiss her overwhelmed him.

Leila pulled her gaze from his and walked toward the door. "Well, thanks for coming over. I think we got a lot accomplished."

He needed a brief second to get himself together, then cleared his throat. "Yeah. I think so too. It was nice spending time with you. Maybe Saturday would work for you to come check out the tents for a dry run, and then you could stay if you wanted. Tristan and I are having friends over for swimming and a cookout. A late 4th of July bash." He stopped next to her at the door. "What do you think?"

She nodded and looked away. "I'll check and see if my dad and Diane can watch Skylar. I'll let you know."

"Great. Thanks for a good time this morning. Maybe I'll see you at the parade." He gave her his crooked, toothy smile. He knew it didn't have the normal effect on her as it did on others, but he didn't want the normal effect. He wanted something real, and Leila was the one he wanted something real with.

Leila's eyes lingered on Adler's shoulders as he walked away, then slowly scanned down to his rear.

"Leila, seriously?" She quickly closed the door and leaned against it. "Not gonna happen. Again, he's not father material. He hardly even acknowledges Skylar. You need to hold out until you find someone better. There's no rush. The perfect man will come along. Someone who wants the best for both of you." She took a deep breath and finished the chores she needed to complete today. Laundry was the first on the list.

As she was hanging clothes, she remembered she had received a text while she and Adler were talking about the tent setup. It was Elizabeth. She and Jessica were meeting in front of the boutique to watch the parade, then planned to grab a bite to eat at the Pizza Place before heading to the carnival. Great. She'd meet them there.

Even though she'd told Adler she wasn't that interested, it did seem like the epitome of small-town life, and she figured if she was going to make this home, she might as well take it all in.

"Okay, Leila, if you plan on going to a 4th of July celebration, you might as well look the part." She changed into a red and white cami sundress and tied her hair with a blue scarf with stars she'd bought the other day at the boutique. She admired herself in her mirror and nodded. "I look cute." As soon as Skylar woke up, she'd bathe her and put her in her red, white, and blue dress, and they'd be ready to go.

Chapter 13

Elizabeth and Jessica were already in the boutique parking lot when Leila walked up with Skylar in her stroller.

"Hey, y'all!" Leila greeted them.

"Hey." Elizabeth gave her a hug and stooped to tickle Skylar. "Hi, Skylar. Don't you look adorable."

"She does," Jessica said as she picked up Skylar from her stroller.

"Where are the guys?" asked Leila.

Jessica tickled Skylar's tummy. "Chad won't be here. He'll try and meet us later at the carnival."

"Brady took Grant to get ice cream. They should be back soon."

The crowd was getting thick when Brady came back carrying a crying Grant.

Grant reached toward Elizabeth. "Aww, baby, what happened?" She rubbed his back as he cuddled into her chest.

"Let's say our little man is not a fan of clowns," replied Brady. "One wanted to give him a balloon hat, and he wanted nothing to do with it."

"Don't worry, Grant. Clowns can be scary," Jessica agreed.

A band could be heard in the distance. "Here comes the band." Elizabeth bounced Grant to the beat as they grabbed a front-row view.

Leila took Skylar from Jessica and held her as the band marched by. She enjoyed herself as she cheered with the crowd at the high school band, which played "God Bless America" and "You're a Grand Old Flag." There were floats and candy being thrown. Grant was given a couple suckers, and they dried up his tears. Skylar's eyes bulged at all the noise and movement.

The girls and Brady walked to the Pizza Place just before the parade was over to beat the crowd. Leila really enjoyed herself. The parade was just as much fun as she'd imagined it would be.

When they reached Pizza Place, it was already crowded. It seemed like most of the town was there, but the four of them and Grant got a booth without a problem. They ate quickly and were on their way to the carnival before too long. Since she'd walked to the parade, Leila walked the short few blocks to the park for the carnival. Jessica joined her, and on the way, they talked about the auction.

"Everything's all set up," Leila told her. "Believe it or not, Adler has everything planned. He came up with some good ideas today for the stage."

"You talked with him today?" Jessica asked.

"Yeah, this morning he came by my house, and we finalized things. I'm going to his house on Saturday to look at the setup and make sure I approve of what he's got planned. It seems like a lot of work to set up tents just to show me, but he insists they do it all the time." She shrugged.

"Sounds like you two have been getting to know each other. Elizabeth told me about your dinner under the trees the other night."

Heat crept up Leila's neck and settled in her cheeks. She turned her head.

"Are you blushing?" Jessica nudged her with amusement in her voice.

Leila bit her lips.

"Oh, my gosh. You are." Jessica's voice was quieter. "Is there anything I should know?"

Leila breathed in deeply. She thought of Adler and how sweet he'd been lately. She still couldn't figure him out. But there was something. "You know, it's a little strange. I don't understand what he's doing. But Elizabeth thinks he's interested in me, and honestly, I get the same vibe."

Jessica's mouth fell open with surprise.

Leila needed to squelch that quickly. "Don't jump to any conclusions. I'm not interested in him, or anyone right now. My focus is Skylar and me. I've got to get our lives together and don't have time to worry about anyone else's feelings or needs."

Jessica's brows raised, and she pursed her lips in thought. "I understand. Your life has changed a lot in the past year. It makes sense that you don't want a relationship right now."

Relief flooded Leila. Knowing that someone agreed with her need to focus on her and Skylar validated her feelings. "Even if I were interested in a relationship, the guy I give my heart to will have to be father material. Not selfish and egotistical. Even though I've seen a different side of Adler lately, he's still too much like Skylar's bio-dad. I don't need to bring another one of them into the picture."

"I get it, and you're right. Anyway, when you meet the right person, you'll know, and there will be nothing you can do about it."

"I hope it's that simple."

"I didn't say it was simple. You'll just not be able to do anything about it."

Leila lifted her brows. *We'll see.*

They made it to the park. It seemed like the entire population of their town and the surrounding ones were all there. It was like she had always pictured a small-town carnival would be. There were kids running everywhere. The sounds of cheers and screams of joy greeted her, and the smell of popcorn and funnel cake filled the air. She loved it already. They found Elizabeth, Brady, and Grant and went off to the kiddie rides.

The night was filled with fun. Leila's dad and Diane hung out with them for a little bit. They took Skylar onto the carousel. Brady played some games, and Skylar's stroller ended up being the home of a few large and small stuffed animals.

Eventually, Jessica went off to find Chad while Leila watched and laughed at Brady, Elizabeth, and Grant on the Scrambler ride, as Skylar bounced on her hip.

Suddenly, a stuffed koala appeared in front of her face. She jumped back and grabbed the koala. "What the heck!" She turned quickly, and there was Adler.

He placed his hand on her arm to balance her. "Didn't mean to scare you."

He had that crooked, almost sexy smile on his face, and his eyes gleamed with amusement. She returned his smile and took in his features. His typical jeans fit him perfectly, and his T-shirt, tonight it was red, was tight and contoured his muscles underneath. Her eyes traveled to his chiseled biceps, and that eagle tattoo, which showed more tonight than usual. Okay, if she was honest, he was hot.

Unfortunately, he knew it.

She put some space between them. "What are you doing here?"

At that moment, Tristan and Stacey joined them.

"Hi, Leila. Hey there, Skylar." Stacey played with Skylar's foot. "I love her dress. It's so cute."

"Yeah, and so patriotic," Tristan agreed. "She looks like a little American flag. She's adorable."

"Thank you, Tristan." She looked at Stacey. "I see you have the sweeter of the two."

Stacey bit her lips while Tristan let out a laugh.

"Hey." Adler held up his hands and shook the koala in the air. "I was going to give Skylar this koala, but that's something only sweet guys would do. So, I guess it's mine." He cuddled it close.

The look on his face caused Leila's heart to skip. Was he really going to give that to Skylar, or did he just say that?

"It doesn't matter. Your mom may not like me, but Skylar, I promise. I'm not a bad guy." He squatted a little to look in her eyes. "Here you go, little beauty." He handed her the koala and closed her arms around it.

It wasn't large, so Skylar was able to hold it and brought it to her mouth. She babbled something at Adler and gave him a toothless grin.

Adler's eyes crinkled at the corners. "She is adorable. See? One of you likes me. Now, Skylar. You need to let your momma know I'm not a bad guy."

Again, she answered him with baby babble and waved the koala in the air. Everyone laughed.

Leila was fixated on Adler's interaction with Skylar. It was adorable, and she couldn't lie. His expression, his smile, was downright handsome.

Skylar stretched her arms toward him.

"Looks like you have a new fan, Adler. She wants you to hold her," Stacey said.

A chuckle came from Tristan. "That would be good. I don't think I've ever seen him hold a baby."

Adler's eyes bulged. "Yeah, that's because I've never held one." He shrugged. "How hard could it be?"

Leila adjusted Skylar. "Let's find out." She held her toward him. "Just take her under her arms and then support her by her bottom. Hold her however's comfortable for you."

"Umm." Adler backed away, and Skylar let out her famous squeal, which could break windows.

"Come on. Try," Tristan encouraged. "You won't break her—well, unless you drop her, so don't do that."

Adler shot him a look and took hold of Skylar. She babbled at him again.

"There you go, and she thinks you're doing just fine." Leila's eyes creased as she backed up a little. Skylar looked totally happy. She giggled and tried sharing her koala with Adler by hitting his face with it.

Adler adjusted her in his arms. "Hey now." He took the koala and held it for her. "See, I got this." He glanced at Leila and wiggled his brows.

Leila's heart stopped, and her hand came up to her mouth. Skylar was happy; it was evident. The more Adler held Skylar and bounced her, the more Leila's heart swelled. Watching them interact with each other caused her vision to become blurry, and she turned her head, blinking quickly as Elizabeth, Brady, and Grant joined them.

Elizabeth's gaze passed between Leila and Adler, who was twirling in a circle with Skylar. "Hey." She placed her hand on Leila's arm. "Looks like Skylar's got a fan."

Leila couldn't answer. Her throat was tight. She gave Elizabeth a small smile and nodded.

"Careful. I wouldn't turn her around too much," said Elizabeth.

Adler stopped and pointed at the carousel. "Want to go on, Skylar? We can get you on your first horse." He gestured to Leila. "Come on. She'll love it. He pulled Leila's arm until she followed him onto the carousel. He stopped by a white ceramic horse. "Hop up on that one, and I'll get on this with Sky."

Leila threw her leg around a brown ceramic horse, while Adler did the same with a baby in one arm. He sat Skylar on the seat in front of him while his arms held her securely. Leila's heart was full. She couldn't remember when she'd been so peaceful and content, probably not since Skylar had been born.

He was right. She did love it, and not just Skylar. Leila did also. "You're really good with her."

"Surprised?"

"Can't lie. Yes, I am."

Adler laughed his deep laugh. "Don't worry. So am I. I've always avoided babies, but. . .I don't know." He shrugged and held Skylar tight as the horse went up and down.

"Well, she seems to like you."

Their eyes locked for a brief moment before Adler looked down and talked to Skylar.

Warmth spread throughout her, and she laid her head on the pole in front of her as she watched the joy on her daughter's face. Adler had surprised her. She let out a sigh.

When the ride was over, Leila took Skylar, and they walked back to their friends. She could feel the pressure of Adler's hand on her back, and her heart fluttered.

"Looks like y'all had fun," Stacey said as they got back to the crowd.

Adler smiled. "Yeah, we did, and I think Skylar enjoyed her first ride on a horse. Maybe soon she can get on a real one."

On a real horse? That would be at his house. Leila wasn't sure if she wanted to do that. "I don't know. She's a bit young."

"Maybe." Adler leaned closer to Leila. She could smell his aftershave. It was very masculine and, yes, sexy. "What do you say you see if someone else can hold her and you go with me on the Ferris wheel?"

Leila's eyes looked up at the tall Ferris wheel. Being alone, that far from reality, with Adler? The fluttering of her heart went into overdrive. "I don't know. . ."

Elizabeth took Skylar out of her arms. "It's okay. You go. I'll hold her. Maybe we'll even take her on a ride with Grant."

"Grant's first date with a girl. I'll chaperone." Brady pulled them to the kiddie section.

"See? Everyone's gone. Just you and me. Come on." Again, his hand was on her back, and he led her toward the line.

As soon as they got there, a seat pulled up, and they were ushered on. Leila had always loved Ferris wheels. She loved heights, and seeing everything from that vantage point always amazed her. "You know, I love being up here. It makes me feel like a bird. Just seeing things from their vantage point is awesome." They stopped at the very top. Her face lit up. This was great. She looked down. "I always thought all the people looked like ants from way up here." She turned toward Adler with excitement in her eyes.

She froze at what she saw. His face was as pale as a ghost, and his eyes were just as wide.

"You, okay?" she asked with concern.

He slowly nodded. His fingers gripped tightly around the bar in front of them, his knuckles white.

A smile grew on her face. "Oh, my gosh. The almighty Adler, fearless with women, actually has a fear."

He glanced at her quickly, with no expression on his face.

"You're scared of heights, aren't you?" She couldn't hide the amusement in her voice.

"No, I'm not." He shook his head, but his breath was uneven.

"Bull. Look at you. Your knuckles are white, and your breathing is fast. You do realize we're totally safe, don't you? We're not going to fall."

He stared off into the distance. "Shhh."

"Look down. Everyone is the size of ants. It's so cool, and everything looks so amazing from here."

He shook his head. "I'll take your word for it."

"If you don't like Ferris wheels, why did you insist we ride?"

"I like them. When they're moving. It's when they stop—at the top—that I don't care for them any longer."

A mischievous grin filled Leila's face. "So, how would you feel if I do this?" She started to rock their car.

Adler went ram-rod straight and gripped the bar tighter, his eyes huge. "Stop, Leila." His voice was calm, deathly calm, but she didn't stop. "Leila. Stop!" His voice became a command, and his hand slapped down on hers and squeezed.

Their eyes met, and both were wide, Adler's with fear, hers with. . .she wasn't sure, but she couldn't ignore how the heat from his hand over hers sent warmth through her body. She moved her fingers to intertwine with his as best she could.

"Okay, I'll stop." Her voice came out in a whisper as her breath came faster. She squeezed his fingers, trying to calm him. The ride jerked to life, and they started to move again.

A shaky laugh escaped her. "There. We're moving."

She could feel him relax, and he turned his hand over and completely intertwined their fingers.

He could have let go. She could have moved her hand. Neither of them did.

Leila looked out over the carnival and focused on calming her breathing. She couldn't focus on anything else because the heat from his touch jumbled all her thoughts.

Finally, it was their turn to get off. The car stopped, and they pulled their hands apart.

She gave him a soft smile. "We made it. Back on terra firma." She stepped out.

He let out a big puff of breath. "Thank God." Again, his hand was on her back. This time, she leaned slightly into it.

"So, was it fun?" asked Tristan as they made it back to the group.

Leila looked from Tristan to Adler and burst out laughing. "He was so scared."

He backed away, his mouth open. "Seriously, you're throwing me under the bus?"

She couldn't stop laughing. "Come, on. It was so funny. The big bad Adler is scared of heights."

"I wasn't scared until you insisted on trying to kill us."

"Oh, come on. I was just swinging us a little bit."

"A little? Really? I think the hinges were creaking and were going to break."

"You're so overreacting."

Tristan slapped Adler on the shoulder. "Well, she knows your weakness."

"Correction." Stacey laughed. "Everyone knows his weakness."

They all broke into laughter, and Adler just glared at them.

"What did we miss?" asked Elizabeth as she and Brady joined them.

Leila gave Adler a sideways glance and winked. "Nothing important."

"Yeah, just my cousin showing his weakness," Tristan replied.

"What?" Brady asked.

"Don't worry about it." Adler took Skylar from Elizabeth's arms. "Come on. It's getting dark. We need to go find a place to watch the fireworks." He walked toward the field.

Leila watched Skylar. She cuddled into Adler's chest, chewing on the arm of the koala. Leila jogged a little to catch up with him. "You good?" she asked.

"Looks like it." He placed his free arm around her waist. "Come on." His mouth ticked up, and her heart swooned.

It was a great night. The fireworks were amazing. They all sat on blankets on a hill with a perfect view. Skylar sat between Leila's legs, and Adler was next to her. Leila leaned back on her hands to look at the sky better, and when Adler did too, their arms touched and she couldn't ignore his closeness, his warmth, or that she noticed the corner of his mouth turn up.

Everything about the night was perfect. The light breeze, which blew away some of the oppressive stickiness of the humid day, the friends who surrounded her, and the man sitting next to her who made sure Skylar wasn't scared.

At one point, Adler took Skylar from between Leila's legs and placed her on his lap, his legs stretched out in front of him. He placed his hands lightly over her ears when the loud booms made her jump. Her eyes were wide at the lights in the sky.

Leila couldn't take her eyes off Adler and Skylar, and her insides flopped as she watched him with her. He was a natural, and Skylar adored him.

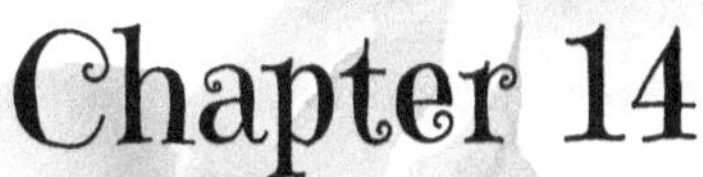

Chapter 14

Too soon, the fireworks were over, and it was time to leave. Adler pushed off the ground with Skylar in his arms. He held out a hand and pulled Leila to standing.

"Thanks," Leila said. When their gaze collided, her pulse picked up speed. They were so close she could smell his cologne, masculine and woodsy. She swallowed hard and rubbed Skylar's hair. "That was amazing. And Sky looks content." She cuddled into the crook of Adler's arm, her koala cuddled close. "I think she might fall asleep."

"She was a trooper," Adler replied.

Leila gathered their blanket and loaded everything into Skylar's stroller. "I can't lie; I'm surprised you held her so long." She took Skylar out of his arms.

Adler pushed the stroller. "I was waiting for her to cry, and trust me, if she did, you would have gotten her back."

Leila chuckled, and they walked behind Tristan and Stacey toward Adler's car. Elizabeth and Brady had already left with a sleeping Grant, and Jessica.

"So," Adler asked. "Where are you parked?"

Leila stopped abruptly as she remembered she wasn't parked any-where. "Umm, I walked here. I totally forgot."

Adler started off again. "Well, looks like you're hopping in with us. Luckily, it's not a far drive since I don't have a car seat."

"No, I can't do that. It's not safe."

"What? Walking home in the dark at night when there are tons of strangers hanging around is?"

Leila shrugged and re-situated the blanket and bag in Skylar's stroller and laid her down carefully as they got to the sidewalk. "It's safer than riding in a car without a baby seat."

Adler sighed. "Fine. I'll take your word for it, as I'm not a parent, but my mom and dad will kill me if I let you walk home alone at night. Lead on, my lady." He bowed and waved his arm through the air.

She stood stunned. *He's hot and adorable.* "Will you stand up!"

"Fine." He stepped around her and pushed Skylar's stroller to-ward the policeman who was acting as a crossing guard. "You can walk home alone at night if you want to, but I'm going to escort the little beauty to make sure she gets there safely. You don't have to follow."

Her heart did that weird-flop thing again. That was the second time he'd called Skylar "little beauty." It was so sweet. *Adorable and sweet—who knew!*

Realizing they were gaining ground, she laughed and ran to catch up with him. "Well, you'll need me to show you how to get her home. You have no clue where you're going."

"Not true. I was at your house this morning. Remember?" They crossed when the policeman waved them on. "I remember passing this park, and I know it wasn't too many turns to your house. Now, which ones exactly might be a challenge, as things do look slightly different in the dark."

She walked next to him, leading. "It's not far. Just about four blocks, but how are you going to get back to your car?"

He stopped and sent a text, then put his phone back in his pocket. That tight pocket, which hugged his ass. *Leila!*

"Problem solved. I sent Tristan your address, and he's going to meet me there and pick me up."

"That seems like a lot of trouble."

"Whatever. You don't have a choice."

She shook her head but enjoyed the attention. A man thought she and Skylar were worth his time, and a man like Adler to top it off. Her eyes traveled over him as they walked in silence. What she saw stunned her. He was perfect. Women gave him double takes all day, and it was obvious why. He could be the portrait in the dictionary next to the definition of tall, dark, and handsome. Add to that the muscles that stretched his shirt and were obvious through his shoulders and back—not overly done, but just enough to make your mouth water—and those biceps which stretched the seams of his sleeves and always left part of that eagle tattoo sticking out.

But also, he was easy to talk to, sweet, and natural with Sky. That was what surprised her the most. When she first met him, she didn't think he was the type that would be good with a baby or even want anything to do with her because of Skylar, but he ended up proving her wrong. What else about him would surprise her? Her heart picked up its rhythm, and she froze in place. She watched as Adler continued walking, pushing the stroller, and talking with Skylar.

She wanted to find out. Was she crazy? *Yes, Leila. Yes, you absolutely are.*

"Ha! I found it." Adler came to a sudden stop and turned to find her a few steps behind. He pointed. "This is your house."

She caught up with him and nodded. They'd made it to her house, and she didn't even realize they had walked so far. She had been distracted. "Wow. You sure did."

"You sound shocked."

She shrugged, and a smirk appeared on her face. "What can I say? I didn't think you had it in you."

His mouth dropped a little, and he feigned looking hurt. "You know there are brains up here." He tapped his head. "I'm more than just muscles and a hot body."

She cocked a brow. Thankfully, it was dark. He wouldn't notice the blush growing on her cheeks. "Yeah, I'm beginning to see that." Her voice was breathy. "Anyway, thanks for walking us home." She took the stroller from him and walked the short distance to the front door.

Adler followed behind, and they stood in front of her house for a beat, their eyes holding on to each other. "So, you're seeing that there's more to me than you first thought, huh?"

"Excuse me?"

He gestured with his head behind them. "What you said back there. You're beginning to see that."

A small smile crept onto Leila's face. "You surprised me with Skylar. You're really great with her, and she likes you."

He shrugged. "What's not to like? She's a lot like her mother. Sweet and adorable."

She couldn't hide the blush that filled her features, and she sighed as she looked away. "I'm not good with compliments."

Adler placed a lock of hair behind her ear, and his hand lingered there. "Well, you'll need to get used to it." His gaze locked onto hers, and he brushed his fingers along her jaw.

His gaze was so intense it caused Leila's heart to pound hard against her chest. She licked her bottom lip as time seemed to stand still and the space between them closed slowly.

Suddenly a car horn blared, causing her to jump back, and the spell was broken. Adler closed his eyes, and a laugh escaped them both.

"Well." Leila had to clear her throat. "I had a great time."

Adler's face shone, and he placed his hand on her arm. "Me too. Will I see you on Saturday?"

She nodded. "Yes. Ten o'clock?"

"Yep, and I want to take you riding, so pack something comfortable, and bring your swimsuit to change into. We're having people over after."

She nodded.

"Goodnight, little beauty," he whispered to Skylar. He kissed his hand and brushed it against her little head, then grabbed Leila's hands and squeezed them in his. "Goodnight, Leila. See you Saturday."

His deep brown eyes melted into hers, causing her stomach to turn to mush. "See you Saturday."

Thoughts of Adler filled her mind as she showered. He certainly wasn't the same guy she'd met back in May at Elizabeth's wedding. That self-absorbed, egotistical man she'd danced with then seemed a far cry from the one she'd seen the past week and especially the one she'd spent time with tonight. There was no trace of the egotistical jerk she thought he was, and he was anything but selfish. The joy on Skylar's face as Adler had spun her around and played with her and that stuffed koala warmed her heart.

Leila peaked in on Skylar. She was sleeping on her side with her little arm around the koala. A smile ticked at the corner of Leila's mouth as she leaned on Skylar's crib. "Pleasant dreams, baby girl." She gently brushed her hand along Skylar's face and heard Adler's voice in her mind saying, "goodnight little beauty." Her insides warmed as she left her daughter to sleep, but she turned at the door. "Love you, bunches, Sky."

Adler grabbed a bottle of water from the refrigerator and settled on the couch as he mindlessly channel surfed. He finally settled on a movie he hadn't seen in a while and laid his head back and got comfortable on the couch as Leila filled his mind.

Everything about the night was amazing because of her. Even the panic on the Ferris wheel was worth it. He balled his hand into a fist at the memory of the warmth of their touch as he grasped her hand in fear.

"Those fireworks were amazing. Don't you agree, Adler?" Tristan asked.

Stacey smirked. "I thought they were, but maybe they weren't the most amazing thing Adler saw all night."

Adler slowly turned his head as Stacey snapped her fingers at him. "Did you say something?" She and Tristan sat in the oversized chair adjacent to the couch. He raised his brows and gave them a look which he hoped would make them leave him alone with his thoughts. Thoughts of long brown hair and hazel-green eyes and the most sweet and most innocent smile he'd ever laid eyes on. But no such luck.

"Just wondering what the most amazing thing you saw all night was." She chuckled. "Gotta admit, I was surprised at how good you were with Skylar."

He pursed his lips and moved his eyes toward the ceiling. *You've brought this on yourself, Adler, but dammit, doesn't anyone think I can change?* A heaviness grew in his chest. "Funny how no one ever thinks anything positive about me." His eyes met hers. "First it was 'be careful, Adler. She's a sweet girl.' Like I'm not good enough to have a sweet girl in my life."

Stacey started to object, but he waved her off. "Then there was a baby, and everyone had shock frozen on their faces when she and I bonded. Look, I realize that because of my past choices it might be hard to think that there's more to me than the playboy persona everyone thinks of when they hear my name, but I want to be loved too. I want marriage and kids. I want someone there for me when things get tough. Why is that so hard for everyone to imagine?" His voice was loud, and his pulse raced. His reaction was probably a bit too much, but it was all true, and he was so tired of everyone not thinking he was worth being with a sweet woman. Okay, he'd probably brought that on himself, but still. If he couldn't have Tristan on his side, no one would ever see he could change.

"Woah, bro." Tristan caught his eyes. "Stacey didn't mean anything by it. We were all surprised that you were so comfortable with Skylar. Admit it, you are too."

Yeah, he was. He had never held a baby before. To be honest, he'd never considered holding a baby before, but Skylar was different. "You're right. Babies always turned me off." His voice grew softer. "A woman with a baby was always a deal-breaker, and honestly, I'm surprised that it wasn't this time. But. . .I don't know. . .when I danced with Leila at Elizabeth and Brady's wedding, something clicked deep in my chest." He pounded a fist over his heart. "She's never far from my thoughts. I want to get to know her, and Skylar's a part of getting to know her."

Another glance passed between Tristan and Stacey. They really must not believe him, or they think he's crazy. Whatever. He knew this was the right thing, and he didn't care what anyone thought.

He breathed heavily. Who was he kidding? He did care what Tristan thought. He was the only one whose thoughts mattered. Tristan knew him better than anyone. "Okay, Calhoun. I see the secret looks you two are passing between each other. The mental telepathy that you both share—creepy, but always there—is bothering me. Be honest. What's on your mind? Do you think I'm crazy? Messing up?"

"You know," Tristan began, "Stacey and I watched you all night. It was quite entertaining."

"Yep," Stacey agreed. "Sure was."

Adler held his gaze on Tristan and lifted his brow.

Tristan sat on the edge of the chair and leaned forward. "Seriously, bro, you were happy. That's what I noticed. You were having a good time and really seemed to enjoy being with Leila and Skylar."

"And. . ." Stacey added, "you looked natural and comfortable with Skylar. With both of them."

Adler was quiet as he thought back over the night. He couldn't remember the last time he'd had such a good time with a woman. Just plain fun, outside, hanging out. Without sex.

He took another sip of water. "Maybe this isn't the right thing to do. Maybe I'm crazy. Or maybe I'm just crazy about Leila." He sat up and leaned forward, like Tristan, but stared at the floor. "I'm crazy about her. She's fun, easy to talk to, beautiful, and calls me out on my shit." He stood. "Skylar's just an added plus. Thanks, y'all. Good night."

Chapter 15

S aturday morning, Leila drove down the interstate toward Adler's. The sun was bright, and thoughts of seeing him made this beautiful day even better. Friday was a long day of work, a doctor's appointment for Skylar, and a meeting at the pregnancy center for the fundraiser. Everything was coming together for the auction, so as long as Adler had the tents squared away, she could sit back and relax for the next two weeks.

She pushed the intercom button at the gate when she arrived. Talk about crazy. One day she found herself homeless and hoping that a father she hardly knew, and his wife would take her in, now she had a guy interested in her and her daughter and he lived behind a large iron gate which opened slowly, allowing her to drive through. Life was strange sometimes.

She drove up the long, winding driveway and went all the way back to the guest house. Adler was waiting for her, and her insides became a jumble of a churning stomach and throbbing heart. He was leaning against a black ATV in tight, faded jeans, a faded red T-shirt which hugged tightly to his body and showed off that sexy-as-hell eagle tattoo, and cowboy boots.

Damn. If she was a dog, she'd be drooling. "Stay focused on the auction, Leila. Business first," she whispered as she pulled up. Maybe she could force her mind to concentrate on the right thing, not on the hot thing standing there with his hands in his pockets, a grin growing on his face, and those dark, sexy eyes. . .*Enough. Focus.*

He was at her door and had it open as soon as she put the car in park.

"Hey," he greeted her.

She found it hard to breathe. He was so close, all man and muscle and pure sexiness.

He grabbed her hand, pulled her away from the car, and closed the door. "Okay. Hop in and we'll go see the tents."

Nothing like getting right to the point.

He led her to the ATV he had been leaning on earlier. "Everything's set up. We'll make sure it's all you want and need, then I want to take you to see the horses and maybe we'll get a ride in."

"Sounds good." She hopped in the passenger seat and held on to the bar in front of her as they bumped along the uneven ground. On the short ride, Adler was all business. He explained what he'd done, the changes he'd made, and what they were going to see.

He was right. Everything was perfect. They walked through the tents, and it was obvious he knew what he was doing. The few changes he'd made would work well. There was a stage for the auction, an area on the other side of that tent for the silent auction items, and the second tent was for dinner and dancing. She hadn't thought of dancing, but like he said, it gave everyone a reason to hang out longer, which would increase the silent auction totals.

He'd thought of everything. "It's perfect. I can't think of anything else we'd need. It's like you've done this before."

"You could say that. I've been to more than my share of fundraisers. Honestly, they tend to get boring. This one, though, seems like the best one yet." His eyes smoldered as he looked at her. Her heart and stomach, which had just gone back to normal, started up all over again. "Let's go. They're calling for storms, but it looks like it should be fine."

"Yeah, one thing I've learned during my first summer in Tennessee: you can never count on the weather. It can rain across the street and be sunny at your house. This weather is crazy, and I've lived through hurricanes."

"Yeah, we'll keep our eyes on the sky, anyway. Right now, though, it looks perfect."

She glanced up, and he was right. The sky had a few puffy clouds, but it was a beautiful blue color. Didn't look like a storm was brewing except far off in the distance. They should be fine.

They hopped back into the ATV, and he took her past the guest house and farther down the driveway. "Have you ever been riding?" Adler asked. His hair whipped wildly in the wind.

"I told you, a little. Never anything serious. Just on trail rides with groups. I'm not a professional or anything."

He chuckled. "That's fine. You'll ride Dandelion. She's the sweetest horse we have."

Just then, they rounded a curve, and her mouth dropped as the largest horse barn she'd ever seen came into view. Not that she'd seen that many.

Adler pulled up in front of the large white barn doors, and Leila's head moved as she took the barn in. "This is beautiful."

"I know something more beautiful."

Leila jerked her head around, and Adler peered at her, his expression hot. Her breath caught in her throat. His gaze dropped to her mouth, and he reached out and ran his fingers through a lock of her hair and rested his hand behind her neck. Her heart beat out of her chest. He was going to kiss her, and that's exactly what she wanted. He slowly closed the space between them. She passed her tongue over her bottom lip and could feel his breath on her face.

"Adler," a voice called out.

"Shit." Adler dropped his head. "Looks like you're meeting Jonathan and Carla, our stable managers."

Leila breathed deeply. *It's for the best. I don't think I'm ready for that.* Maybe if she said it enough, she'd believe it.

Jonathan was the epitome of a cowboy. He was a tall, thin, older man who wore jeans, a plaid shirt, cowboy boots, and a cowboy hat. His wife Carla had shoulder-length brown hair and a wide grin on her face.

"Hi, Adler. I hope we didn't interrupt anything." Carla wrapped Adler in a hug.

"Nothing that hasn't been interrupted before," Adler answered as he moved next to Leila.

A blush crept up Leila's neck and over her face, and Jonathan let out a deep, hearty laugh.

"Jonathan, Carla, this is Leila. Leila, these are the best barn managers around."

Jonathan shook Leila's hand with a pat on her arm. "Let us know if you want to hear any embarrassing stories about this one. We have a bunch."

"Okay, Jonathan. Be nice." Carla pushed her husband away and shook Leila's hand. "Ignore him. It's nice to meet you, Leila."

"Thank you. Nice to meet you both, and I might have to take you up on that offer one day."

"Okay, enough of this. I have horses to introduce her to. Come on, Leila." Adler wrapped his hand around hers and pulled her through the barn doors.

As they entered the barn, the rich earthy scent of hay enveloped them. Leila was instantly enthralled with the comforting atmosphere. At each end of the barn where the doors were open, golden sunlight snuck through, casting a warm glow that danced through the dusty and musty air. Adler clicked his tongue and was answered by a couple of horses up and down the aisle. "Are you the horse whisperer?" Leila asked softly.

Adler's face lit up. "Guess I could be. I grew up in this barn. These horses are like my family." He stopped in front of a huge midnight-black horse. The horse stuck it's nose over the gate of its stall, and Adler scratched it. "Meet Thunder."

"Thunder?" He was huge and, she couldn't lie, a bit intimidating.

"He might be big, but he's really a gentle giant. Go ahead and scratch his nose."

Leila bit her bottom lip and reluctantly scratched his nose. Thunder shook his head and let out a soft nicker.

"See, he's gentle."

Leila wasn't sure she agreed with that but didn't want to say anything negative. She thought she'd heard something about horses being able to sense fear and taking advantage of it. Better to say nothing and act confident.

She followed Adler as he introduced her to more of the horses, then they stopped in front of a brown horse who was not anywhere near as majestic as Thunder. "Leila, meet Dandelion."

"Now, that's a sweet name that seems to agree with this one." Leila confidently scratched Dandelion's nose, and Dandelion nudged her lovingly.

Soon they had the two horses saddled and ready to go. Adler gave her a lift onto Dandelion, and he hopped up on Thunder.

"Ready?" Adler asked.

"Where're we going?"

"Just follow. Dandelion knows this land well. She'll follow behind Thunder. Enjoy the scenery."

And that she did. The sky seemed endless against the green hills thick with velvety tall emerald grass. Again, she noticed gray clouds in the distance, but she wasn't worried about storms. She wasn't worried about anything. Birds swooped over the field, and bees buzzed in the wildflowers growing throughout the pastures. She breathed in deep, and grass and fresh air filled her lungs.

She couldn't remember the last time she had felt this relaxed. Her gaze fell on Adler's back, and the graceful way his body moved with his horse. Her heart fluttered with a now familiar flutter. She also couldn't remember the last time she had felt these feelings for a man.

Chapter 16

She and Dandelion caught up to Adler and Thunder, and when they stopped at the top of a hill, her breath caught in her chest. The hills led to an iconic scene stolen from a painting. There was a pond in the center of the meadow with a large oak tree which was reflected in the calmness of the pond. Next to the tree was an old log cabin whose wood was rustic, yet well cared for.

"It's amazing," she said breathlessly.

"It is." Adler looked up at the sky. "And I think we may actually get some of that rain after all. Come on." He kicked Thunder to a walk.

Leila glanced at the sky, and he was right. What was once blue sky and puffy white clouds a minute ago now churned with thick and gray.

As the horses ambled toward the pond, a flash of lightning was followed quickly by a crack of thunder. The horses picked up their pace to a trot, and Leila grasped the reins with both hands as her body bounced uncomfortably up and down in the saddle. They got to the oak tree just as the sky opened up. Adler helped her down from Dandelion, and they took off for the cabin as a torrential downpour hit.

It wasn't a long run, but it was long enough. They were both drenched by the time they made it to the door of the cabin.

Leila squealed as another crash of thunder boomed overhead, and Adler laughed a deep laugh as he pushed them through the door out of the rain.

"Oh, my gosh. That came out of nowhere." Leila's hair was plastered to her head. She pulled her tank top away from her body. It was suctioned to her as if she'd gone swimming with her clothes on. She shook her arms, trying to get some water off them, and froze as Adler's thick laugh filled the small cabin. "Is something funny?" She asked as she glanced at him through wet lashes.

What she saw took her breath away. His hair was stuck to his head, and he scrubbed his fingers into it, causing water to spray everywhere.

"Hey!" she squealed. "You're worse than a wet dog."

"Really. You should see yourself. You're no better."

She slapped his arm. "Rude."

He moved away from her, laughing.

"Okay, umm." She looked around the small cabin, hoping to find towels or something they could dry off with. There was a wooden bench, two rocking chairs, and a small table with chairs around it. It was a cute area, and surprisingly clean, but also not surprisingly, everything was wood. "This is cute." She said as she walked around the small space. "But there wouldn't, by any chance be towels or blankets?"

"Nope. Sorry."

She walked to the window, which looked out on the large meadow. The horses had taken shelter under the extended roof. It was as if they knew where to go to get out of the rain.

The rain poured down outside, and the thunder continued to crash. Luckily, it was a hot day, so being wet wasn't so bad.

Leila turned quickly and smacked right into Adler. His arms wrapped around her, and her hands rested on his chest. She could feel the warmth of his skin through his damp T-shirt which, when dry, stuck tight to his body. Now that it was wet, it clung to him like Saran Wrap, showing off all the curves and contours of the muscles underneath.

Her eyes left the muscles of his chest and traveled up to his throat and then rested on his lips.

Her breath hitched. She imagined those soft-looking lips on hers.

Her pulse picked up speed as Adler's grip tightened around her, and he pulled her closer. Her pulse continued to race until she needed to open her mouth a bit so she could breathe.

Don't look up any higher. Don't meet his eyes. She kept her gaze fixed on his chin, on the slight stubble that was there. On his lips that parted just a little.

Suddenly his thumb and finger rubbed against her chin, and he was nudging it up, and up, until her eyes finally collided with his.

He was so close she could feel his breath on her, and she could smell his cologne, and damn, he smelled good. Their gazes held each other, and the pull she felt between them on the Ferris wheel and on her porch Thursday night held her in place, and a familiar heat in her gut grew just as it had earlier today on the ATV. The only difference was they had people to interrupt them then, but here there was no one else.

His hands held her face, and his thumbs traced over the bridge of her nose, down under her eyes and over her cheeks. "I love those freckles." His voice was a thick whisper.

Her stomach turned to mush.

The heat searing from his brown eyes melted hers, and she no longer heard the rain against the roof or the thunder crackling through the sky. It was like time stood still as she became caught in those deep brown eyes, like a riptide in the ocean. She was being pulled away from the shore but hoped she wouldn't be released.

All she could think of was closing the space between them, burying her fingers in the hair at the nape of his neck, and feeling those lips on hers. Warmth spread throughout her body as his hand went behind her neck, and he held her tightly.

Then his lips met hers.

The kiss was gentle and sweet, and his lips were as soft and warm as she'd imagined they'd be.

Her heart throbbed against her chest. This was crazy. He wasn't right for her, but she didn't want to stop.

Then he pulled away, and her eyes slowly fluttered open.

Their eyes searched each other again, and she slid her hand behind his neck and lifted up on her toes. She needed to feel his lips against hers again. She pulled him to her, closing the gap between them, and their mouths met again. Not as soft this time, but full of desire. Full of need.

Her mouth opened as his tongue pushed its way in, and their tongues danced together, deepening the kiss.

Her arms wrapped tightly around his neck. One of his arms gripped her tightly against her lower back. The other was grasped behind her neck, and his fingers were wrapped in her hair, holding her tight. Her insides melted under his kiss as a throb of desire tore from her toes to her head.

Their breathing became gasping, and his lips moved down her throat, causing her to arch her neck as a soft groan escaped from her, followed by a deeper, manly one from him.

Finally, his lips found their way to hers again, and they devoured each other as if they would die if parted. Adler backed her up against the wall, and Leila's pulse raced as heat roared to life in her groin.

Adler suddenly broke their connection, but their mouths were millimeters from each other. Leila caught her breath but wasn't ready to be separated from him. She pressed her lips against his again in a long, deep single kiss. They broke away, and he leaned his forehead against hers. She breathed in deeply, needing to get control, and slowly opened her eyes.

His were on fire, desire evident in their depths. "Thank you for that," he said in a breathy voice. He kissed the tip of her nose. "That was more amazing than I had imagined."

Leila backed away a little bit but didn't want to break the spell that tied them together. "You imagined kissing me?"

He ticked his eyebrow up. "Oh, yeah." His voice was raspy. "That and so many other things."

Heat crept around her neck.

"But those other things can wait. This couldn't." He brushed her hair behind her ears and held her head in his hands. "I wanted to kiss you Thursday, but my cousin spoiled that, then today—well, thank you, Jonathan."

A laugh escaped her gut and broke the spell between them. "A kiss Thursday night might have been nice, but this was perfect."

"Might have been nice?"

She shrugged. "Well, you know, then I wasn't sure if I was that into you. You're scared of heights. I don't know if I can be with a guy who's scared of something as simple as heights."

"Really?" Laughter filled his eyes as they roamed her face. He brushed her cheek lightly with the back of his hand. "Thank you."

He became serious, and she leaned into his touch. "For what?"

"You tore down all the tough-guy walls I built around myself and gladly hid behind for years." He cupped the back of her neck in his hands. "You made me fight for you. I appreciate that more than you know."

She swallowed, and her expression grew serious to match his.

"Leila, meeting you has done something to me, made me realize a relationship can be so much more than. . .than just—" He sighed. "Then just sex. I want more with you. I want to spend time with you, get to know you. Get to know Skylar. But there's something I'm scared of more than heights."

"What?" she whispered. This man, who just a few short months ago was an egotistical womanizer, now admitted to being afraid. She placed her hand on his cheek and could feel the stubble against her skin. Scratchy, yet soft. Just like his heart.

He took her hands in his and intertwined their fingers. "I'm scared that you won't be able to see me as someone you can be with." He glanced out the window.

"Hey." She jerked his arm until he looked at her again. "That kiss should have shown you I think differently now. You're so much more than what I thought. Honestly, I think you're surprising yourself too." She stood on her toes again and pressed her lips to his gently, willing him to understand that she no longer saw him as the egotistical, self-absorbed asshole she once did. He was much more than that.

His hands held hers tight, and he touched their foreheads. She could feel him breathing as if he were sorting through feelings. That was good. She needed to as well. She gave him an extra minute.

"The rain stopped," she whispered.

"Yeah, we should go. Everyone will be at the house, and who knows what they'll think." His smile was confident and all Adler once again.

"Yeah, who knows." She grinned widely.

He pulled her hand to his mouth and kissed her knuckles. "Let's go, beauty."

Her heart melted.

Chapter 17

Adler took the ride back to the stables slowly. He didn't want his time with Leila to end. It was a typical July after a harsh rainstorm. Bright, clean, hot, and extremely humid. A dip in the pool would be welcome.

As they rode in silence, he stole glances at her. Most of the time, she was taking in the scenery. How he wished he could get inside her head and hear what she was thinking. Their time in the cabin was better than he had hoped. He silently thanked the storm for making it perfect. He'd wanted, no, needed, to kiss her for days, and things between them were so intense on the 4th of July that he couldn't wait for today to see her again.

He'd dreamed of holding her and kissing her, but the dream was nothing compared to reality. She made him feel things, real things, that he didn't realize he wanted to feel. He had an intense need to be near her, to talk to her, to touch her. He loved the warmth that radiated through him from deep in his gut when they were together. He'd felt it for the first time when they danced at the wedding, then again at the carnival. Today in the cabin, he was drawn to her like a moth to a flame, and he couldn't take his eyes off her. Even now as they rode in silence, and he watched as her body moved in a gentle rhythm with the horse, there was a connection which bound him to her and made his stomach clench with need.

She caught him watching her. "What?" Her smile lit up her face when she uttered that one simple word.

God, she was a picture of perfection, and she had no clue what she did to him. His heart skipped, and he shook his head. "Nothing."

"You're staring at me. It makes me uncomfortable." She looked away shyly.

That made her even more beautiful. The flush that crept up her neck and splashed color on her cheeks when she got embarrassed was endearing. She didn't realize how amazing she really was. "Get used to it. I can't keep my eyes off you." The corner of his mouth ticked up when she turned toward him.

She rolled her eyes toward the sky, and he laughed a deep, guttural laugh. She blushed and squirmed in her saddle.

When they were almost to the stable, he kicked Thunder to a trot, knowing that Dandelion would follow, and quickly dismounted before Thunder got to a complete stop and went to Dandelion to help Leila down.

"Here, let me help you." He placed one hand on Leila's back while he held Dandelion steady. Heat radiated through her tank top, and she smelled of roses.

"Thanks." She patted the horse's neck. "That was a lot of fun. I can see myself doing this again."

He was glad to hear that and stood a bit taller. "I'm glad. You looked like a natural."

She laughed, and the sound rang in his ears. "I wouldn't say that, but it wasn't as bad as I thought." She tipped her head to the side and combed her fingers through her hair. "Gosh, I'm sure my hair's a mess."

Adler lightly brushed her face with his hand and tucked a lock of hair behind her ear. "I think you look amazing." His voice came out as a whisper, yet thick with emotion. She froze, and a small smile grew on her face.

His gaze fixed on her lips, and he placed his hand on the back of her neck and pulled her mouth to his. Heat seared through his chest as the kiss became more intense. She moaned in surprise, but it didn't take long before she kissed him back, deepening the kiss. His heart flipped when her mouth opened and welcomed his tongue. She was delicious. Everything about her was perfect.

Their lips broke apart, and he held her close. "I'm crazy about you, Leila." She stiffened under his touch, but he tightened his hold on her so she couldn't pull away. "I know this seems strange and off." He cupped her face. "I can't explain it, and I'm sure it makes you uncomfortable, unsure, but the moment I saw you at Elizabeth's wedding, everyone else disappeared."

"Stop, Adler. Look, I know there's something between us. I felt it at the carnival and just now at the cabin." She pulled out of his hold. "But you don't need to say those things."

He held on to her arm. He needed her to believe him and to know she was the reason he couldn't be with Desiree any longer. He couldn't be with anyone else. Just being with a woman was no longer enough. "Listen, please." He placed his hand on her shoulder. "Please, Leila." His voice shook.

She turned. Her eyes looked damp, and she bit her bottom lip.

He bent his head to force her to look at him. "You're the reason I couldn't be with Desiree." Her eyes narrowed, but he pressed on. "Yes you. Once we danced, something clicked, and I suddenly needed more out of a relationship than just sex."

"What?" Confusion shrouded her eyes.

"I don't know what I feel, and I sure don't want to rush things, but I know I want to be with you. Just you. I want to get to know you and Skylar more." He rubbed his hands on her arms. "But there's no hurry, I promise. If you'll be with me, we'll take things at your pace."

They stood there, and their eyes locked. His heart stopped. He didn't know why he'd told her this now, but he suddenly needed her to know. This wasn't going to be a sex thing. Sure, he wanted that; he wanted all of her, but he wanted more than a quick tumble in the sheets, and he needed her to understand that.

"If you're not ready for a relationship, if it's still too soon, I'll wait for you. If you want to just spend time getting to know each other, that's what I'll do. I don't want to pressure you into anything."

Now, that was something new for him.

"You really want a relationship with me?" Her voice was a whisper.

"Yes, more than anything." He slid his hands down her arms and wrapped her fingers with his. "And I won't rush you. Just knowing you're mine is enough."

Her face lit up, and she squeezed his hands. "I'd like that."

He released his breath, and his heart started again as relief flooded him. "Thank God. Come on. I want everyone to see me with my girl."

When they pulled up to the house, it was a small group. Really small. Just Tristan and Stacey. They climbed out of the ATV, and he took her hand. "Well, not many people will be meeting my girl."

Leila met his smile. "I guess not. Their loss."

"So true." Adler pulled her to a stop and drew her close to place a kiss on her lips. A long, deep kiss. When they separated, their gazes held until some catcalls got their attention. He ticked up his brow. Her smile was soft and genuine, which caused his pulse to race.

"So, I guess the cabin did its job once again, huh?" Tristan laughed.

"You're blushing," Adler whispered to Leila.

"I'm sure I am. It's still a little new."

He winked and pulled her close.

❦

What a night. Leila totally enjoyed getting to know Tristan and Stacey and being there with Adler. She watched him as he and Tristan joked about things they'd done growing up. He was relaxed and so sure of himself.

She studied him as they talked. She'd always thought he was hot—you'd have to be blind not to think that, with his eyes large and deep, his skin soft and warm, his body muscular and strong, his hair always messy, his smile crooked and wide. He was pure perfection, and he cuddled her next to him with his arm around her shoulder, holding her tight.

But it was getting near dinnertime, and she had been here all day. She had to get home to Skylar. She sat up.

His hand rubbed her neck. "You good?"

"Yeah." She nodded. She didn't want the night to end, but it had to.

"You've got to go, don't you?"

The look he gave her warmed her insides and gave her chills at the same time. She nodded. "I've got to get home to Sky. I told Diane I'd be home around six." She stood, and he followed as she smiled at Stacey and Tristan. "Good night. It was great spending time with you."

Stacey stood and gave her a hug. "Good night. Give that baby a hug."

"I will."

Adler held her hand as they walked to the car. "Can I see you tomorrow?" Adler asked. "Maybe I could come over and spend time with both of you?" He wrapped his arms around her.

She placed her hands on his chest. That hard, warm chest. Butterflies stirred in her stomach. She still couldn't believe he wanted to be with her and her baby. Why would he, when he could be with anyone? She had so much baggage. It wouldn't be easy.

"Hey." He gave her a gentle shake. "You've gone somewhere. You need to be right here."

His voice was calm and caring. She gazed at him, and the familiar pull melted her heart. "You really want to spend time with me, a mother with a baby?" It was hard to believe. "Why? You can have anyone. Anyone who doesn't come with so much baggage."

"Stop." His hands grasped her arms. "I don't know what kind of baggage you think you have, but I know what I think, and I think you *and* Skylar are awesome, and I want to get to know you both better. Enough said." He lifted her chin. "I don't want to hear anything else. Got that?" His gaze was intense, and her heart fluttered.

Should she open her heart and life to him and give him a chance? She really wanted to. The cabin popped into her mind. The kiss, the heat between them, her desire for him. Yeah, she really wanted to.

"Leila?" His voice was a question. His lips met hers.

The kiss sent her head spinning. Her breath became rapid as he pressed deeper into the kiss and sent her to the next level of need, of desire. Her hands slid up his chest and grabbed his neck desperately, pulling him closer.

Yes, she wanted this. If he wanted her *and* Skylar, she wanted him. All of him. He pressed her against her car and deepened the kiss. His mouth devoured hers until it was hard for her to breathe.

Finally, she found the strength to pull away. Her heart pounded in her chest, and her body was warm. She had to go. If she didn't go now, she wouldn't want to go at all, and Skylar needed her. And she needed Skylar.

"I know," he said as he reached around her and opened her door. "You need to go. I'll see you tomorrow. Noon? I'll bring lunch."

Noon sounded great. "I'm looking forward to it," she said as she got in her car.

"Me too." He leaned in and pressed his lips to hers in a kiss that was soft and lingering. "I'll see you tomorrow. Drive safe."

She waved as she pulled out. The warmth that spread through her continued as she drove down the driveway. He liked her. Really liked her. It was like she was living in a dream, and if she was, she never wanted to wake up.

Chapter 18

"I'm home." Leila floated through the front door, and there was Skylar, playing on the floor with Tom. Skylar squealed when she saw Leila, and Leila scooped her from the floor and planted kisses all over her face. Skylar's grin was wide and toothless and melted Leila's heart.

"Someone's in a good mood," Tom said as he hoisted himself from the floor. "I guess you had a good night."

"I did, Dad." She kissed his cheek. "Thanks for watching her."

Diane came in from the kitchen, drying her hands on a towel. "You know it wasn't a problem. She's the sweetest girl ever.'"

"Thanks, y'all are the best."

"Hey." Tom wrapped his arms around them. "We're family. We love you."

Leila relaxed in the warmth of his embrace. "I know, and we both appreciate all you've done for us." She sniffed. "I need to get this baby ready for bed. Good night." She hugged Tom and Diane, and kissed them both, then took Skylar to their apartment.

Skylar quietly played with her koala and sucked on its nose while she cuddled on Leila's lap.

The corner of Leila's mouth ticked up as she thought of the fair and the uncomfortable and unsure look which filled Adler's face when he met Skylar for the first time and gave her the koala. Tears filled her eyes when she remembered how Skylar cuddled against him during the fireworks, when he held her.

He definitely surprised her by being so considerate, thoughtful, and absolutely sweet to Skylar. She let out a contented breath and blinked back the tears. *Get a grip on yourself.*

Even though she'd tried hard to ignore the connection between them at the carnival and the current that ran through her skin when he slapped his hand over hers, begging her to stop rocking the car on the Ferris wheel, she couldn't ignore it anymore.

He was nothing like she thought. His egotistical and self-absorbed personality was just an act. After tonight, she was sure of that. She wanted to get to know Adler better and find out all there was to know about him. He'd pushed his way into her heart, and there was nothing she could do.

Her phone's video call ring sounded. It was eight o'clock. Who could be calling?

She reached for her phone, and warmth flooded her. It was Adler. She took a deep breath and answered.

His handsome features filled her screen, and his smile lit up her world. "Hey, beauty."

She willed the tears to stay away. "Hey."

"Is the little one there? Can you put her on the phone, or is she sleeping?"

Leila laughed. She couldn't help it. Tears filled her eyes. He wanted to see Skylar. After meeting her once, with no reason to be attached to her, he asked to see her. She turned the phone toward Skylar and wiped away the tears that fell.

"There she is. Hey, little beauty."

Skylar let out a high-pitched squeal and hit the phone with the koala.

"She seems to like that koala." Adler released a deep laugh that made Leila relax.

"Yep. She's had it with her all day and cuddled it last night."

"She's lucky. I wish I had something to cuddle."

Leila's breath hitched, and their gazes held each other through the phone. "I wish I did too." Her voice came out thick with emotion as a lone tear fell down her cheek. *Shoot.* She brushed it away quickly.

"What's wrong?" Adler's brow creased.

Leila shook her head. She didn't mean to cry. Damn tears. "Nothing. It's just been. . ." She sighed back more tears that welled in her eyes.

"What? Leila, do I need to come over?"

He would drive the twenty-minute drive for her, to what? She shook her head.

"Leila, don't do this. You're upset. Something happened. Don't lock me out. If you need me, I'll be there."

She took deep breaths to calm herself and sat Skylar on the floor with toys. "Everything's fine, I promise. Nothing's wrong at all." She took a deep, shaky breath. "If you really want to know, I'm just overwhelmed by how lucky we are." She shrugged it off. "I've gotta go. Skylar needs to be changed and fed. It's almost her bedtime. Good night, Adler." She blew a kiss into the phone and hung up.

Leila picked up Skylar and got comfortable on the couch as she prepared to nurse.

There was a knock on the upstairs door, and Diane came downstairs. "Do you mind if I join you?"

Diane was so sweet. Of course, Leila didn't mind. She waved her down.

"I don't mean to pry, but who were you on the phone with?" Diane held up her hands. "You know what? Don't answer that. It's none of my business."

Leila chuckled. "It's not a big deal. It was Adler. You met him at the carnival."

"Adler, which one was he?"

"He wore faded jeans, and a faded red T-shirt. Dark hair."

"Really handsome?" Diane added.

"Oh, my gosh." Leila's mouth dropped as her face lit up and a blush crept up her neck. "Diane. He's a little young for you. Don't you think?"

"Of course, I've got your dad. But he's about perfect for you, isn't he? And from what you say, Skylar's already approved."

Leila changed the subject and filled Diane in on the pregnancy center's fundraiser. The last thing she wanted to talk about was her feelings for Adler. She couldn't put them into words anyway, so she took up some time with all the details of the silent auction and the live auction.

"Knock, knock." Her father walked down the steps.

So much for her usual quiet solitude.

"Sorry to interrupt, but there's someone here who says he's a friend." Tom walked down the rest of the steps as Leila adjusted Skylar over her shoulder and fixed her shirt.

She froze. Adler was there. Her heart leapt. "Adler. What are you doing here?"

"You looked upset." He sat next to her. "I know you said you were fine. But. . .I was worried. I hope you don't mind."

He left her speechless. She shook her head.

He smiled at Skylar. "Hey, Sky."

Skylar gave him her wide, toothless smile, and he took her from Leila and bounced her on his knee.

"You two have fun." Diane smiled and pulled Tom up the steps.

He was here on the floor now with her daughter. She watched as he stacked the blocks and had the koala knock them down. Skylar waved her arms and bounced in response.

Leila laughed. It felt good to laugh. It took a huge weight off her shoulders. "She really seems to like you."

"I don't know. She seems to like everyone." Adler built the blocks up again and made the koala knock them down.

"Maybe." Her voice was soft.

Adler glanced up and caught her eye just as a small tear escaped again. *Seriously Leila?* He jumped up from the floor and wrapped his arms around her.

"See. I knew something was wrong." His voice sounded irritated, and he pushed her back. "Talk to me."

Just at that time, Skylar started crying.

"She's getting tired." Leila picked her up and walked her to the bedroom. Adler followed. Leila changed Skylar's diaper and got her ready for bed before laying her gently in her crib with the koala. She watched her for a bit as her sweet girl settled in for the night.

She gestured for them to leave and watched as Adler stood over Skylar's crib and a small smile filled his face.

"Goodnight, little beauty," he whispered, so low Leila almost didn't hear it. She watched as he kissed his hand and placed it on Skylar's head. Skylar's eyes followed Adler as she chewed on the koala.

A lump formed in Leila's stomach. As soon as the door was closed, tears silently fell. Adler saw and placed his hands on her arm. The heat of his touch calmed her. She was so glad he was here. She melted into his gaze, her eyes shining.

"Tell me what's wrong, and don't say nothing. I can tell there's something. You left me happy, and now you're in tears." This time when he held her arm, he didn't let go.

Leila shook her head. "Trust me, nothing's wrong. Everything's just about perfect. Us living here with my dad and Diane, and you." Her gaze met his. "I don't understand how you could possibly want to be a part of us when you could have anyone you want, yet you want me and someone else's kid? That doesn't make sense."

Adler brushed the tears from her cheek with his thumbs. "Leila..."

She held up her hand to stop him. She needed to say it all while it was top of mind. "You've totally surprised me, and you're so great with Skylar. When we danced at the wedding, I never thought this would be a thing. I never thought you'd be here." She rested her hands on his chest, and warmth radiated into her hand and throughout her body.

He closed his hands over hers. "I'm here because I have to be. Something inside me came alive when I saw you at the wedding. I can't explain it, and yes, I'm surprised that Skylar didn't scare me off, but she's just as amazing as you are."

His eyes searched hers. She could feel them embedding into her heart.

"I'm here because I want to be, and I need to get to know you. I care about you, Leila."

Her heart soared. She gripped his shirt and pulled him closer. They held each other's gaze, millimeters from their lips touching. Her breath picked up, and her hand caressed his face.

"I'm glad you're here. Thank you for coming over," she whispered. She could feel his warm breath on her face.

His eyes searched hers, and he combed his fingers through a strand of her hair. "I'm glad you want me here."

Their lips met softly.

Leila could feel the tidal wave of emotions rolling off Adler and washing her fears and doubts away.

He pulled away and brushed some hair from her face. "Do you think your dad and stepmom can listen for Sky? I'd like to get you out of here for a bit."

She nodded and grabbed the baby monitor. After talking with Diane and her father, she followed Adler out into the night. She didn't know where they were going, but getting out and getting some fresh air seemed like a good idea.

She stopped dead in the driveway. Adler didn't come in his Mustang. He stood in front of his motorcycle. "Umm." She looked at him, then back at the motorcycle, and pointed. "Do you expect me to ride on that?" she asked as fear engulfed her. She didn't like motorcycles, or what she referred to as "death machines." "There's no way I'm getting on that."

He laughed that deep laugh as he hooked a helmet on her head. "Yes, you are. I'll be careful. I promise. And we aren't going far."

She stood there, not breathing, or at least it seemed like she wasn't breathing. She couldn't get on that. She couldn't move.

"Hey." He held her arms.

She moved her gaze from the monstrous bike to his deep brown eyes.

"I'll be careful. Trust me." He dipped his head. "Do you trust me?"

She searched his eyes and felt nothing but trust and safety. His hands caressed her arms. Did she trust him? She pushed her gaze deeper into his. Yes. She trusted him. She nodded, and he kissed her, a quick, gentle kiss which wiped away her last bit of doubt.

Adler climbed onto the bike and straightened it. "Okay. Just get on. Put your feet there and hold on to my waist. As tight as you want."

Hold on to his waist tight. That wouldn't be hard. She swung her leg over the bike, secured her feet, and wrapped her arms around his chest. His warmth instantly relaxed her. She scooted a little closer to him and rubbed her hands over his shirt, feeling his tight muscles underneath. Yeah, she would enjoy this.

"Mm. I like this already," Adler said as he closed a hand over hers. "Hold me tighter if you need to."

She kissed his neck and squeezed him tighter.

He kicked the bike to life, and a tingle started in her groin. Was it from the vibration of the motor, or the closeness to Adler? She didn't know, but she held on tight for the ride.

Chapter 19

A dler wasn't sure where he was going, but with Leila's arms tight around him, it didn't matter. As he rode, her grip loosened, and she relaxed. She still held her body against his, her chin tucked over his shoulder, and occasionally she would rub her palms against his chest, sending electricity through his body which settled in his groin. *Ignore it Adler. Focus on the road.*

He drove on and finally pulled off onto a gravel lane. He slowed, being careful on the rough terrain. He knew where this led and came to a stop at an overlook. He secured the bike and turned off the motor.

"Wow. Where are we? It's beautiful."

Leila was right. It was. This dead-end road overlooked the sprawling valley below. The scattered lights of the small towns glittered like a Christmas village below them, and off in the distance, the light of the moon reflected off the water from the river that meandered through Orlinda Valley, the town that sat between his hometown of Copper Springs and Leila's.

They dismounted from the motorcycle. Adler observed the growing wonder on Leila's face, and a smile ticked at the corner of his mouth.

"It's beautiful." Her eyes danced in the moonlight.

She was breathtaking. The simplest things brought her joy. He looked out over the cliff and saw things differently. It really was an amazing sight, made more so because of the company he was experiencing it with.

He took the helmet from her, laid them both on the bike, and led her to a fallen log. They sat there, and he watched her as she took in the surrounding scene. He could watch her forever, and he wanted to. The thought struck him like a slug to the gut. He inhaled sharply but couldn't deny it. It was true, and it shook him to his core.

"What's wrong?" She turned toward him, and her brow creased.

His smile ticked up another notch, and he brushed her hair from her shoulder, grazing her neck with his knuckles. "Just watching you." His voice came out in a thick, husky whisper.

The smile that played on her lips left him breathless. His gaze fell on those lips, and a need to kiss them filled him. He slowly lifted his eyes to meet hers as his pulse picked up speed. The spell that went between them was broken when Leila looked away. "This view is breathtaking. How did you find it?"

Fuck. He yearned to taste those lips again. To feel her skin under his hands. He was dying with desire for her. He closed his eyes and took a deep cleansing breath, willing his body to calm itself. And shrugged. This was his place. His place to get away from the world. "I like to ride sometimes when I need time to think." He looked out at the sky, and it unfolded forever above them. It was a clear night filled with stars, and the moon was full. "I found it years ago. I don't really remember when, but I come up here a lot by myself. It's like my secret spot."

She turned to him and lowered her eyes. "By yourself? You've never brought anyone here with you?"

He didn't miss the doubt in her voice. "Nope." His gaze met hers. Even Tristan didn't know about this place. "No one. I never brought the guys here to party, and to answer that unspoken question swimming around in that head of yours, no. No girls either. You're the first person I've ever shared my secret place with." His palm brushed her cheek. "It's my place to be at peace and to think. It's hard to be the one everyone expects to have no feelings, no desires, no wants. Up here, I can pretend I'm watching over the world and have all the answers I need. This has always been my refuge." There was nothing left to say. He'd already said more than he'd ever said to anyone, even Tristan. She brought out a side of him he hadn't known existed, didn't realize could exist. In the short time he'd known her, she had already made him a better person.

Leila covered his hand with hers. "Thank you." Her voice was soft.

He raised an eyebrow. "For what?" he asked as he massaged her neck.

"For bringing me here and checking on me tonight. You didn't have to, but you did anyway."

Adler watched as her eyes glistened with tears. "Hey." He wiped a stray tear. "Talk to me."

Leila sighed deeply and blinked quickly as she turned away. "I promise you, nothing happened. I'm just being emotional." She laughed. "I always wanted unconditional love from a parent, but I never got it from my mother. All she gave me was criticism. When I walked into my house tonight, I was overwhelmed with the feeling of home. My dad was playing with Skylar on the floor, and it was so obvious how much he loved her." She breathed a shaky breath. "Then when I was sitting with Skylar, I was thinking of you. How great you are with her. How sweet you've been to both of us. Ben was never like that."

Ben? Ben must have been someone important to upset her this much. He could feel the heat rising in his body. There's no way he'd let any man make Leila feel this bad. "Who's Ben?"

Leila sat up tall. "He's Skylar's biological father and hasn't ever been in her life. He gave me money for an abortion when I told him I was pregnant and has ignored all my calls since I left Florida when I was four months pregnant." Her voice was clipped and a bit harsh.

The sudden tenseness of her body was obvious, and Adler rubbed her back.

"Girls were always hanging all over Ben. He had a nice car and money. He was ruggedly handsome and a smooth talker. When he started showing me attention instead of the other girls, I thought I was something special. As you can see, though, I was wrong. I was thrown out like garbage, and so was his unborn child." She stood and leaned on a tree. "When I got on the plane from Florida, I swore to myself I'd never let myself fall for someone like him again."

Wow. Adler's eyes went wide. That hit hard. It was like a kick in the gut with a steel-toed boot. *That's why she had issues with me when we first met. I'm a lot like Skylar's dad. Or at least I was. I need her to realize I'm not that person. Not with her.*

Adler walked behind her and placed his arms around her waist, resting his chin on her shoulder. "Now I understand why your first impression of me was negative. I promise I'm not really egotistical, or self-centered, or an asshole. I just played one for a while." She leaned back in his arms, and he relaxed against her. Good. Maybe she did see he was different.

She turned around and flashed a small smile. "I know. You proved I was wrong about you."

His crooked smile emerged, and he raised his left brow. "I'm glad." He tightened his hold on her. "And I hope you know I'm nothing like Ben, and I will never not want you or Skylar."

Leila wrapped her arms around his neck.

He feared he might scare her off telling her all that, but she was still here, with her arms wrapped tightly around him. The warmth of her skin seeped into his pores. He breathed deeply and inhaled the strawberry of her shampoo and the rose scent of her perfume.

His pulse raced, and he finally did what his lips had been begging for since they got off the bike. He kissed her.

Slow and tender at first. He loved the softness and warmth of her lips. His tongue swept inside her mouth and tangled with hers. Then carnal need took over. He deepened the kiss, and she leaned into it and threaded her fingers in his hair, causing a moan to escape from his throat. God, he needed her. He needed this. He pulled her neck closer with one hand while his other found its way beneath her shirt and touched her bare back. Shock waves filled his body from the warmth and silky softness of her skin.

His need to feel all of her took over, and his lips left hers and traveled down her neck. His tongue delicately explored her skin, and he playfully nipped her shoulder.

"Adler."

The breathy whisper of his name from her caused his pulse to race even faster. He shifted just enough so his hand on her back found its way to her stomach and up. He stopped as he traced his fingers along the edge of her bra. She shifted just enough so he could cup her soft breast in his hand. He throbbed with anticipation. Their desire increased, and his hand pushed her bra up and he touched her soft warm skin below.

The moan and soft "Yes" that escaped from Leila caused his growing erection to push uncomfortably against his jeans.

"Leila." Her name came out in a deep moan as his mouth found hers again and devoured it. He couldn't get enough of her. She was sweet and tantalizing. And so irresistible. He ached for her, and their kisses turned desperate.

"God, Leila." He pressed his hand against the soft, warm skin of her breast, then brushed it down along her stomach, relishing in her shudder beneath his touch.

His breath was coming in gasps, like he'd just run a marathon that he didn't want to end. He rested his forehead against hers, his eyes closed tight, and tried to memorize how soft her skin was under his touch and embed in his mind her warm and tender kiss. "I can't get enough of you."

When he finally opened his eyes, hers were soft and watching him. Her smile ignited him all over again, but he fought the urge to devour her, to tear her clothes off and take her right here. She was worth more than that. Yes, he wanted her. He needed her, but not here. Not now. Not until he was sure it was what she wanted, that he was who she wanted. When they had sex, it would be special and perfect, and possibly forever.

Leila held on to Adler's waist as they flew down the road. She was already getting used to the free feeling of riding on the back of his bike. Maybe it was the closeness and warmth radiating from him that made it easy for her to relax. Her body was still reeling with the feelings from his kisses and his touch. His lips on her neck, his tongue on her skin, his hand on her breast. She shivered thinking about it.

The ride didn't last nearly long enough before they were getting off his bike in her driveway. He started up the front walk, but she stopped him. "It's late. Let's go around back." She grabbed his hand and led him to the back of the house and the door that led to her and Skylar's apartment. "If you come over, you can use this door." She unlocked it and let him in. A dim light was on in the corner.

Adler entered the small room but didn't leave the tiny entryway.

"Take a seat. I'll be right back." She went to check on Skylar. Seeing that she was sleeping peacefully helped her heart to feel at ease. She went out and expected to see Adler on the couch, but he was still in the entry. "What's wrong? Why aren't' you coming in?" She held his hands in hers. Her heart sped up at his touch as his warmth seeped into her skin and calmed her heart some more.

His hand went up to her neck and held her head. "I can't." His eyes held hers.

Her heart fell. What had happened since they had left the over-look? The spark between them was unmistakable, and she was sure he felt it also. Every time their skin touched, or their eyes met, her skin tingled. Maybe she was mistaken.

"I don't understand why you don't want to stay. I know we have a connection. I know there's something here." Maybe she misread him. Maybe it was just how he was. But she didn't believe that.

The corner of his mouth ticked up in that sexy crooked grin, causing her stomach to flutter. "Oh yeah, there's something here. That's why I'm not coming in any farther. If I sit on that couch and kiss you, I won't stop." He squeezed her hands. "You have a lot to sort through, and I don't want us to rush into anything. We have all the time in the world. I promise."

A soft chuckle left her. She couldn't believe that Adler, the playboy, the ladies' man, had just said that to her.

He raised a brow.

She chuckled. "I can't believe you're the same guy I danced with a couple of months ago. The guy who acted all sexy and gruff when he slid the garter on my leg. The guy who I was told was a player and took girls to bed with no expectations."

His eyes left hers and stared at the floor. She saw the muscles in his jaw clench. He shook his head and opened his mouth to speak.

Quickly, she covered it with her hand. "It's okay. I'm sold on this new Adler, and after tonight, I'm pretty sure this is the real you. The one who doesn't have to be someone he's not." She removed her hand and wrapped her arms around his neck and stood on her toes so their eyes could meet. "This Adler is sweet, and kind, and loving, and hot." She brushed her lips against his in a soft, gentle kiss. "Thank you for showing me this side of you," she whispered.

He kissed her lightly. "Thank you for bringing this side of me out."

They stood there basking in the warmth of each other's presence for a beat.

"I have a question." Leila took a breath and bit her bottom lip.

"What's up?"

"I'd love to see you tomorrow morning. Would you meet me at church?" She held her breath, not sure what he'd think of that. Was church even something he did?

Adler's brows popped up. "It's been a while since I've been to church." He shrugged. "Sure. If I get to spend more time with you, there's nowhere else I'd rather be."

She released her breath, and her face lit up. "Great. It starts at eight-thirty. Text me when you get there."

"I will. Now I really gotta go."

Leila reluctantly agreed. If he stayed much longer, they wouldn't be able to resist the temptation growing between them. She kissed him lightly and closed the door behind him, making sure to lock it tight as she leaned against it.

She wrapped her arms tightly around her body. "That was amazing. He is amazing." Her heart swelled as memories of Adler and his kisses, his touches, filled her thoughts. The most amazing thing was he thought of Skylar also. "How did I get so lucky?"

She pushed away from the door and was on cloud nine as she brushed her teeth and got ready for bed.

Chapter 20

"Where are you going at this hour" Tristan asked as he filled his coffee cup and eyed his cousin, "dressed like that?"

It was eight o'clock on Sunday morning, and much earlier than Adler usually crawled out of bed on the weekend. He understood why Tristan was so confused but ignored the interrogation as he leaned around him, filled a to-go cup to the top with coffee, then adjusted his gray tie. "I'll see you at the Pizza Place after church. I'm sure you're meeting Stacey there. I figured Leila and I would come by and eat with you. Save us a seat." He slapped Tristan on the back, smirked at the shocked look on his face, grabbed his coffee, and left.

He had the top of his Mustang down and enjoyed the warm mid-July breeze as he drove down the interstate. The morning was thick with humidity, and the clouds were low and gray, like it might rain. Before long, he pulled into the parking lot of Community Church, where Leila attended, found a spot to park, and closed his roof just in case. He adjusted his tie again to loosen the constricting feeling it gave him and combed his fingers through his wind-blown hair. His heart raced nervously.

"Calm yourself, dude. It's not like you've never been to church before. You did grow up in one." Yeah, he had, but it had been a long while since he'd walked through the doors of any church. He took a deep breath, lifting his shoulders as he climbed out of the Mustang. "Relax, it's not like you'll be hit by a bolt of lightning."

He sent Leila a text and stepped out of the car as a small roar of thunder sounded. He glanced up at the darkening sky. "Okay then, maybe a lightning strike is a possibility." He picked up his pace and followed the small crowd through the glass doors and down a hall. They had to know where they were going.

Large doors opened ahead, and there she was. Leila looked beautiful in a yellow and white flowered sundress that fell just above her knees. When she saw him, the corners of her mouth lifted, which caused his heart to race. Her tanned skin looked soft and perfect against the yellow of the dress, and the green of her eyes popped.

He gave her a tight hug and kissed her gently on her cheek. Was that appropriate? He wasn't sure. This was church, and the last time he'd attended a service, the only woman he wanted to hug was his mother, and his grandma if she was with them.

"I can't believe you actually came." She squeezed his hands.

"I promised you I'd be here." He wasn't that much of a heathen, was he? "It's been a while, but this isn't my first time inside a church, and I'll take any reason to spend more time with you."

"I'm glad you're here." She pulled him into the sanctuary, and they found seats behind Jessica, Chad, Jacob, and Kristen. He said hi to them and didn't miss the surprised looks they gave him. *Seriously, I'm not that bad of a person.*

A giggle escaped from Leila as they sat down, and Adler shot her a look, which caused her to smirk and wink. That was sexy. Adler had to force his attention to stay on the front of the church, to the hymns, the prayers, the Bible readings, and the message from the pastor. It was difficult. So many other things caught his attention. The church was a traditional church with cushioned pews and an altar up front, a lot like the church he grew up in.

When the service was over, they walked hand in hand to the nursery, and Leila signed out Skylar while Adler waited in the hall.

He watched as people passed by, many acknowledging him with words of good morning or head nods, and after a bit of smiling awkwardly to total strangers, Leila came out with Skylar in her arms. She was the most adorable baby with her soft, dark curls around her face, and her light hazel eyes, exactly like her momma's.

He stepped next to Leila as she walked down the hall. "Hey, little beauty."

Skylar let out a squeal of joy.

"That's such a high note she can reach." He shook his head.

Leila laughed, her face lighting up. "Yeah, well, she only greets you that way."

He pursed his lips and reached for Skylar's finger, but instead of getting her finger, she leaned toward him, shaking her arms.

Leila stopped in the hallway. "I think she wants you to hold her."

Adler lifted Skylar from Leila's arms and placed her at his side before he walked outside. The rain had stopped, and the sun was out, causing the summer day to be hotter than usual and thick with humidity. "Come on, let's get you into an air-conditioned car quick. It's *hot* out here." Adler shook his head when he said hot, causing a belly laugh from Skylar. "Her laugh is adorable." He smiled wide and said "hot" again the same way. She gave another belly laugh.

"It's so funny what makes her laugh. I really don't understand it." Leila unlocked her car, and Adler opened the door.

He waited until she got Skylar strapped in the back seat, then twirled her toward him before she could get in the car. "I was thinking." He brushed her hair from her face and stared at her. His gut clenched as she stared at him. It amazed him how she made him feel. Like there was no one else in the world but her. "Why don't we skip the Pizza Place today and grab a bite to eat and go back to your house. Enjoy the day together. You, me, and Skylar. Do you want pizza or sandwiches?"

"Sandwiches would be great. That Italian you bought last time was mouthwatering."

"I know something else that's mouthwatering." His gaze held hers, and their connection was hotter than ever. He leaned toward her, and his lips were almost on hers when Skylar let out a blood-curdling scream.

He jumped back as his heart leaped in his chest. "Shit."

Leila laughed. "You'll get used to her need for attention." She climbed into her car.

When Leila got home, she laid Skylar on the floor to play and cleaned up the kitchen. For a place that held just two people and one didn't do anything yet, things grew messy rather quickly. She made her bed, picked up clothes, swept the floor, and just finished cleaning the kitchen when there was a knock at her door. She opened it, and there was Adler leaning against the doorjamb. He pocketed his phone and gave her a sexy-as-hell grin. He had his tie off and his top button unbuttoned. He looked relaxed and damn sexy. Her heart swooned. "Hey."

"Hey, back," he answered as he stepped in, wrapped his arms around her, and covered her mouth with his.

The kiss was sweet and deep. It took her breath away and left her weak in the knees.

"I've wanted to do that since I first saw you this morning." He brushed his thumb along her jawline.

There was a whoosh deep in her stomach. "Well, it was worth the wait."

"You're worth the wait."

She could feel herself start to blush, so she pulled him in and closed the door.

"There she is." Adler set the bags on the counter and went to Skylar and swooped her in his arms. She squealed with excitement.

They spent time on the floor playing with Skylar. Leila rested her back against the couch and watched them interact. They were so comfortable around each other, and Skylar was enthralled with Adler.

The feeling's mutual, baby girl. The lightness of Leila's heart was hard to ignore. She would not have believed that of all the men to steal her heart, it would have been this one.

He came out of left field and was determined to get her to see him differently, and, as usual, Adler Warfield got his way. She was head over heels in. . .well it was something, but she was not going to put a name on it yet.

He glanced up and shot his crooked grin at her and winked. Her heart melted, and a shock burned deep in her gut and sparked sensations in her nether region, which hadn't come alive in a long time. Her breathing picked up pace, and when a deep manly laugh came from Adler and he picked Skylar up far above his head, causing her to squeal with excitement, that was it. Everything about this man made Leila want him. Not only was he handsome, sexy, and sweet, he was a natural with Skylar.

Her stomach growled and diverted her attention.

Adler placed Skylar on the floor and chuckled. "Was that your stomach growling?"

"You heard that?"

"Yeah, it was loud enough I'm sure your neighbors heard it."

Leila pursed her lips. "Whatever."

Adler stood with Skylar in his arms, then put his hand out. "We need to eat. You're hungry."

He grabbed her hand and pulled.

"Yeah, I am." When she stood, she ended up inches from him and wasn't sure if it was food she was hungry for, or Adler.

Skylar leaned toward her. Right now, all she had time to be hungry for was food. She couldn't do anything about her other appetite until Skylar was napping.

As they ate, they talked, and Leila fed Skylar sweet potatoes and baby rice cereal. She ate so well, even though the stench that came from the food disgusted Leila, but she wasn't the one eating it, and Skylar sure didn't seem to mind.

"Tell me more about what your dad does." Leila was curious. She knew they owned and operated Warfield Meats and they had acres of land, but it was hard to believe the small herd of cattle they had could lead to a business large enough to give them the ability to live like they did.

He told her all about their company, how many cattle they had in Tennessee and then about their ranch out in Texas. As she listened, it made more sense. Skylar started fussing, so Leila cleaned her with a wet cloth and got her ready for a nap while Adler cleaned up their lunch.

"She went right to sleep. I think all your playing wore her out." Leila watched in awe as Adler cut up fruit. She sat at the counter. "What are you doing, and where'd you get all that fruit?"

He placed strawberries, apples, and peaches in a pitcher that already contained some liquid, stirred it, and poured his concoction into two large wine glasses and passed one to her.

She stirred it around and lifted a brow. "Sangria?"

"Yep." Adler took a sip.

"I didn't take you for a sangria kind of guy." She took a sip. It was really good. And refreshing.

"I'm not, usually. I'm a beer guy, but on a really hot day, sangria tastes good."

She narrowed her gaze and tilted her head. It still didn't seem right.

"Okay." He shrugged. "And my mom loves sangria and taught me how to make it." He took another drink. "I've added some twists of my own, and here you go." He held his glass up. "Here's to us, and an amazing future."

Us? What did he mean by that? "You want there to be an us?" Heat filled her.

Adler bit his lips and placed his glass on the counter.

Leila watched as he walked toward her. Did she turn the air conditioner up too high? It was really getting warm in here.

He pulled her from her seat. "Leila." He held her hands in his. "I want there to be an us, and I really hope it's what you want."

His gaze seared into hers, and the heat from a moment ago ignited throughout her entire body. He wanted them to be an us. The heat ignited a flame. She wanted nothing more right now than him. All of him. "Oh, yeah. That's exactly what I want too." She couldn't hold back from him anymore.

She placed her hand behind his neck and pulled him to her. When their lips met, the flame that burned inside her became an inferno of passion. Their lips devoured each other, and their hands groped and squeezed.

There was nothing Leila wanted right now more than him. She wanted to feel all of him and wanted him to feel her. "Adler." She pulled slightly away and got lost in the desire that radiated from his eyes. Their breaths were heavy. "I want you to make love to me."

He leaned away. "Are you sure? We don't have to."

"Yes. Yes, we do." She closed her lips on his again and kissed him deeply. She made sure he understood her words were true. When she backed away, she pulled him to her room and closed the door behind them.

They stood focused on each other for a beat, then Adler's hands cupped her face. "Leila."

Her body became weak, and she held on to his arms, not breaking their connection. "Adler." She whispered his name.

He kissed her gently, and her heart fluttered wildly. While they kissed, his hands traveled to the straps of her dress, and he slowly pulled them down.

Her heart beat out of her chest, and she broke away. Adler's lips separated, his mouth open slightly, and she felt his breath on her face. She slipped her arms through her straps and watched his face as her dress fell to the floor. She stood before him wearing only navy blue, lace panties.

His stare was so intent as it traveled down her body, like he was scrutinizing every curve, and she became self-conscious. It didn't last long though, as his hands brushed softly against her skin, caressed her side, and glided over her breasts. She shivered beneath his touch, sucked in a quick breath, and exposed more of her neck, pleading silently for his lips to touch her again.

His lips quickly found the skin right below her ear, and a tingle rushed through her. His tongue blazed a trail down her neck and over her breast and fondled her nipple. She couldn't hold back the groan from her throat or his name as it escaped from her.

He slowly found his way back to her mouth and caught hers in an intense and passionate kiss. Before her knees could give out, he scooped her up and laid her gently on her bed.

His eyes traveled down her body, and she wiggled under his gaze, suddenly feeling uncomfortable. She placed her arm across her stomach to hide her stretch marks and the small pooch that was now her stomach. "Don't." His voice was deep and thick, and he gently moved her arm. "Don't hide from me, Leila. Don't ever hide from me. You're perfect."

His gaze on her body made her pulse race, and she gasped for breath. "Come here then. I'm lonely. I need you next to me." Her voice pleaded with him.

He yanked his shirt over his head, unhooked his pants and let them fall to the floor, then climbed on the bed next to her.

He was a work of art. She rubbed her hand against his hard muscled chest and caressed his firm pecs. God, he was flawless. His skin was dark from the sun, and his muscles rippled under her touch. She kissed his chest and heard him take a quick breath. Her gaze traveled over him and rested on his well-defined biceps and the eagle tattoo that adorned one. It was always sexy as it peeked out from his shirt sleeve, but now it was just plain hot. She traced it with her fingers. "This is an awesome tattoo." She brushed her lips against it.

"Leila." He said her name in a deep and throaty voice.

The tingling sensation pulsed between her legs again, and she pushed herself up to meet his lips. Their kiss intensified, and their hands wandered and fondled each other's bodies.

Heat built inside Leila, and she was ready to explode. It had been a long time since she had been touched by a man, and even with Ben, she never desired him like she desired, needed, and wanted Adler. "Adler, please."

"Are you sure?" His gaze burned into hers.

She had never been so sure of something in her life. She needed to feel him inside her. "Oh, yeah." Her mouth ticked up.

Just then, Skylar started crying, and her body deflated. She placed her head on his hard chest. Maybe she'd go back to sleep. "Please, baby girl. Go back to sleep."

Skylar's cries got louder and more demanding. She let out a heavy breath.

"Hey, it's okay. I'll get her." Adler kissed the top of Leila's head and climbed out of bed. He stepped into his boxer briefs and left her room.

Leila laid her head on a pillow and watched the ceiling fan go around. "I can't believe her timing," she moaned.

Disappointment flooded her, but her feelings changed quickly as she watched Adler come back into her room, shirtless, and cuddling Skylar close to his chest. He was whispering to her, and she was totally content and calm. Her head rested on his, and her eyes fluttered closed as the tears dried where they fell.

Chapter 21

I t was finally Tuesday night, and Leila was ecstatic to get out of the boutique and head for home.

She hadn't seen Adler since Sunday, and every nerve ending in her body was at attention whenever she thought of what they almost did. Even though she was exhausted, she couldn't wait to get home. Adler was coming over. Her stomach fluttered just thinking of him.

When Leila pulled into her driveway, his Mustang was already there along with a couple of other cars. Diane was having some of her friends over for book club tonight. They must still be there.

Leila walked through the front door and was greeted with a belly laugh from Skylar. Leila loved that sound. It was a constant source of peace in her hectic life.

The scene in front of her caused her to lean against the door and put her chin to her chest. There were four women seated around the room, and Adler seated on the floor playing with Skylar. He glanced up, and the side of his mouth crept up. "Skylar, look." He pointed toward Leila, and Skylar turned her head. As soon as she spotted her mother, she bounced on her bottom with a wide grin.

Diane and her book club friends sipped wine and were watching Skylar and Adler.

What the heck. In the short time Leila had lived with her dad and Diane, she was always told that no one was allowed to bother book club, especially men. Why was Adler there, clearly where he shouldn't be? Leila laid her purse on the table by the door and sat next to Skylar, scooping her in her arms and plastering kisses on her face, causing Skylar to wiggle and laugh. "Okay, I've got to ask." She scanned the room. "What is Adler doing here? Doesn't he break the 'No men allowed' rule of book club?"

"Well, he hasn't been here long," Diane said. "And as soon as he came into the house, Skylar's face lit up. He sat on the floor and played with her. It was so much fun to watch, we had no reason to ask him to leave."

"And it's so heartwarming to see such a handsome man be so good with a baby," Kaye, a fifty-something married woman, said.

"Absolutely," Tonya, a short lady with long grayish-blond hair, agreed. "Not to mention he's very easy on the eyes."

"Totally agree," Ruth replied as she lifted her wine glass.

Tonya, Kaye, and Diane lifted theirs.

"Book Club!" Ruth exclaimed.

"Woo!" answered the others. They all took sips of their wine.

Leila's eyes became wide as saucers. Which caused guffaws around the room.

Oh, my God. Leila looked at the bar table in the corner. Yep. There were three empty wine bottles, and one was half empty on the end table by Diane. "I am so sorry," she said to Adler, with her hand on her forehead.

He chuckled. "You have nothing to be sorry for. These women are a blast." He leaned over and planted a kiss on her lips. It was soft and deep and lingered.

"Don't mind us, you two. We were young once also," Tonya remarked.

"We're not old, Tonya." Kaye replied as she filled their wine glasses and held up another empty wine bottle.

"Pushing sixty isn't young," Diane said, sipping her newly refilled glass.

"It doesn't matter." Tonya waved her hand through the air. "Age is just a number, and the ability to have fun with a hot man knows no age." Tonya winked at Adler.

"True that." Ruth replied as she clicked her glass against Tonya's.

Leila broke away and shook her head as a blush rose on her cheeks. "What do you say we go downstairs?" She pursed her lips.

"Sounds good to me." Adler rose to his feet and helped her up. "Ladies, it was wonderful meeting all of you."

"Yeah, we're heading to my apartment." She gave Skylar to Diane to say goodnight and rushed quickly out of the room, trying not to hear the comments coming from the book club members.

Adler chuckled as they walked downstairs. "Those are some fun ladies."

"Yeah, they're great." Leila turned on the lights as she got into the living area. "Just a little crazy sometimes." Suddenly she was pulled against Adler. "What?" she asked as she faced him.

"I just want to see my girls."

Her free hand traveled over his chest. Her mouth watered at the memory of kissing that chest. Her eyes traveled up, and her heart skipped. His hair was its typical organized mess, and his shirt was perfectly tight in all the right places. She stepped back to continue her perusal of his body. His jeans clung to his thigh muscles, and his smile was wide. He was a perfect specimen of a man. Tall, dark, extremely handsome, and surprisingly sweet.

"Hey, you done looking?" He brushed her hair lightly from her face, and his hand stopped behind her neck. The warmth of his skin seeped into her body, and a bolt of electricity shot through her.

"For now." Her gaze met his for a beat before his lips covered hers in a soft kiss that caused her surroundings to disappear. He was warm and smelled so good.

Skylar started babbling and patted Leila's cheek. She pulled away from Adler as a grin grew on her face. "I think someone needs attention."

"Yeah, and she's not used to seeing her mom kiss her boyfriend."

Leila pulled in a breath. Her boyfriend? Is that what he thought? Her heart pounded in her chest. He thought that much of her to call himself that? She remembered how he'd called them an "us" Sunday night, and the corner of her mouth crept up. "You're my boyfriend?" She could get used to that.

His brown eyes pulled her in.

"I sure hope so." His gaze was smoldering. "I've thought of you constantly since Sunday, and there's nothing I want more than you and me together." His thumb traced her jawline.

Her heart skipped. "It's only been a couple of days." She tried to play it off like she wasn't concerned, like their time apart wasn't a big deal. But in reality, it scared her how much she thought of him and how much she missed seeing him.

"Really? You didn't miss me?" His hands cupped her face, and his lips claimed hers in a heart-stopping kiss, which made her knees weak.

When he pulled away, she had to remember to breathe. "Maybe I missed you. Just a little." Her voice was a breathy whisper.

"And are you on board with us being an item?"

Everything inside her melted. "Yeah, I am."

His smile met his eyes, and Skylar let out one of her ear-splitting squeals, which could wake the dead.

"Well, I think someone else approves." Adler took Skylar from Leila and sat on the floor and picked up the koala. "Hey there, little beauty. No need to squeal like that. I promise you'll get all the attention you need, and now that your momma and I are an item, I plan on being here more often."

Leila's heart swelled as Skylar's face immediately lit up and she bounced on her bottom, waving her arms with joy. It amazed her that Skylar always had that reaction with Adler. She wasn't the only one who saw him as amazing.

They had a great night. Adler played with Skylar on the floor or held her in his lap, and Leila couldn't tear her eyes from them.

Watching Adler with Skylar filled her with peace. When he caught her watching them, he grinned, and her heart fluttered. His smile caused her to go breathless. This was another perfect night. They laughed at Skylar and talked about so much, Leila couldn't really keep up.

Skylar rubbed her fists against her eyes. She was getting tired. "It's late. I need to get her ready for bed," said Leila.

She and Adler gave Skylar a bath and dressed her for bed.

Leila sat in the glider rocker in Skylar's room with a warmed bottle. She loved watching Skylar eat. Her little eyes closed, making her look angelic. Skylar's fingers closed over Leila's as she held the bottle. It wasn't long before she was sleeping, and the bottle's nipple slipped from her mouth. Leila carefully laid her against her shoulder and patted her back.

"I thought you nursed her." Adler had been leaning in the doorway watching.

"I was, but now I pump more and use bottles." She shrugged, and suddenly a little burp came from Skylar's chest. Leila caught Adler's expression as his eyes got wide. She laughed quietly and placed Skylar in the crib.

"She's an angel," Adler whispered.

"Yeah, she is." Leila nodded.

When they left Skylar's room, Leila grabbed two waters from the refrigerator in her kitchenette and sat on the couch next to Adler. She melted into the cushions as soon as her body hit them and let out a sigh. "This has been a day." She took a deep drink and thought back to work. It had been an unnaturally busy day at the boutique. There was a Christmas in July celebration throughout the stores downtown, and people were taking advantage of the sales and door prizes offered. Even though it was during the week, people were out in droves.

Adler placed his hand on her neck and started rubbing. "You're tight." Her head rolled to the side as he massaged out the kinks in her muscles.

"Here." Adler situated her so she was between his legs. He placed his water bottle on the table and massaged her neck and shoulders with both hands.

His hands were strong and warm. The stress she held melted away at his touch. She moaned. "That feels *so* good."

"I'm glad." He leaned closer. She could feel the heat radiating from him. "You should never be stressed," he whispered. His breath against her ear made her shiver. His lips touched just below her earlobe and caused a ripple to course through her body. "This is how you should always feel."

His voice was breathy, and his kisses were light as they traveled across her skin. She leaned against him, and his hands continued to massage away her stress as his lips made her forget all about the day.

"Leila?" Her name was a question as his hands left her shoulders and rubbed across her chest gently and slowly, making their way toward her breasts.

Her chest lifted to accommodate his hands as she whispered his name in answer to hers. His tongue left a trail from her shoulder and across her skin as he sucked and kissed. A shiver traveled through her body, and her head fell to the side, exposing as much of her neck to him as she could. His hands traveled down and cupped her breasts.

She breathed in a shuddering breath, and her skin exploded with electricity as his lips continued to taste and devour her. The need she experienced on Sunday ignited once again. She turned, and her gaze met his.

His eyes were smoldering with need and desire.

Her heart skipped a beat. That look was for her. This Adonis of a man, who could have any woman he wanted, had that look for her. She swallowed against the lump in her throat.

He brushed the hair from her face and off her shoulder. "Leila, you are so beautiful." His voice was thick, and his face was filled with emotions. "You don't know what you do to me." His eyes searched hers, bore into hers.

Her breath shuddered. "Adler…" She couldn't find the words she needed. Her thoughts were muddled. Instead, she rested her hand on his cheek and kissed him, softly at first until the need she had erupted like a volcano and a tingle of desire set her body on fire. She pressed her mouth harder against his and allowed his tongue to dance with hers. She wrapped her arms tightly around him, bringing him closer.

Things went from slow to Mach 4 in the blink of an eye. His hands found their way under her shirt, then it was over her head and flung across the room before she could say no. But no was nowhere on her mind. She wanted him like the earth wants the sun. She needed him like flowers need rain. "Come into my room," she whispered.

He pulled away. Their gazes held, and he pulled her to her feet. His eyes traveled down.

She stood in front of him in her lacy black bra and shorts. She watched his chest lift and fall rapidly. Time stood still. She laid her hand on the side of his face.

He kissed her palm and took her hand in his. He pulled her toward her bedroom. As soon as he closed the door, he devoured her with new desperation. The heat that was between them on Sunday was mild compared to the inferno that exploded when his lips pressed to hers in the hottest kiss she'd ever experienced.

She needed to feel his skin against hers and tore his shirt from his body, gasping at the beauty that was Adler. Yes, she'd seen him

Sunday, but it was different now. Now they were an item, and she could no longer deny her feelings for him. He made her feel things she'd never felt with a man, and it was so worth the wait. His gaze made her heart do somersaults. His kisses on her skin blazed fires over her and caused her insides to turn molten. The touch of his hands made her tingle in places that had not been alive in so long.

"Leila," he growled, catching her off guard. "I need you now." His voice came from deep within his chest.

The desire in those words, in his look, was all she could take. She unbuttoned her shorts and slowly stepped out of them, stripping off her bra and panties also. He followed her by doing the same, and her heart stopped. Her eyes wandered slowly down his amazing chest, and her breath caught. She took his hand and pulled him to the bed, and they lay down together.

His hands slowly traced a path down her arms to her hips. His eyes followed. "God, you're perfect." Their lips met again until finally his left hers. He pushed her gently on her back and kissed a trail down to her breast. First one. He sucked gently, then went to the other.

This was heaven. Her hands traveled over his skin to the curve of his hips and gripped his firm, tight ass. Then up his muscular back and across his strong shoulders. His skin was smooth, hard, and warm.

Finally, his kisses left her breasts and traveled down her chest. Her breath caught as he dipped still lower. The speed of her heart made it difficult to breathe. His lips halted on her skin just below her belly button.

"Don't stop, Adler, please." Her voice was so low and desperate, she wasn't sure she'd said those words out loud.

She sat up a little, and his eyes peeked at her.

"Your wish is my command," he said as he gave her that sly, crooked grin, which set her heart aflutter, and dipped between her legs.

She held his gaze until she could no longer, and her head hit her pillow as her lower body bucked in answer to his tongue. She didn't realize his tongue could do those things, make her feel this way. He did things to her that she didn't know were possible. He made her feel things she didn't realize she could feel. He sent her to places she didn't know existed. Her breath raced as she climbed the summit and reached the peak of ecstasy again, and again...and again.

Even though what he did to her was addicting, she needed more. He was like crack, and she was hooked. "Adler," she begged. "Come to me."

He crawled up to her, and she pulled him to her mouth. Her body yearned to feel him inside her. It had been so long. The last time she'd been with a guy was the night she got pregnant with Skylar. But that was Ben. He'd never made her feel like this. This wanted. This needed, and this desired.

Adler left her for a second, picked up his pants from the floor, and dug in his pocket.

Leila couldn't keep her eyes off him, his perfect, sculpted body, which was all hers. Her body tingled with anticipation and need.

Finally, he was back next to her, tore open the condom, and rolled it over his pulsing erection.

She closed her eyes and scratched a trail down his back.

His warm lips closed on hers softly. "Leila, look at me," he whispered.

Her lids fluttered open, and as their gazes met, he thrust into her.

She gasped and dug her nails into his back, willing him deeper and deeper. It hurt a little, but it was a good hurt, an amazing pain. She lifted her hips as he drove into her.

She couldn't contain herself any longer. Her eyes closed, her head tilted back, and she moaned his name. She clutched his ass as he gave one last thrust.

"Yes," he moaned.

"Adler," she answered.

Then she came. It was like an explosion as her body convulsed. She didn't think she had anything left, but man, was she wrong!

He pushed one last time, and as he moaned, their eyes met and then their lips crushed against each other as they finished together. He collapsed onto her chest.

Her breathing was rough, and she breathed deeply, trying to gain control again. "Stay the night with me?" She wasn't sure if she should have asked, but she didn't care. She didn't want him to go. She wanted to wake up with his arms around her and kiss him goodbye before he left for work.

He moved to his side and laid his head on a pillow. His arm draped over her, his fingers traced circles on her arm, spreading goosebumps over her body. "Are you sure?"

"Yes." She nodded and turned to face him. "I want you here."

"Then I'll stay." He kissed her lips. "I'll be right back."

The bed became empty as soon as he was gone, but luckily it didn't last long before he was back. She rolled over, and he pulled her up against him, and pressed a kiss below her ear.

He snuggled closer, until there was no space where his body ended and hers began. It was like they were one person. It was perfect.

"Good night, beautiful, and thank you for an amazing night."

She brought his hand to her lips and kissed his knuckles, hugging them tight. "Thank you, Adler." She'd never slept so soundly in her life.

Chapter 22

Leila woke the next morning and could still feel the warmth of Adler's fingers on her skin, his lips on hers. A smile crept up the corners of her mouth, and she reached out, but her hand met an empty pillow. She blinked the sleep from her eyes. Adler's clothes were gone from the floor where they were haphazardly thrown last night, and her heart fell. She had been looking forward to morning kisses and morning sex. He must have left early for work yet didn't even kiss her goodbye.

She let out a sigh and rolled over on her back, frustrated and alone, her eyes on the ceiling fan as it twirled and hummed.

Cabinets banged shut in the kitchen, and Skylar let loose a happy squeal.

Adler didn't leave. Leila's pulse picked up pace. She tied her silk robe around her and went out to the kitchen.

The scene before her took her breath away. She leaned against the wall and quietly watched Adler and Skylar. Skylar was in her highchair, with oat cereal on her tray and a bib around her neck.

Adler sat in front of her in his jeans and a white T-shirt, with a jar of baby food, trying to feed a little girl who was doing her best to take the spoon from his hand, causing the mushed—it looked like sweet potatoes—to go everywhere.

Leila brought her hand to her mouth to quiet the laugh that threatened to escape from her lips.

"Okay, little beauty. You're making this more difficult than it should be." He scooped more baby food onto the spoon, making it to Skylar's mouth before she grabbed it and pulled it from his hand. She gnawed on the spoon and smiled around it, causing the sweet potatoes to ooze out the side of her mouth and down her chin. Adler let out a puff and flopped back in his seat.

Skylar's eyes flashed to where Leila was standing, and a shrill squeal exited her lips along with the baby food.

The laugh that Leila was holding in escaped as Adler slowly turned to face her. When their eyes locked, her heart melted. How was it possible the world's most gorgeous guy could possibly look even hotter with bed head and baby food on his white T-shirt? His smile made her pulse race. She grabbed the towel that hung on the oven and sat in his lap. She wiped food from his face and shirt and laughed. "What are you doing?"

He brushed her hair off her neck. "I woke up and heard Skylar playing in her bed, so I got her up, changed her, and thought I'd feed her. I didn't want to wake you."

She wiped more mashed food from his cheek. "Well, that is the sweetest thing ever." How could she let him know how much his loving her daughter meant to her? She covered his lips with hers. "Thank you, so much."

His eyes held hers. "For what? Turning your daughter orange?"

She chuckled. "No, for being you. Being amazing." Her heart was so full she thought it might explode. "Let me finish breakfast. Don't you need to be getting to work?"

"Unfortunately, yes." He moved her from his lap and stood. "I need to go home first and change." He wrapped his arms around her. "Do you think Diane and your dad could babysit tonight? I want to take you on a date."

"I'll ask, but I'm sure that won't be a problem. I work until five-thirty."

"Then I'll see you here at six." He placed a quick peck on her lips. "Oh, and I plan on spending the night again, if that's okay with you. I want a repeat of last night." He winked and kissed Skylar's head. "Goodbye, little mess."

Skylar offered him her baby food-crusted spoon.

"No, thank you. I'll let you keep that." He waved and walked out the door.

Leila peeled a banana and gave a piece to Skylar and sat at the table. "Sky, how did we get so lucky?"

Skylar gave her a toothless grin filled with mashed up banana and sweet potato.

"You are a mess. I need to get you cleaned up." Leila got Skylar in the bath and herself ready for work.

Leila's step was lighter as she went through her workday. She was on cloud nine and didn't think she would ever come down from the high.

"Leila, could you go in the back and look for the rest of the candles to fill this display?" She and Barbara Stanzel, the shop owner, were working on the floor and stocking shelves.

"Sure. I saw them yesterday." She placed the pictures she was holding on their stands and went into the back. It took her longer than expected to find the boxes she was looking for, and she grabbed a few others that Elizabeth must have just ordered. She placed them on the rolling cart and pushed them to the front. Barbara was talking to someone near the door when Leila went back to the front.

"Thank you so much. They're beautiful." Barbara turned to Leila.

Leila's eyes went wide. Barbara had a vase in her hands filled with a dozen pink and white roses. Leila hadn't realized her boss was seeing someone. As far as she knew, Barbara hadn't seen anyone in years. "Wow, Mrs. Stanzel. Those are beautiful. Who's your secret admirer?" She joked, yet was interested. Did her boss have a hot man hiding in the wings somewhere? Someone she didn't know about?

Barbara walked toward Leila. As she got closer, the spicy, floral smell radiating from the roses filled Leila's senses. "Those smell amazing." She couldn't help herself, and when Barabara got close enough, Leila put her face close to the bouquet and breathed in a deep breath. "They smell wonderful. Who's the guy who sent these?"

"I don't know. They aren't mine." She held them toward Leila. "Someone must really know how special you are."

"No way." They couldn't be hers. No one had ever sent her flowers before. Leila took the bouquet to the checkout counter, and her pulse raced in anticipation. She took the envelope from the pick and pulled out the card. As she read the short note, her pulse raced. Adler was so sweet.

"So, is this that handsome guy I heard you and Elizabeth talking about?" Barbara asked.

Leila met her gaze as a flush rose from her neck and filled her face, and a lopsided grin ticked up the corners of her mouth. She nodded.

Barbara laid her hand on her arm. "Well, you left a mark on him. He must realize how amazing you are. Now, let's get this place closed up." She patted Leila's arm and walked to the back.

Leila pulled her phone from her pocket, took a picture of the roses, and sent a thank you text to Adler. It was sweet of him, and the card just said a simple thank you for giving him the time she did. He'd enjoyed spending time with her and Skylar.

Chapter 23

Leila walked around the back of the house to enter her apartment. She didn't want Diane or her father to make a big deal about the flowers.

She placed them on the corner of the kitchen counter and rubbed a petal between her fingers. She loved the velvety texture of rose petals. Between that and the amazing aroma, her senses were filled and so was her heart.

She ran up the stairs, still floating with excitement. Eighty's music filled the air along with Diane's somewhat melodic voice. Leila laughed as she caught Diane dancing at the counter while she prepared a salad. Skylar's gaze was fixed on her. This was exactly the life she wanted for Sky. Filled with people who loved her and lots of fun.

Leila joined in the chorus of the song coming from the speakers, causing Diane to glance up.

"Hey, you're home. Come help me finish this salad."

Leila danced her way across the room and leaned over her daughter, kissing her on her forehead. When Skylar saw her, she squealed and started bouncing in her seat. "I think she likes it." She pulled Skylar from her seat and danced with her in her arms.

"Well, who doesn't?" Diane answered as she shimmied her hips and cut tomatoes to the beat.

"Right?" Leila agreed as she turned circles with Skylar, whose head fell back a little and she let out a belly laugh.

"This is probably the best sight I could ask for when I walk in from work. All my best girls enjoy spending time with each other." Tom entered the kitchen, and everyone stopped dancing as he placed a kiss on Leila and Skylar's heads and wrapped Diane in a tight hug, planting a deep kiss on her lips.

Their affection made Leila grin from ear to ear. Watching them together gave her hope that love was real and could work out. That was a thought she'd never had in Florida as she watched her mom go from one relationship to another and never find a guy who loved her and accepted her for herself. A knock on the door caught her attention, and she danced her way to the front room and pulled open the door.

Adler stood there and instantly took her breath away. The smile that was on her face was now there for a different reason. His hands were in the front pockets of his just-tight-enough pants, and his button-up shirt showed off his muscular body perfectly. He looked handsome and ready for a night out. Shoot. She'd forgotten to ask Diane and her dad about babysitting.

"Well, it's the two most beautiful girls in the world." His smile filled his face and placed adorable creases at the corners of his mouth.

Leila's heart fluttered madly. "And we're glad you're here."

He stepped inside and greeted her with a soft kiss as his arms pressed carefully around her. When they broke away, he took a reaching Skylar from her arms. "And hello to you, little beauty."

Skylar's face lit up, and she laid her head against his chest, which melted Leila's fluttering heart. This guy was too much.

"Hi, Adler." Tom walked into the room. "I figured it was you. Diane just finished dinner. It's simple. Grilled chicken and salad, but she makes a mean skinless chicken breast. You're welcome to join us."

Adler raised a brow at Leila.

"Dad, I totally forgot to ask if you and Diane would babysit. Adler wanted to take me out."

"Well, then you'd better get ready. You don't want to keep him waiting."

"Seriously? But I forgot, and if you both have plans. . ."

"Nonsense. Go change or do whatever you need to do. We'll keep Adler entertained."

"Thanks, Dad. You're the best." She kissed his cheek. "I won't be long." She said to Adler.

He was walking into the kitchen with Skylar in her arms. "Don't worry, I'll be hanging out with your dad. Take your time. Our reservations are at seven thirty."

Reservations. She ran down the steps and into her room. She'd never been to a restaurant that needed reservations. She changed into a knee-length dress and sandals and freshened up.

They drove to a steakhouse Leila had been past before but never thought she'd be able to eat at. They walked in, and the smell of garlic and steak filled the restaurant and caused Leila's mouth to water. It was just before seven thirty as she followed Adler, her hand intertwined with his. The hostess's face lit up when she saw him.

"Adler Warfield. It's been a while."

Leila looked between Adler and this pretty blond. She could not miss how her face lit up when she talked to Adler, or how Adler's brow ticked up and a small smile played at his lips. "Hi, Becca. How you been?"

"Oh, you know. Been busy with work and waiting to hear from you." The giggle that escaped her made Leila's stomach churn.

"Yeah, well, I have a reservation for two." He pulled Leila next to him and wrapped his arm around her waist.

The hostess—Becca—raised one brow and took a quick glance at Leila before turning back to Adler. "Yes, right this way." She placed her hand on Adler's arm as she passed him and winked.

Seriously! Leila couldn't believe this woman was openly flirting with Adler while it was obvious he was on a date.

Adler's eyes met hers. "I'm sorry," he whispered.

"No problem," Leila answered with more confidence than she felt. She couldn't help feeling inadequate in the wake of this woman. Becca wore a little black dress that fell just above her knee and was tight enough to show off her perfect body, which Leila was sure saw a lot of hours in a gym and had never had a baby. Her skin was porcelain perfect, and even Leila couldn't deny she was drop-dead gorgeous. Every muscle in Leila's body tensed up.

She let out a sigh as she pulled out a chair.

"Can I get you a drink? A Manhattan, or your favorite—a Cape Codder?" Becca asked as she placed their menus on the table and never took her eyes from Adler. Was Leila invisible?

"Nope, I think we'll take a bottle of. . ." He glanced at Leila. "Chardonnay." He raised his brow in question, and Leila nodded.

"Really? You don't usually drink wine." Becca batted her eyes.

"We're the customers; it's what we want. Now, if you'll excuse us." He laid his hands on the table, palms up, and his attention turned to Leila.

Becca was dismissed. A jolt of happiness shot through Leila, and she placed her hands in Adler's. His warmth washed away the uncomfortable feeling Becca's flirting had caused.

He squeezed her hands. "Don't let that get to you."

"What? It didn't."

He raised a brow. "Really? You tensed up as we walked to the table." His thumbs traced circles on her palms. "Becca was no one special. She had a hard time when I never called her back."

She smiled what she hoped was a believable smile. Becca was no one special. Did that mean they went out, or did they sleep together? Did she have the right to ask, or should she just brush it off?

Just then, Becca came back with the bottle of wine and two glasses of water. She was the hostess. Did she always deliver the drinks?

"Here you go." Again, Becca smiled widely at Adler and ignored Leila. Adler pulled his hands from hers and took the glasses.

This was crazy. Leila cleared her throat as Becca grabbed for the bottle, and Leila caught the woman's arm. "You know what? We can handle this on our own. I think you need to get back to the hostess stand." She gestured to where a group of customers stood waiting. "Thanks for your help, Becca, but I'd like to spend some private time with my boyfriend." She shot her a grin, then turned away to dismiss her. Becca got the message, turned abruptly, and stormed away.

Leila poured them both wine, and Adler snickered and raised his glass. "Here's to the most beautiful girlfriend, who is even more beautiful when jealous."

"I'm not jealous," she said as she clinked her glass against his. "I was just finished with her ignoring me and flirting with you. I think you'd react the same way."

Adler sipped his wine. "Nope. I would not act that way."

"Really?" Maybe she'd gotten the wrong impression about what being Adler's girlfriend meant to him.

"Yep. You were calm. I would have been rude and probably used some cuss words to get my point across."

"Yeah, I remember how you acted when William showed interest in me, and I didn't even like you then."

"Really? Come on. You felt something. I think you just didn't want to admit it."

She thought back to her feelings that night when Adler was jealous and acting like a jerk. He'd really annoyed her. Maybe it was because she had feelings she was ignoring. She shrugged. "Doesn't matter. We're here together now."

She enjoyed dinner and their time together, though she continued to question how serious he had been with Becca.

Finally, they left the restaurant. There was a coffee shop in the next shopping center, and Leila loved its caramel macchiato. "Could we run over to the Roasted Bean? They have great coffee."

"Sounds good."

They walked hand in hand across the parking lot, but Adler stopped abruptly when he opened the door. His face fell.

Leila followed his stare. Standing at a high tabletop were two girls. Both were beautiful brunettes who looked like they could be swimsuit models. She glanced back at Adler.

Seriously? Which one had he gone out with now, or was it both? A rock took up residence in her stomach, but she pushed her shoulders back and breathed in deeply. "You good?" she asked as she wrapped her arm around his waist.

He gathered himself and gave her his sexy smile. She stood on her toes and planted a kiss on his lips. If someone was watching them, they'd get the clue that he was no longer available. Neither of these girls said anything as they waited for their coffee, but the looks they shot their way were pure ice.

They walked to his car in uncomfortable silence. Leila sipped at her drink to calm the lump in her stomach.

As soon as they got on the road, she turned toward him. "What was that about?"

"What?" He glanced at her, then put his eyes back on the road.

"Did you date one of those girls too? Or both of them?" She needed to know, though couldn't ignore a feeling that squeezed at her heart.

"It doesn't matter. Leila. They're in the past."

They. She couldn't ignore it. Three girls in one night. Plus, if she thought of Desiree, that would be four women she'd met, or run into, that he had been with. He hadn't admitted to sleeping with them, but he didn't have to.

He wrapped her hand in his, and she turned toward the window, blinking back the tears that made her vision blurry.

Finally, they made it to her apartment. She had received a text from Diane saying she'd put Skylar to bed, so she put her finger to her lips as she unlocked the door. As soon as she closed it behind them, she was engulfed in Adler's strong waiting arms. This was where she loved to be. His presence always affected her, and his brown eyes pulled her into his hypnotic gaze, but tonight it seemed different. She knew she needed to ignore the women they saw. That was a different Adler. This one saw only her. But ignoring his past was easier said than done.

"I'm sorry about tonight." His voice was deep and throaty and made a small smile crawl up the corners of her mouth.

Her hands were on his chest, and she could feel his muscles beneath his shirt as his warmth radiated from it, but even his warmth couldn't help relax the squeezing that still constricted her heart, making breathing difficult. Her eyes held his. "Can I ask you something?"

"Of course. You can ask me anything." He squeezed his arms tighter around her.

"Please be honest."

He raised his eyebrow.

"Did you have sex with all those girls? Becca at the restaurant and the two in the coffee shop?" There. She asked. She wasn't sure how knowing details about his past would make her feel better, but maybe she was wrong. Maybe they just went out a couple of times and there was nothing serious. But her memories of her first impression of him came back and slammed into her, reminding her how much like Ben he was. She knew the answer before she saw it on his face.

His jaw flexed, and his gaze fell from hers. "Leila." His voice was flat.

That's all she needed. Why was it a surprise? She knew everything about him before she fell hard. *You promised yourself you wouldn't get involved with an egotistical asshole again, yet here you are.*

She walked away and leaned on the counter.

"Leila. You knew you weren't my first. You heard about my past. Those women meant nothing. Why are you letting it bother you?" His voice was calm, yet his words were clipped.

Leila didn't know what she disliked more. The fact that he didn't deny having sex with them, or the fact that she knew this about him but fell for him anyway.

Adler moved next to her. "They don't matter. The only ones that matter to me are you and Skylar. You know that. I've told you, you made me a better person." He placed his hand on her back. "If anyone should be concerned and jealous, it should be me."

What? Her eyes went wide, and she backed away.

"I might have slept with those women, but I don't have any babies with them. You have a connection with a man I won't ever be able to sever."

His words leaped at her. She didn't like his tone at all. "Seriously? Ben isn't now, nor will he ever be, a part of Skylar's life. I learned too late that sex and women were just a passing interest for him. As soon as he got what he wanted, he moved on to one of the many waiting in the wings. Women meant nothing to him either."

She spat out the words blindly. "Anyway, it's not at all the same. Ben was only the second man I ever slept with. I don't have a history a mile long showing up in every corner of every town I go to." There, she said it. Now Adler knew how inexperienced she really was and how different their backgrounds were.

Adler took a step away from her and blinked rapidly. "You really think that way? You're still comparing me to Ben. I thought you said the old Adler was gone. I thought you saw me here and now."

Leila's pulse raced. All the feelings from the restaurant came back to her like a whirlwind. How she'd been invisible in the other woman's presence. How she could see the impeccable Hollywood beauty in her and the two at the coffee shop. She was nothing like them. There was no way Alder could like her after being with them.

She swallowed the lump in her throat as her emotions threatened to get the best of her. "What I see now, and reality are totally different. I see those women, and I also see I'm nothing like any of them. I don't know what this is, but you can't really be interested in me, not after being with them."

Adler raked his fingers through his hair and linked his hands behind his neck. "How can you say that after last night, after how I've shown you how much I care for you and Skylar? You're being so irrational right now. Those women meant nothing, which is why I'm not with them." Irritation oozed from his words, and his voice became louder.

A tightness formed in her chest. *How dare he?* "They meant enough for you to sleep with, or was that just sex for you? And if it was just sex, how do I know that this won't turn into the same thing? That one day you won't get bored with me and go back to how you were before we met?"

"You really think it's possible for you to mean nothing to me? God, I thought I explained how much I care about you."

She leaned on the chair in front of her. Her gut was heavy, and her feelings were all over the place. Could she trust his words? Was it fair to Skylar to let him get close to her, only for him to wake up one morning and decide they no longer meant anything to him, and he no longer wanted to be tied down? Her heart was raging against her chest, and her breathing became faster.

She needed to calm down before she said something she would regret. He didn't understand what it was like growing up thinking his father didn't want him. He had an amazing father and mother who loved each other. Leila understood what it was like with a single mom, and it was bad enough Skylar would have to know her father didn't want her. It was Leila's duty to protect her daughter. Her body and her heart. This was why she didn't want to get involved in a relationship. *Leila, why were you so stupid? Why did you let this happen? Is this man really the kind of man you want to raise your daughter?*

No, he wasn't, and she needed to end it now. It would be hard, but tonight was what she'd needed to open her eyes to what he was really like deep down in his soul. "Adler, I knew I wasn't ready for a relationship." She struggled to hold back the emotion bubbling its way to the surface. "You, though, are nothing but a bad decision, and I'm sure once the reality hits that this is a forever commitment, you'll be running for the hills. You aren't ready for the commitment of being a family man, and even if you thought you were, you sure aren't father material, and you're not someone I'd ever consider for being the father of my daughter."

His eyes widened, and he backed away from her.

What did she just do? Leila took a step forward as her heart crashed in her chest. She grabbed his arms. "Adler, I didn't mean that. I'm so sorry." She was pleading and sounded desperate, but she didn't care.

He bit his bottom lip as he nodded. "Yeah, you did. You said it." He jerked away from her grasp like her touch burned him, and he cleared his throat.

Leila's heart pounded.

"I'm sorry too, Leila. I thought you saw me. The man I desperately want to be, but I guess I was wrong. I won't waste your time anymore since I'm not someone you'd see as a father figure." His voice was thick, and he stomped to the door and closed it softly behind him.

Leila stared at the door as if she watched it long enough, it would magically open and Adler would reappear, but he left. He walked out.

What did she do? Her shoulders slumped forward, and she leaned on the door as tears ran down her face. Maybe he was still outside. Maybe he hadn't left after all. Maybe she could stop him and beg him to come back.

She yanked the door open, ready to yell for him, but she heard an engine come to life and then speed away. Her heart stopped, then tore in two as she stood in the dark. "Leila, you really screwed things up."

Chapter 24

Adler opened the convertible top and sped away, trying to leave behind the hurt and dread eating away at his insides. Speed was what he needed, and the wind blowing his hair helped to keep him focused. As he flew down the road toward the interstate, he compelled speed to take over his thoughts. The wind whipped through his hair, waking him from the shock Leila's words caused.

She'd never consider him being Skylar's dad. What bothered him the most was that he hadn't thought of being her dad until those words were spoken. It was like a sword through his heart. That little girl meant so much to him. He loved her as much as he loved Leila.

Shit. He smacked his hand against the steering wheel. He didn't need to think that. He had never loved anyone before. Tears stung his eyes. He blinked hard and pressed the gas pedal down. Picking up speed, he hoped the wind would blow away the burning hurt growing in his chest.

He turned off the road and finally came to a stop. He wasn't at home. He was at the overlook, and thankfully there was no one else there. He pulled the Mustang carefully up the uneven gravel road, got out of the car, and sat on the log where just a couple weeks ago he'd sat with Leila. How did things go so wrong? He rested his elbows on his thighs and hung his head low. The tears that had stung his eyes while he was driving slid slowly down his cheeks. He let them fall and dry in the air. He sat there for a while, watching the lights become brighter as the moonless night closed in around him.

Leila's words churned in his head. She'd said he wasn't ready for the commitment of being a father.

She'd said he was a bad decision.

Anger rose in his chest as her words swam through his mind. "Fuck!" he yelled at the top of his lungs. That single word echoed off the nothingness of the overlook. He had never hurt like this before. His chest ached as if it were being split in two. He needed to get control of himself before he got back in his car and headed home, because he couldn't stay here much longer. He had to work in the morning.

Eventually, he was calm enough. It was only nine o'clock, though it seemed like a year had passed since he left Leila. When he reached the gate of his driveway, he punched in his code—his birth-date—and wound his way up the driveway. As he approached his parents' house, they were getting out of the car. He remembered it was Wednesday, the night they went out with friends after their church service.

He couldn't explain why, but he parked next to their car. When his mom turned, his heart finally split. He was thirty. Why did he need his mother right now? That made no sense. He was a grown man.

He got out of his car and walked to her with long strides.

"Hey, Ad." Her smile was wide, but once he was close, she could see the expression on his face. "What's wrong?"

He wiped roughly at the tears he didn't realize were falling and wrapped his mother in a tight hug. She was the one woman who, no matter how many times he screwed up or how many bad decisions he made, would always love him. She wrapped her arms around his chest. He squeezed her tight as his heart slowed down to a more even rhythm.

"Adler, what happened?" She pulled away from him and cupped his face like she used to when he was little, but this time she needed to angle his face down to her.

"I was with Leila. I'm crazy about her, Mom, and I thought we had something, but she said I was a bad decision and wasn't someone she wanted to be Skylar's father."

Elisha's eyes popped. "Wow. Okay. Let's go into the house and talk about what happened."

Adler took a deep breath, held it for a beat before exhaling. Good. His emotions were finally under control. It was amazing that even at his age, a hug from his mom made everything okay. He shook his head. "No, Mom. I'm good now." He gave her a small smile.

She held his eyes for a minute. "Look, I don't know why she said that, but the fact that you're this upset tells me you really care about her and her little girl."

Adler tilted his head slightly so he could see his mother better. His heart beat wildly. "I. . ." He met his mom's gaze again. "I love her and Skylar. The first time I saw Leila, there was something different. Then, when I found out about Skylar, I tried to let it bother me, but it didn't. As soon as I met her, it was just. . ." He sighed and shrugged. Wow. Did he just tell his mom he loved Leila? "I gotta go. Thanks, Mom."

"I didn't do anything, but I'm glad I could help." She pulled him into another hug. "Remember, I'm here if you need to talk."

Adler kissed her cheek and drove around to his house.

The next two weeks were a blur. Leila handed the vendor fair and silent auction over to Stacey and Jessica. She wanted nothing to do with anything involving Adler. She needed to focus on her life and keep it as uncomplicated as possible.

"Jessica and I are going to dinner. Want to come?" Elizabeth asked as they were closing the boutique Tuesday night. "We're going to talk about the fundraiser and hang out."

Leila decided she could use some girl time. "That would be great. Let me ask Diane if she minds watching Sky a little later." She called Diane and wasn't surprised that she quickly agreed. "Okay. I'm in."

She met the girls at the local diner and gave Jessica a hug when she met them at the table.

"So, just over a week and it'll be the auction." Jessica bubbled over with excitement. "We're meeting at the center Saturday to work on the silent auction baskets and print the papers for them. Are you two able to help?"

Elizabeth quickly said yes.

"Yep. Count me in," replied Leila.

"Great." Jessica said and fidgeted with her napkin.

Leila glanced between the girls. Something was going on. She could feel how things had changed. "Okay, what's up? Jessica, one minute you're about to bounce out of your seat, now you look like you stole your best friend's boyfriend and need to let her know."

Elizabeth and Jessica raised their eyebrows.

Leila could tell there was something they weren't saying. "Just say it."

"Okay." Jessica's body leaned forward. "How are you?"

Leila tilted her head to the side. What did they know?

Jessica sat up taller. "Okay, fine." She exchanged a quick look with Elizabeth. "I've seen Adler a couple of times when I've met with him about the fundraiser. He's not as chipper as usual and has lost his self-confident air. When I ask him about the two of you, he won't talk. I thought you two were a good thing. What happened?"

A lump formed in her chest. She'd tried hard not to think about Adler over the past couple of weeks, and it'd been pretty easy to avoid him since he didn't live in town. "Yeah, well, I realized he wasn't good for us."

"Us? What do you mean?" Elizabeth asked.

"Skylar and me." Leila let out a breath and pushed her plate away. She'd suddenly lost her appetite.

"Explain. How wasn't he good for you?" Jessica asked. "He seemed to be really good for both you and Skylar. Honestly, he seemed to be great."

Leila didn't want to talk about this. She'd spent the past two weeks trying to forget Adler and avoided any place she might run into him. "It's simple." She put her hands on the table and picked at her fingernails. "I realized I was getting too involved, and he isn't the guy I need in my life. Because of Skylar, any guy I choose to be with has to understand that we're a forever commitment."

"Oh." Elizabeth exchanged a look with Jessica.

"Come on. You both told me what he was like. You know he doesn't stay focused on a relationship. I don't want Skylar to get attached to someone only for him to decide that being tied down to a woman and someone else's baby isn't for him. That would break her heart, and she needs someone she'll be able to count on. She doesn't need to have daddy issues like I did growing up, and Adler isn't the type of person to take on someone else's baggage. He's too focused on himself. He's too much of a ladies' man, and like I've said before, he's too much like Ben. Skylar—and I—need someone better."

"Well, you sure were happy when you spent time together, and he seemed pretty into you and Skylar," Elizabeth answered.

"It doesn't matter. Let's get back to talking about the fundraiser." Leila needed to change the subject and get focused on the purpose of their dinner.

Chapter 25

It was the Friday night before the fundraiser, and Leila had just gotten back from the final planning meeting. She leaned against the front door as she entered her house. It had been a long night, and she'd had a hard time keeping her mind on the discussions going on around the room.

Adler had been at the pregnancy center with Stacey, filling them in on what Warfield Meats was bringing and how the tents would be set up. She'd sat in the back of the room to avoid his gaze as much as possible, and the entire time he talked she tried to keep her mind on what he was saying and not how amazing he looked.

Even though he didn't look as rested as usual, and his words lacked the excitement that was typical Adler, he was as handsome as ever. Leila's heart became heavy the longer she watched him. Every now and then, his gaze would find hers and linger for longer than necessary, causing that familiar tingle throughout her body. If only things could have been different with them. She couldn't deny they had feelings for each other, but feelings weren't enough when it came to becoming part of her life and having Skylar get attached.

Finally, they finished their meeting and had been dismissed. As soon as Adler left the stage, his eyes locked on hers and he walked in her direction. Luckily, Deloris Green grabbed his arm and started talking with him. Leila had taken that opportunity to sneak out. Now here she was at home, and she breathed easier.

"Hey, glad you're home." Diane met her at the door. "You look exhausted. How'd things go?"

Leila took Skylar from Diane and sat heavily on the couch. She hugged her close and laid her head on the back of the couch, closing her eyes. "Everything's in order, and we're about ready."

"I'd figured you'd come home happier. You've been excited about the fundraiser for months," Tom said as he sat on the other end of the couch with a cup of coffee.

"Adler was there. It was the first time I've seen him since we stopped seeing each other. It was just a little awkward."

"I know it's none of my business, but you both seemed really happy. What happened?" asked Tom.

Leila shook her head and let out a sigh. She had avoided telling her dad and Diane much about this, but it couldn't be avoided forever. "Let's just say he wasn't the right man for us. He isn't dad material."

"Dad material? Was it getting that serious already?" Tom asked.

"Tom!" Diane slapped him. "You need to stop. Our job is to support Leila. Your job is to keep your thoughts to yourself."

Tom lifted his hands in surrender. "Fine. I'll try my best to stay out of it, but babies know who they can trust, and Skylar seemed to love Adler. Maybe you should listen to her." Tom replied curtly.

Leila changed the subject and talked about the night, leaving out the heaviness of her heart and the change she'd noticed in Adler.

Diane listened and asked basic questions, and her father was unusually quiet and just grunted occasionally. Her father's behavior bothered her. She could tell he wasn't happy about her decision with Adler, but it was her choice who she allowed in her and Skylar's life. He needed to stay out of it and let her be.

Leila pushed herself off the couch. "Well, it's late, and this one needs to go to bed."

Tom handed Skylar her stuffed koala, and she hugged it tight while sucking on the paw. "She's always really loved that koala." He hugged Leila, and she relaxed.

Diane's gaze was soft and understanding. "We love you both, Leila. But promise me something."

Leila met her intense gaze and nodded.

"Never settle just because you think someone is the right one for Skylar. Make sure you choose someone who loves and appreciates both of you. It won't be easy, but if a man says they want to be a part of your life and has accepted you as a package deal, maybe you need to give that person a chance. He may not seem to be the perfect person in your mind, but no one's perfect." Diane placed a kiss on Skylar's head, and her voice became softer. "Find someone who loves you both, but don't settle. Promise me."

"Of course. I promise." Leila returned Diane's smile.

"Good. Also remember that love isn't easy. It's work, and when you find the right person, it's worth doing whatever you need to make it work." Diane gave her a soft smile before she left the room.

She wouldn't settle. She and Skylar both deserved someone who loved them and would treasure them. Skylar squealed happily, oblivious of the feelings swimming around her, the koala still clutched in her grip.

She walked down to her apartment and dressed Skylar for bed, then got comfortable in the glider rocker to nurse her.

Adler's handsome face flashed in Leila's mind with his smile that caused her heart to race. She remembered how he'd touched her, kissed her, made love to her, and her pulse kicked up a notch.

Then the words she'd said to him came flooding back to her, and her heart fell. Those words filled her with dread. The shadow that had shrouded his face sent a dagger into her heart and made it hard for her to catch her breath. She remembered how he'd backed away from her touch, and her heart broke all over again.

Her eyes filled with tears as Diane's words echoed in her mind. *She told me to find someone who loved and appreciated both of us, and that's exactly what I wanted. Adler did.* She didn't know if he loved them, but he cared a lot. She did not doubt that.

He wasn't the egotistical man she had met in May. He was anything but. Yeah, he had a past, but she shouldn't judge him by his past choices, not when he was trying so hard to be different. "You really screwed this up." Skylar stopped eating and babbled, then went back to her bedtime snack. Leila laughed, and some of the stress of her feelings lifted. "I know, baby girl. I'm sorry."

She doubted she could fix the mess she'd created, but she had to try. She wiped the tears from her face. Like Diane said, when you find the right person, it's worth it to make things work. Adler was the right person. No matter how much she fought it, she knew deep in her heart it was the truth. Now she hoped she wasn't too late to make things right.

Chapter 26

The morning of the fundraiser was a perfect first Saturday in August. It was slightly overcast, and without direct sun, the temperature would actually be bearable.

Adler wasn't far from Leila's mind. She had considered sending him a text multiple times last night but hesitated. What would she say? What could she say? "I'm sorry" seemed weak. She was more than sorry, but she couldn't figure out what she was feeling, so she wrestled with it the rest of the night and slept awfully.

Now she sat at her kitchen counter, pushing eggs around her plate with one hand and scrolling through social media with her other while Skylar ate oat cereal. She was tired and irritable, not a good combination to start her day.

She needed to send him a text at least. Ask him to meet her. Tell him they needed to talk. If she didn't, it would be on her mind all day, and she wouldn't give the silent auction the attention it needed. Fear that he'd ignore her sat like a brick in her gut. He had every right too. She had been awful, rude, and hurtful. *Why did you say those things to him?* "Skylar, what should I do?"

Skylar babbled to her and offered her some soggy oat cereal.

"Thanks, but no thanks, baby girl." Leila pushed away from the counter and placed her plate in the dishwasher. She needed to clean up and get going.

She arrived downtown early, and it was already bustling with activity. She and Marge, another volunteer, oversaw making sure the vendors knew where to go, and later she needed to assist with the silent auction.

Butterflies filled Leila's stomach. Adler would be here at some point, and she didn't know what she would do when she saw him. Things would be awkward and uncomfortable.

She should have at least apologized in text and asked him to find time today to talk. She took her phone from her pocket and scrolled again to his number. She couldn't do it. *Dammit.* Luckily, she didn't have time to worry about it because as more vendors showed up the morning became chaotic.

It was twenty minutes to eight. More vendors had arrived and were setting up, and people were starting to meander around. Things were a jumble of chaos and joyful noise.

Jessica walked over with a clipboard. "How're things going?"

"Things are good," Leila said. "We've had some minor issues with one of the vendors needing electricity, but they didn't reserve a booth with electricity, so they weren't put in that area. I found someone willing to change who no longer needed it. So that minor problem was solved."

"And Leila has dealt with all the little stresses of planning a fundraiser perfectly," Marge added. "This is where her sweet and relaxed personality shines. Event planning might be her thing."

Leila shrugged. She was tired but was enjoying herself and agreed with Marge. She thrived in this chaotic atmosphere. Maybe event planning was her thing.

"Well, that's great to hear, and I hope your sweet personality can help problem-solve the next issue." Jessica gestured for Leila to follow her. "Marge, I need to borrow her for a bit. Will you be okay by yourself? Just for a few minutes."

"Of course, you go ahead."

Leila followed Jessica. "What's going on? Anything wrong?" They were walking toward the tents and passed a temporary fenced area. There was a horse trailer in the corner. "I didn't know we were going to have pony rides."

"Yeah, well, that was Adler's idea. He thought something for the younger kids would be good. They're two dollars a ride, and all proceeds will also go to the center. It'll also add to one of the live auction items."

"Oh, really?" Leila's heart skipped at the mention of Adler. She was at the last meeting, and she didn't remember anything that had to do with horses. "What is it?"

Jessica quirked her eyebrows. "The Warfields are offering horseback riding lessons, and Adler's giving them."

Her stomach twisted uncomfortably. She'd have to see him at some point today. She knew that and had been preparing for it, but now with this knowledge, it was totally unavoidable.

"It looks great. What did I have to okay?" Leila asked as she glanced around the tent. There was a dance floor at one end and tables all around. There were food trucks set up in the courtyard at the other end. Patrons would be able to grab food, take a seat out of the heat of the day, and listen to the live band or DJ, depending on the time, and dance if they wanted to.

"It's the silent auction area. We have only one large tent, and then a smaller tent for the auction. We're out of space, and still have items coming in."

They entered the other tent, and Leila's mouth gaped. There were tables everywhere, and they were full. One table was crowded with gift certificates from local businesses. Another overflowed with baked goods, and another with gift baskets. "Where did all these items come from? There's so much." She was in awe.

"That's what's great about all the towns that surround ours. So many people wanted to donate things. Do you think you could help Mrs. Parks organize these and the ones still coming in?"

"I'd love the help. This is a lot for one person," Charlotte answered.

Leila beamed. "Of course, Mrs. Parks, but what about Marge? We told her I'd only be gone a little while."

"I'll find someone else to assist her. Most of the vendors are here, so there isn't much more to do in that area," Jessica answered.

Leila got right to work helping Charlotte organize items, take in new items, and find places on the appropriate table. She stopped to look over the table for the live auction items. This had a list of the big-ticket items, along with a list of the people and groups who were putting themselves up for auction for their services so attendees could plan what they might be interested in bidding on.

Leila was talking with Barry, the owner of the local jewelry store, Gold and More, when laughter filled the air. She knew that laugh. It was Desiree. She had volunteered to bring baked goods and gift certificates from her bakery, but Leila hadn't noticed any of her items yet. She had planned to bid on some cinnamon rolls.

She looked up. Her pulse picked up speed, and her heart stopped. She had been so busy all morning that she had forgotten about the heaviness of being without Adler until this moment.

Charlotte was taking a basket from Desiree's arms, and there he was, standing with his arm around Desiree's waist. She couldn't hear what they were talking about, but Charlotte pointed them to the table for homemade items, and they walked in that direction. Leila watched them. They looked like a happy couple as Adler kept his hand on Desiree's lower back and led her to the table. The memory of when he led her off the Ferris wheel with his hand on her lower back popped into her mind, and her stomach churned. She suddenly remembered the electricity that was impossible to ignore when they held hands, or when he wrapped her in his arms and kissed her lips. Heat crept up her neck.

For someone who was as hurt as he'd been when she said she knew he wouldn't be able to change his ways, he proved her right. He had gone right back to what he was doing—or better yet—*whom* he was doing before her. Jessica and Elizabeth were mistaken if they thought he missed her. From what she saw, he looked perfectly fine. Thank God she hadn't sent that text this morning.

"Hey you." An arm wrapped around her shoulders, and she turned to see Jessica.

Leila cleared her throat and pulled her gaze away from the show across the tent, gave Jessica the most sincere smile she could muster, and looked like she was focused on the clipboard in her hand. "Hey. I just got a last-minute donation from Barry. He donated a gold watch and jewelry—a matching gold necklace with a diamond pendant and matching earrings."

"That's awesome and so generous." Jessica glanced quickly at the new items on the table in front of Leila. "So, are you going to bid?"

Leila's eyes went wide. That was laughable. She couldn't afford the starting bid on the jewelry, and what would she do with something that fancy? "Yeah, no. I can't afford that."

"I'm not talking about the jewelry. I'm talking about what had your attention across the tent." Jessica gestured with her head in Adler's direction.

Leila glanced across the tent again, and bit the inside of her cheek to hold back the emotion that threatened to spill from her eyes. He was so handsome. He had on jeans and his typical tight T-shirt. His back was facing them, and her eyes traveled from his tight glutes up his V-shaped back to his sculpted shoulders. Her fingers tingled as she thought of the warmth of his skin beneath her touch, and that familiar tingle started in her groin. *Wake up, Leila.* She shook her head hard.

"Maybe you should. You want to talk, and you can't keep your eyes off him. It would force him to give you the time of day." Jessica replied as she squeezed her arm tighter around Leila's shoulder.

"He can't be that upset about us. He ran back to her." Her voice was quiet.

"I don't think so. When you were talking with Barry, he was watching you."

Leila's head shot around to Jessica. Her eyes were wide. "Seriously?"

Jessica nodded.

Leila bit her bottom lip. Maybe she should bid on his lessons. She had some apologizing to do, anyway. It was her fault they weren't together.

Her gaze traveled across the tent as Adler and Desiree left. He was no longer touching her, and before they left, he turned casually, and their eyes met. His gaze was void of emotion, which ripped at her heart. Her stomach somersaulted as he walked away.

Leila spent the early afternoon working with Charlotte and Marge in the silent auction tent. People strolled in and out, often wandering around the tables and writing down their bids. Leila walked around, checking on how things were going. She was pleased with all the money items were already bringing in, and it was still early. The silent auction closed at five, right before the live auction started.

"Look who it is, Skylar." Tom's voice bellowed through the murmur of voices in the tent.

Leila turned, and her face lit up when she saw Skylar. She took her from her father. "Hey, Sky." She showered her daughter's face with kisses.

Diane hurried up to them. "My gosh. I think I might spend our mortgage in this tent. There are so many great items."

Tom wrapped his arm around her waist and pulled her close to his side. "Yeah, I think I may need to keep you close. Our bank account is important, and we need to be able to afford that mortgage payment."

"You're right." Diane kissed his cheek. "But did you see how much my hair salon's gift certificate is already up to? That's almost double what a cut and color would normally cost."

Leila beamed. This day was already so successful for the pregnancy center.

"So," Diane continued. "Think you could get a break and come eat something with us?"

Leila glanced around. It was quiet, and Charlotte had just gotten back from her break. She didn't see why that would be a problem. "Sure. Let me go tell Mrs. Parks. Could you order me a cheeseburger and fries with a Sprite? I'll be right there."

Leila talked to Charlotte and passed her the clipboard, then wandered to the picnic tables. She wanted to eat in the sunshine. She'd been under the tent all morning.

She sat down at a picnic table with Skylar as she waited for her dad and Diane to join them. She glanced around the park. People were wandering everywhere. Many of the vendors had full tents of customers, and everyone seemed to be having a good time. She beamed. This was part of her vision, and she loved seeing it come to fruition. Maybe event coordinating was something she should look more into.

Her stomach let out a low roar. "Dang. Did you hear that, Sky?"

Skylar's eyes grew larger, and she leaned away a little. She chuckled at Skylar's expression.

Leila didn't realize until now how hungry she was. She was starving. She'd been working hard all day and was so busy the day flew by. She hadn't even had a snack today and had hardly touched her eggs at breakfast. "I hope your granddad gets back soon. I could eat a whole house."

She tickled Skylar's side, and she giggled and tried to wiggle away. "I love you, Skylar." She said, laughing. Skylar started bouncing with joy, up and down. "Wow, what are you so excited about? Is Grandpa coming back with our food?" Leila turned to tell her dad thank you and grab the tray of food from him but stopped suddenly, and her heart fell in her chest.

It wasn't her father that caused the excitement Skylar just experienced. It was Adler. He stood close to the table. His large brown eyes caught hers and held on. Leila's heart caught in her throat. Her breath stopped. What could she say to him? What should she do?

She did the only thing that came naturally and smiled. "Hey, Adler."

He walked slowly over to them. "Hi." Skylar held on to the finger he held out and smiled her gummy smile. "You look just as beautiful as ever, little one."

His gaze slowly met Leila's. He was so sweet and handsome and perfect. *Say something. At least tell him you need to talk.* Her tongue was frozen, and she didn't know what to say. *You've gotta say something.* She cleared her throat.

Just then, Desiree called his name. He gestured for her to wait one minute. "I gotta go. I just wanted to say hi and see her." He brushed his hand over Skylar's hair and walked away.

Leila swallowed a lump in her throat as she watched him. Leila's dad passed him, and they greeted each other kindly. Leila's stomach churned as her vision became blurry. She'd really screwed up and didn't know how to fix it.

Tom set the tray on the table. "Hey, here's your food."

Diane sat next to her and started pulling food off the tray. She caught Leila's gaze. "So, how did that go?"

Leila shook her head. "Sylar was excited to see him, but he wasn't over here long before Desiree called him. I guess they're together again. So much for what I meant to him."

"I don't know," Diane answered. "From what I could see, it looked like he wanted to talk to you. Maybe you need to do something about that."

"Yeah, I don't know, maybe." She picked up her burger and handed Skylar a fry, pointedly ignoring the looks Diane and her dad exchanged.

The sun was getting low in the sky, and it was time to get the auction started. Leila left Skylar with Diane and her dad and went to the stage with Jessica and Elizabeth.

Jessica bounced on the balls of her feet. "I can't believe how awesome the day's been. The silent auction items brought in so much money. The center has already reached its goal. Deloris is ecstatic."

Elizabeth took the clipboard from Leila. "It's been great. Now let's hope the live auction does as well."

Deloris Green joined the girls and clapped her hands together. "Everything has been going amazingly well all day today. We've already raised more than I hoped." Her face was lit with joy.

Her excitement was contagious and caused a rush of exhilaration to flow through Leila. "Everyone has been so generous."

"And it's only the beginning. Now it's time for the auction." Deloris wrapped an arm around each girl. "Thank you so much."

Elizabeth laughed. "I think I speak for Leila also when I say that we'd never be able to repay all that you and the center have done for us. We're more than glad to help."

"That's what the Crisis Pregnancy Center is for. Elizabeth, are you ready to get the auction started?"

"Absolutely." Elizabeth wore a giant grin on her face as she and Deloris took the stage.

Leila and Jessica stood off to the side to take part in the auction.

Steve Gregor, the auctioneer from Gregor Auction and Realty, introduced Elizabeth as she took the stage. "Thank you, Mr. Gregor. And thanks to all of you for coming out and supporting Crisis Pregnancy Center with your time and money."

There was loud applause from the crowd.

"I also want to let y'all know that the pregnancy center has already reached its goal. . ." The crowd cheered and clapped. Elizabeth held up her hand. "I agree. That's amazing, but remember, that was just a goal. Now it's time to smash that goal to pieces and help the center even more. It's time to get started!"

The tent vibrated with excitement as the crowd filled it and spilled out into the humid night. People were elbow to elbow as they jockeyed for a better spot to observe the items as they were presented on stage. The enthusiasm of the crowd was contagious. Hopefully, they were all as enthusiastic about bidding.

Everything about the night filled Leila with joy. She was part of something bigger than herself. The pregnancy center had been there for her when she was lost and scared, and seeing these people there to support it helped her stand taller.

Jessica nudged her in the ribs and handed her an auction card. "Here's your number."

The auction got started. Steve Gregor was off and running, his voice rambling out words faster than Leila could keep up.

They started big, with a Vulcan 900 Classic. The motorcycle, which was rolled onstage, got lots of attention from the crowd, and the bidding started quickly.

Steve Gregor kept things going at a rocket pace, and items flew off the floor. The amount of money being thrown out was astonishing. Leila and Jessica laughed often at the excitement of it all. With the speed of Steve's babbling, and the bidding numbers being thrown up and down, Leila found it hard not to be a part of the excitement. She almost raised her number in the air a couple of times, but luckily, she held herself back because the bidding was way more than her paycheck at the boutique could afford her.

Finally, it was time for the services auction, and the first ones out were the Christian Church youth. They were being auctioned to help with any outdoor chores people needed and were separated into two groups.

The crowd loved this. A group of teen girls auctioned off their babysitting services, and a piano teacher offered lessons. There was a professional house painter, someone to clean pools, and then finally Brady, Jacob, Tristan, and Chad were up to build an outdoor deck. They were dressed in tight jeans, tight white T-shirts, work boots, and toolbelts which rested low on their hips. They got lots of laughs and catcalls as they strutted onstage.

"Okay, okay, everyone." Elizabeth tried her best to get the crowd's attention. "These *handsome* men are here to build one lucky person a deck."

Brady strutted to her and placed a kiss on her cheek and winked, causing her to laugh and the crowd to jeer.

Brady leaned into the microphone. "Our emcee is beautiful, don't y'all agree?" Elizabeth turned redder than a rose and grabbed the microphone from him, hip-bumping him out of her way.

Jessica and Leila had tears streaming down their faces from laughing. Leila thought her side was going to split as the bidding on the guys got higher and higher. Finally, the bidding on their services was complete, and they strutted back off the stage, waving and playing to the crowd.

"Okay, everyone." Elizabeth had her hand up to get the attention of the crowd. "Our last item to bid on is a horseback riding lesson with the one and only Adler Warfield."

Leila turned, wide-eyed, toward Jessica.

"You need to bid. He can't ignore you if you win the lesson," Jessica said with a wicked grin on her face.

Adler strutted onto the stage, and Leila's heart stopped. He looked better than she'd ever seen him—if that was even possible. He must have changed since she saw him earlier. He was wearing dark blue jeans, tight as usual in all the right places, and a light blue button-up shirt, tucked in allowing his belt buckle to be seen. He had on his normal cowboy boots, and his face was sexy with a day's worth of whiskers.

Leila turned to Jessica. "Yeah, I need to win my man back." She pushed her head up and held tightly onto her card. She was ready.

Chapter 27

"This is Adler Warfield," Elizabeth announced.

Adler forced the biggest smile as he strutted across the stage. He didn't want to be there, strutting and being judged like cattle. The thought made him chuckle. Now he knew what it was like to be one of their steers on the auction block. *I can't believe I was talked into doing this.*

He scanned the crowd. There was Desiree, looking hot as usual. He smiled a crooked grin her way and winked. At least she helped him see the fun in this.

He continued scanning the crowd. Maybe he'd be able to catch a glimpse of Leila. He didn't see her, but close behind Desiree were Tom and Diane. Diane had Skylar in her arms, and Adler's heart softened. Skylar looked sweet and absolutely adorable. Her eyes were wide. The noise and commotion must have been a little overwhelming for her. He thought back to earlier when he'd said hi to them. He was hoping to get an apology from Leila, or a little acknowledgement at least, but it didn't seem like she had anything to say to him. Elizabeth's voice brought him back to the business at hand.

"Adler Warfield is offering his services to give horseback riding lessons, or if you already know how to ride and don't need lessons, he will be your guide for a trail ride through the back country at Warfield Acres." Elizabeth twirled her finger in a circle in the air. "Turn so they know what all they're getting."

He dropped his chin and glared at her. *You've got to be kidding me.* "Seriously?" he whispered.

"Of course, I'm serious," Elizabeth said into her microphone. "Don't y'all want to see what you'll be getting for your money?"

There were loud cheers and claps throughout the crowd, with whistles coming from the front.

Adler turned and shot daggers at the guys. *Assholes.* He moved his gaze toward Elizabeth, shook his head, and rolled his eyes. He stuck his arms out and gave a sneer to the crowd as he turned in a slow circle. Again, the cheering and whistling continued. Adler wanted to choke someone, but whatever.

"So. Who will start the bidding?" Steve Gregor asked, and he started rambling in his auctioneer voice.

The bids started slowly. A little embarrassing. Adler couldn't stand up here and listen as his services went slowly from $20, to $25, then $30—really? Okay, this was ridiculous. He was worth more than this.

He strutted to the edge of the stage, put his arms out, palms up, and gestured to the crowd. "Come on, people!" he yelled at the top of his lungs. "It's for charity, and I'm worth more than this!" He turned again, slower this time, and made sure to flex when he was finished. The noise became deafening, and a loud "fifty dollars!" came from somewhere in the crowd.

The bidding was off and running. Adler couldn't keep up, and luckily, he didn't have to. That was Steve Gregor's job, and he was a pro.

It seemed like there were at least four people causing a bidding war. One older woman who kept winking when she caught his eyes. That was a little creepy, but he smiled at her anyway. Desiree was another. She could get his services for free, but he winked at her when their eyes met. One woman he didn't know, but it looked like she was bidding for the teenage girl standing next to her, and the fourth person, Adler couldn't see.

It was a battle back and forth, until finally there was a "five-hundred dollars" shouted above the noise. Everyone, even Steve Gregor, froze as silence engulfed the crowd. Steve's eyes were wide. "Did I hear right? Five-hundred dollars?" he asked in his thick southern drawl as his gaze darted around.

Adler's did as well. Who would possibly pay that kind of money for a horseback riding lesson?

Then he caught the winning bidder's eye. It was Desiree, but who did she outbid? Adler glanced around, searching for the fourth bidder. And the fourth bidder finally came into view. Leila lowered her head as she walked away from the auction.

Leila couldn't believe it. She'd gotten caught up in the bidding and was excited about the possibility of winning. She could see how people got addicted to the adrenaline rush of gambling. Her heart was palpitating fast, and her body was alive. Then a bidder yelled out, five-hundred dollars. A crazy sum, and she immediately recognized Desiree's voice.

Every muscle in her body tensed. She couldn't compete against her in any way. And she was tired of trying.

As soon as that amount was said, Leila glanced at Adler, and caught the wink he sent Desiree's way. She was crazy to think he would ever be interested in her over Desiree. She deflated and had to get out of the tent. All those people made it so claustrophobic and stuffy. She needed air.

She pushed her way to freedom and fell onto the bench of a picnic table. It was better out here because the noise of the auction was muffled, and the night was warm, yet comfortable. She sat staring at the mostly empty downtown, the lights in the trees causing a romantic glow over the streets.

I totally screwed this up. He was amazing and sweet. And so out of her league. Tears slowly carved a path down her cheeks.

"Hey, Leila, are you okay?"

Leila looked up as Stacey and Tristan walked toward her. Just what she needed—Adler's cousin reporting back to him that she was out here crying. She turned her head and wiped her cheeks. "Yeah, I'm good." She gave them what she hoped was a believable smile.

"I saw you leave, and I wanted to come talk to you." Tristan sat next to her. "I don't know what Adler's doing, but I can tell you he misses you."

Leila kept her eyes on the ground. It didn't seem to her that he missed her. "I don't know if I believe that."

"Look." Tristan gently placed his hand on her leg. "He told me what happened, what you said to him. He was hurt. He still is. I've never seen him like this before. He's never cared for anyone as much as he does you, so he's never been hurt like this either."

Leila's heart tore into a million pieces, and she had no clue how to piece it back together. Her words had forced him away, and he seemed pleased with where he was now. "I saw him earlier with Desiree. They looked like they picked up where they left off." Heat grew in her chest. "I know what I said was hurtful, and I wish I could take it back, but if he's happy. . ."

Stacey sat next to her and grabbed her hand. "He and Des aren't together. I'm sure she'd like to be, but he's not interested in her. They're just friends."

She glanced at Stacey. "A friend who just spent five-hundred dollars on something she could do for free."

"Look, I'm sure he'd accept your apology if you gave it. I know he misses you." Tristan stood. "That's all I wanted to say."

"Thank you," Leila said in a soft voice.

Stacey squeezed her hand before they left.

Leila watched them until they disappeared around the corner, then stood. She needed to stop feeling sorry for herself and get back to the auction. She pushed her shoulders back and took one step, then stopped. Frozen to the spot. Adler had just walked out of the tent, and their eyes met. *Go talk to him, Leila.* She coaxed herself and put a shy smile on her face. Before she lost her nerve, she walked to him at a fast pace. "Adler. Can we talk?"

His face was void of emotion.

"Please?" She was close enough that she closed her hand over his bicep. A tingle shot through her, and her gaze fell on his eagle tattoo. She brushed her fingers over it and suddenly became desperate. She squeezed his arm lightly. "I'm sorry. I'm so sorry. What I said was mean and so wrong." She was rambling, she knew it, but she was scared if she didn't get what she wanted to say out quickly, something would stop her. She squeezed his arm a little more. "I don't know why I said you wouldn't make a good father. I was. . ."

Adler pulled away. "I know why you said what you said. You don't believe people can change." He shook his head, and a shadow went over his brown eyes. "No matter how much I tried to convince you I cared for you, you didn't believe it. I want you to know that we weren't a game to me. I thought we were real." His eyes were glistening under the lights, and he tipped his head up and sighed deeply.

The sight broke Leila's heart. She had this handsome and sweet guy upset because of how she'd treated him. She had never been on this side of things before. "Adler, I know you cared for me. I was stupid and insecure. You're so amazing, and I didn't understand what you could see in me when you could have anyone. . ."

"Adler?"

Leila jerked her head to the side. It was Desiree. Just the woman who didn't need to be there.

"Hi, Leila." Desiree's concerned eyes bounced back and forth between Adler and Leila.

Leila pressed her lips together. "Hi." Her voice was barely audible.

"Good, I guess you paid, Des? We gotta go." Adler's eyes never left Leila's and shot daggers into hers.

There was no way she would ever repair her heart now. "Adler, please. We really need to talk." Emotions choked her. He couldn't walk away. Not now.

He shook his head. "I'm done here. Nothing else here is important." He gestured with his head. "Come on, Des."

Desiree's brow creased. "Adler, maybe you should stay. Clear things up."

He let out a heavy sigh, and his words were harsh. "Stay if you want. I'm leaving." He walked away and didn't look back.

Leila looked at Desiree as tears fell from her eyes.

"Leila, I'm sorry. I'll talk to him." Desiree gave her a quick hug and followed behind him.

She didn't want to stay and watch them walk away together, so she took a deep breath and entered the tent. She needed to find Skylar and head home.

The drive to his house seemed longer than usual, and Adler turned up the radio loud. He wished he were on his motorcycle going ninety around the sharp curves toward his house. That always calmed him, but instead he had to be okay with the wind blowing his hair because he had the top down to his Mustang. When he'd left Desiree at her car, they'd made a date for her riding lesson and trail ride. He wasn't looking forward to it. He didn't enjoy the day at all.

When he'd pulled up to the fair, the first person he saw was Desiree, and she'd asked him to help her carry her baskets of baked goods to the tent for the silent auction. He had planned on spending the day with Tristan and Stacey, but getting rid of Desiree became more difficult than he'd expected. Unfortunately, she seemed to want to be with him again, but that was the last thing he wanted. Then, seeing Leila, made him automatically flirt more with Desiree.

Idiot. Now you led Desiree on and didn't allow Leila to apologize. You're a dumbass.

Chapter 28

A dler let out a sigh as he got ready for his lesson with Desiree. He had a hard time believing she'd spent that kind of money to have a lesson with him. What did she want? That wasn't hard to figure out, and how he'd flirted with her the night of the auction didn't help. He was being childish, trying to make Leila jealous. Who was he?

Now it'd been two additional weeks since he'd seen Leila. He'd spent the time working, avoiding Desiree, and deleting texts he started to Leila. She'd looked sincere when she apologized at the fundraiser, and there was no doubt she was upset seeing him with Desiree.

Every time he saw her, his heart ached. He pictured her sitting at the table holding Skylar. Before she turned toward him, her face was glowing, and she was beautiful. He had been drawn to her, like the first time he danced with her at the wedding.

Then after the auction, the sadness that radiated from her ripped his heart out. She apologized, and he wanted to accept it and wrap his arms around her, but instead he was immature and hurt her just like she'd hurt him.

Someone would have to give in, or he'd be miserable forever.

Oh, well. Gotta get going. He slipped his feet into his boots, grabbed his sunglasses off the kitchen counter, and filled a small cooler with waters. He refused to drink beer. He didn't want his inhibitions to be diminished, allowing him to make a stupid decision. He rode his motorcycle the short ride to the stables where Desiree was meeting him for the riding lessons she didn't need.

Sure, she may not have been a professional, but she'd been here with him, and they'd been on the trails. He really hoped she didn't think this was how they would get back together. Right now, he didn't want sex. His heart hurt, and he wanted Leila.

Finally, a car pulled up, and Desiree got out. She wore jeans and a tight shirt, which showed off her belly button ring. There once was a time he'd thought that was so hot. Now it did nothing except make him think that outfit was not something you should wear to go riding.

"Hey, sexy," Desiree purred as she sauntered toward him, her hips swaying and her auburn hair up in a high ponytail.

He gave her a small smile and hugged her without the enthusiasm of her squeeze.

She pulled away and cocked her head to the side and looked up at him with her green eyes. "You good?"

"Yeah. Are you ready for a lesson? Let's get it started. What do you want to learn? You already ride pretty well."

She shook her head, her auburn ponytail flopping from side to side. "Honestly, I don't want a lesson. I just wanted time with you."

That's what he was afraid of.

She placed her hands on his arms and looked up at him seductively. There once was a time that look would have gotten him worked up and he'd have had no problem taking advantage of her, but not this time.

"Des. Don't." He backed away, putting space between them.

She dropped her arm and chuckled. "I can't believe it." She stood there, shaking her head.

He quirked an eyebrow. "What?"

"You have serious feelings for her, don't you?"

He froze and slid his gaze over her. Desiree was hot, and any guy would want her, but she didn't have that sweet innocent beauty about her. She didn't make his insides heat up with her smile and with her touch. Leila did. His shoulders met his ears. He couldn't deny it.

"I know you like each other. Hell, it's obvious. Everyone can see it. What I don't understand is if you like her this much, why didn't you accept her apology at the auction?"

He shrugged. "I don't know. I've been wondering the same thing." His vision started getting blurry. He turned away and blinked quickly.

Desiree's voice was soft and gentle. "You love her."

Adler's heart stopped. "Excuse me?"

"Leila, dumbass. You love her, and don't deny it. It's written all over your face. I know we stopped seeing each other because you had feelings for her, but I didn't really think they would last." She chuckled again. "I guess I was wrong." She shook her head as a smile broke across her face.

He couldn't be sure he loved Leila. He had never loved anyone before but his family. Love wasn't a word he used ever. But these weren't feelings he'd ever had either. "I don't know if I love her, but I do miss her. Not that it matters."

"What do you mean?"

"She doesn't think I'm good enough. She can't forget my past." He walked away as anger rose from his chest.

"Did she tell you that?"

"Yes. The night we stopped seeing each other." He slumped against the fence.

"Well, she seemed really sorry at the auction. I heard the way she spoke to you. I heard the desperation in her voice." Desiree stood next to him and leaned on the fence as well.

"Yeah, well, I don't know what to do." Adler gazed out over the hills. Was it just a few weeks ago that he realized his feelings for Leila? That they rode across these hills and got caught in the rain? "She wants someone who will not only love her but also be a good role model and father figure for Skylar. I don't fit the bill."

"Well, I don't think that's true. I bet she'll figure things out sooner than you think."

"Yeah, right." He could only wish.

"I know she misses you terribly. She knows she made a mistake and wants to fix things. She just doesn't know how. She'd love to talk to you, but she thinks we're a thing and you aren't interested in her anymore."

He stood up straight. Did he just hear her right? His heart stopped, and his pulse picked up. "What? How do you know all that?"

"Well, let's just say I was with the girls, and you and Leila came up in conversation. She was also upset that you wouldn't accept her apology at the auction."

"Yeah, I was rude, but in my defense, I was still hurt. She said some shitty things."

"You're right, she did, and she knows it." Desiree laid her hand on his shoulder. "Look, I think you two have something special. Go to her. She's at her house."

"What if she doesn't want to talk?"

Desiree laughed. "The ladies' man is nervous and insecure. You *are* crazy about her." She walked to his motorcycle and handed him his helmet. "Go and talk with her."

His pulse picked up speed. He wanted to see her more than anything. Boy, he wanted to, but Desiree paid for these lessons. "You paid good money. . .well, ridiculous money for this date. I can't just walk away from you."

"Be honest with me. Do you really want to spend time with me today, or would you rather go and try to work things out with Leila?"

He looked at her, and her green eyes pulled him in, but not like they used to. He started getting antsy.

He grabbed his helmet. "Thanks Des. We can still do this date. You did pay good money for me."

She laughed a laugh deep from her gut. "Look," she said. "Even though I did pay ridiculous money for this date, it wouldn't be worth my time. It was a donation to a great cause." She pushed her hands against his chest and pushed him toward his motorcycle. "Go to her."

"What if it's too late?"

She gave him a shove toward his bike. "Just go. Make this right. Like I said, you're both crazy about each other, and everyone can see that."

"Thank you, Des." His heart raced, and he kissed her cheek as a silly grin ticked up his mouth. He put on his helmet and jumped on his bike.

He rode like a bat out of hell toward Leila's house, his thoughts going back and forth like crazy. Three months ago, he was just having fun. Having sex with a beautiful woman, doing what he wanted. Now here he was, stressed over whether a woman—a single mother—was interested in him, and surprisingly he needed her to be interested in him more than he could admit.

Chapter 29

Adler pulled to a stop in front of Leila's. There were trucks and cars parked along the street, some of which he recognized. Tristan, Jacob, Chad, and a couple of others were there. Leila's father had "bought" their services at the auction. They were building a back deck for him. Great. He'd have an audience. Just what he needed.

He turned off the engine and took off his helmet. Suddenly his stomach started churning. *Dammit. What the hell!* Adler couldn't believe how his heart reacted at the thought of seeing Leila.

Leila had burrowed deep beneath his skin, and even after she got rid of him, here he was, still always thinking about her, not able to keep his eyes off her when she was around. He pictured her in his mind. Her sweet personality. Her long brown hair, those hazel-green eyes, and soft skin. Her adorable daughter. Ever since he saw her at the wedding, she'd filled his every thought, and ever since he saw her at the auction his heart was empty, alone, and lost.

The banging of hammers and buzzing of saws traveled in the air as he walked down the driveway. He took a deep breath to calm his nerves. The last time he was here, she didn't want him around. He wasn't good enough.

What if Desiree was wrong, and she still thought that? Or even worse, if something could be worse than that, what if she was with someone else, someone she thought was good father material?

He froze as the front door opened, and Leila walked out. Her brown hair floated behind her, making her look like the angel she was. She was breathtaking. Adler's pulse raced as he sauntered cautiously toward her.

He cleared his throat. "Leila?" Nerves took over his insides and made his churning stomach go into overdrive.

She looked up, and their eyes met. Hers went wide.

The side of Adler's mouth ticked up a little, and his pulse raced.

He saw her eyes flick quickly up and down, then back to his face. "I thought you had your date with Desiree today," she said, her voice soft.

"I did, but plans changed." He was so close he could smell the strawberry scent of her shampoo. He could touch her if he wanted to, and his fingers itched to reach out. "We talked about things, and this was where I wanted to be."

Leila's eyes flitted across his face. "Why?" Confusion shrouded her features.

Adler's heart stopped. Maybe Desiree was wrong. "I thought maybe. . ." His voice trailed off as she backed away. God, he was stupid. He combed his fingers through his hair and held his hands behind his neck. She'd told him she didn't want him. That he wasn't good enough. Why was he here? He pressed his teeth tightly together, and anger rose from his gut. *Don't get mad at her. It's not like she led you on.*

"Adler." She pulled his arms from behind his head. The warmth of her touch slowly seeped into his skin. His gaze met hers, and the familiar pull was there, bringing them together. "I'm surprised you're here after how I treated you."

He tried to say something but couldn't think of any words. It was okay. He didn't need to.

"I need you to believe that I'm sorry." She squeezed his hands.

Adler breathed in deep and pushed his shoulders back. *Keep your feelings in check.* He worked hard to hold himself back. He wanted to reach out and wrap his arms around her so badly he could taste it, but he needed to keep his head on his shoulders.

"Adler, when Skylar's dad asked me to take care of my pregnancy, I was so frightened and alone. I swore that I'd never put myself in a situation where I was blindsided by a man again." She placed her hand on his cheek, and her warmth seeped into his skin. "But you blindsided me, and it frightened me. Why would a man like you be interested in me? Then when we went out and all those women, beautiful women, talked to you, it took me back to Ben."

Her eyes filled with tears, and his heart lurched. "Leila?" Instinctively, he closed the space between them.

She put up her hand. "Let me finish, please."

He stopped and gently placed his hands on her arms.

"You and Ben are so much alike. You're both handsome, and you both have a magnetism that attracts women to you. In my mind, I pictured you walking away from us and breaking both our hearts, but I was wrong. You're nothing like Ben, and I shouldn't have compared you to him."

Adler tucked her hair behind her ear. "I'm sorry. . ."

She laughed lightly as she pulled away. "You have nothing to be sorry for. You've been nothing but amazing and wonderful to me and Skylar, and I treated you so badly. So awful. I'm the one who's sorry. I can't believe you're here after what I said to you." She paused and stepped closer reluctantly. "I thought I was doing the right thing for Skylar. I was so stupid." She placed her palm on the side of his face. "I wish I could take back all the things I said. I don't think you'd be a bad father. Skylar adores you. I adore you. I think you're amazing. You aren't the person I thought you were, and I was so wrong to say those things."

He studied her face and put a space between them. He knew she was sorry. He could see it in her eyes. "Leila, I hope you realize how wrong you were. I'm not the person I used to be, but I could have just forgotten us today. I'll be totally honest. Desiree didn't want the lessons she bought. She wanted me again." Her eyes bulged. "But she knew I wasn't available. My heart is taken."

Leila rubbed her hands on her face. "Adler, I really hope you can forgive me."

His gaze traveled across her features. Her beautiful eyes, her porcelain-like skin, her soft pink lips that he really wanted to feel against his. His heart filled with emotions he didn't know existed. "Of course I forgive you." His voice was thick. This woman made him feel more than he thought possible, and the only thing he was sure of was that these last few weeks without her were a nightmare, one he didn't want to relive. He swallowed hard as his pulse picked up speed. Their gazes held.

Leila's soft whisper broke the silence. "Kiss me, please. If you want to."

Adler's mouth ticked up at the corners. "I don't want to, beautiful. I need to." Without waiting another second, his mouth devoured hers. Finally, his heart grew calm, whole, and complete.

Chapter 30

"Well, it looks like we have another set of hands, guys."

Adler and Leila pulled apart slightly, and a blush crept across Leila's face as she met Adler's smirk.

There were Tristan, Jacob, and Chad, tool belts on, baseball hats on backwards, and water bottles in their hands, standing and watching them.

Adler gave such a small shake of his head that she almost missed it, and his lips met hers again, lighter this time, gentler.

"I don't think he's very interested in working right now," said Tristan.

"Has that pretty boy ever even held a power tool?" asked Chad.

Adler pulled away. His eyes were pointed at the heavens, and he had his bottom lip sucked in. He was so adorable and hot that Leila laughed. She couldn't help herself.

"Sorry," he said to her as he flipped up his middle finger and turned toward the guys. "I'm busy here. Shouldn't y'all go back to work?"

"I thought maybe you decided to come help us when we heard your bike pull up, but it looks like something else got your attention." Tristan said with a smirk.

"Anyway, Leila, Jessica sent me a text and said she's on her way and you hadn't answered. Now I know why."

"Thanks, Chad." She wanted to keep Adler a little longer before she went to the pregnancy center with Jessica. "Want to see Sky?" she asked. "Then, when I go with Jessica, you can help the guys. That way you'll be here when I get back." She raised her brow in question.

"Let's go." He pulled her toward the door. "I'll show y'all my skills with power tools once the girls are gone."

Adler opened the door for her, and she walked into the living room and smiled at Diane, who was sitting on the floor playing with Skylar.

"Adler." Diane jumped up from the floor and gave him a hug. She stood back and looked between them. "I'm so glad to see you. What are you two up to?"

"He stopped by and wanted to see Sky," Leila answered, as Skylar let out a happy squeal. Leila's heart swelled as Adler sat on the floor and Skylar bounced up and down and flapped her arms, a wide toothless grin on her face. Her dad was right. Babies can pick out the good ones.

"Hey, little beauty." He picked her up and placed a kiss on her cheek.

Skylar gave another high-pitched squeal.

Diane's arm went around Leila's waist. "He's the good one."

Leila's face shone. There was an amazing man sitting on the floor, her daughter laughing in his arms. Leila could still feel the pressure of his lips on hers. Warmth filled her. "Yeah, he really is."

Leila and Jessica left the Crisis Pregnancy Center and went back to Leila's, meeting up with the guys just as they were cleaning up. The deck looked great. Tom could have done it himself, but why when there were capable and willing young men to do it for him?

"This looks great," Jessica said. "I'll know who to call when my Grams is ready to have her deck redone."

"I think we could help her out," Chad replied as he gave Jessica a kiss. "We're done. Would you mind taking me home?"

"I think I can do that," Jessica answered with a smile. "Bye, y'all."

"Tristan, are you ready? The girls are having dinner for us," Jacob said as he gathered the last of his tools into the back of his truck.

"Yep. I'll be right there." He looked between Adler and Leila. "You staying?" he asked Adler, his brow raised.

Adler smiled and wrapped his arm around Leila's waist. "Yeah, bro. I think I am." Leila's heart skipped a beat when their eyes met. Her smile grew, and she leaned into his side.

"Alright. You two be good." Tristan grinned wide and climbed into his truck.

When he was out of sight, Adler turned to her. "I guess I should've asked you. Is it okay if I stay awhile?"

Her desire for him was intense, and her heart beat wildly. "I'm glad you want to." She grabbed his shirt and pulled him closer.

His crooked smile melted her heart, and whatever issues she had were gone. His lips met hers, and her breath caught as she was lost in everything Adler.

His kiss was warm and a little desperate. She slid her hand behind his neck and kissed him harder. Suddenly, very aware that she had almost lost him, she pulled herself against him in a desperate plea to feel him and taste all of him. Finally, they pulled away, their breaths rapid, and her hands rested on his shoulders.

He wrapped his arms around her waist and pulled her closer. "Can we go inside? It's a little dark out here, and I'd love to spend some time with Skylar."

He wanted to spend time with her and Skylar. What was she thinking, pushing him away? "Sounds great. Let's go get her."

They went to Leila's apartment with Skylar, had sandwiches for dinner, and enjoyed being with each other. They sat on the floor of Skylar's room playing with her before she had to go to bed.

"I almost forgot. I have something for you both." Adler stood and put his hand in his pocket. "Here."

He placed a bracelet in Leila's hand. It was the turquoise bracelet with dolphins that he purchased at the boutique a while ago. "I forgot you bought this." She looked at him, confused.

"It's for Skylar. One day we'll take her to swim with real dolphins. Until then, she'll have this one."

He was looking into the future, and it included her and Skylar. She let out a breath. "Thank you. That is so sweet of you." She leaned over and kissed him, then stood with Skylar in her arms. "It's late. She needs to go to bed." She placed the bracelet on Skylar's dresser, then laid her in bed. They both kissed her lightly and left her room.

As soon as Skylar's door was closed, Adler pulled her to him and wrapped his hand around her arm. "Here." He latched the other bracelet that he'd bought from the boutique onto her wrist.

Leila touched the pink and white roses, read the plaque that now adorned her wrist. *You are enough*, written in cursive, and the Bible verse she loved on the back. She blinked back the tears that threatened to fall. "Adler. . ." She glanced up at him, her vision blurry.

He wiped a tear from her cheek. "I need you to know and realize. You are enough. You are everything I never knew I wanted, and everything I didn't know I needed." He laughed a little. "Does that even make sense?"

It made sense. It made perfect sense. Her voice caught, and she nodded.

Adler placed his palms on both sides of her face and held her in an intense gaze. "The moment I saw you at the wedding, I knew you were the one."

Leila's hands went to his wrists. "Adler?"

He shushed her as he placed his thumbs over her lips. "I love you, Leila. I've never said that to anyone before, and I've never needed to be with anyone like I need to be with you."

Her breath caught. He loved her. This amazingly perfect man loved her. Her heart swelled. She wrapped her arms around him and crushed her lips to his. The kiss went from zero to sixty in zero seconds flat. "I love you too," she whispered as they pulled away. Her stomach was filled with butterflies, and her pulse raced. "I want you to stay with me tonight," she added breathlessly.

Adler's gaze was intense, his breathing deep and quick. "You don't have to ask me twice."

His smile was seductive as he pulled her into her room, and warmth flooded her. "I think your 'melt their panties off smile' has finally started working on me," she said, her voice filled with desire.

"Really?" He smiled, his eyes hot.

She nodded as she undressed.

He quickly followed, and they met on the bed, wrapped in each other's arms.

Epilogue

It was a perfect Saturday afternoon in late February. There wasn't a cloud in the sky, and the sun shone brightly. Leila climbed out of the ATV when Adler stopped in front of the small tent set up beside the horse pasture and barn. "Adler. This is too much." There were pink and silver balloons everywhere, with two very large pony balloons.

Adler held Skylar. "Ne, Ne," Skylar said.

His smile filled his face. "Yes, little beauty, those are pony balloons, just for you." He draped his free arm over Leila's shoulders. "It's not about you today, beautiful. It's all about this little beauty, and she loves it." He leaned over and gave Leila a quick peck on the lips, then walked ahead and placed Skylar on the ground. She batted at the balloons and squealed, then toddled on wobbly legs toward Diane and Elisha.

Leila stood back, taking in the scene. The tent was set up with a buffet table at one end. They were having chicken tenders, vegetables, and macaroni and cheese. A one-year-old's heaven on earth.

Nico and his kitchen staff worked hard serving the guests who had already arrived. Next to the buffet was a cake table with a cake in the shape of a horse. That was not her idea, but like Adler said, this wasn't about her. It was all for Skylar.

"Hey." Tom wrapped his arm around her shoulder.

"Hi, Dad." She sniffed back tears.

"It's a lot."

She nodded. "Yeah, but he wouldn't have it any other way. It's all for Skylar, as he's told me millions of times since we started planning this. He said his girl only turns one once, and it was reason to celebrate." Leila chuckled. "Makes me wonder what he's going to do when she turns sixteen."

"He's going to love you both." Tom squeezed her shoulders.

Leila smiled, and her heart swelled.

Her dad was so right. She glanced down at the ring on her left hand. The round diamond reflected the sunlight and reminded her of how much Adler loved them. Even though she tried to get him to reign in his purchases and asked him to not go overboard on her engagement ring, the ring was a total of four carats, even though as Adler pointed out, the center ring was "only two carats" the surrounding diamonds made up the rest, and according to him, they don't count.

She laughed to herself and shook her head slightly. She knew everything he gave them was given out of love, but how was she going to get him to realize she didn't need big and extravagant? She just needed him, and she had that.

She gazed off in the distance where two houses were being built on the hill overlooking the stable and pastureland. One for them, and the other for Tristan and Stacey. Their house was the closest to the horse barn. Adler was adamant about Skylar loving horses, and it seemed that he was getting his wish. The houses were enormous and, like her ring, a bit much, but this was her life now, and a life with Adler would always be exciting and extravagant. She would have to get used to it.

She and Adler were having a double wedding with Stacey and Tristan in May. Since Leila and Stacey have very small families, and mostly the same friends, it just made sense. The houses were on track to be completed and ready to be moved into by the end of May. They better be. The four of them were coming home from their honeymoons then and would need to live somewhere.

"Babe, come on." Adler called and waved her down.

"Let's not keep him waiting. I'm sure he has more surprises for Skylar and you." Tom pulled her forward.

Leila laughed. She was sure Adler had planned many things he didn't fill her in on. She joined Adler and Skylar, who were sitting at a table at the front of the tent. Skylar already had her hands in a plate of macaroni and cheese, with a mouth full of chicken.

"I got you a plate." Adler pulled out a chair for her and kissed her softly.

"Thank you. It looks delicious." She commented as she wiped cheese from Skylar's face and placed the bib around her neck.

They ate and talked and laughed at the kids. It was a great afternoon surrounded by family and friends. Skylar got more toys than any one-year-old could ever use in ten lifetimes, but all she cared about were the boxes and bows. Grant helped decorate her hair with the bows from her packages until she was covered and there was nowhere left for anymore, so he decorated Elizabeth.

"Okay." Adler stood and pulled out his phone.

"Who are you texting?" Leila asked.

He held up a finger, gesturing for her to wait a second. "Skylar has one more present."

No way. "What did you do?" What else could he possibly give her? "She has enough."

Adler grabbed her hand and pulled her out of her chair. The excitement on his face was contagious, but also a little overwhelming. "Nope. Every child who is a member of my family gets this on their first birthday." His smile filled his face as he picked up Skylar and turned Leila around.

Her mouth fell open. "Oh, my gosh. Adler." Her heart stopped. There was a beautiful brown pony with a jet-black mane and jet-black tail being led toward them by Jonathan and Carla. It had a pink ribbon braided throughout its mane and tied around its tail.

"Come on, Sky." Adler almost ran to the pony with Skylar in his arms.

Skylar squealed as she reached out to pet the horse softly on its neck. "Ne, Ne."

Adler laughed. "Yes, Skylar. A pony. All for you."

Leila wrapped her arms around Adler's waist and laid her head on his shoulder as Jonathan took Skylar and held her on the pony's back. Her heart swelled. "You're too much, Warfield," she whispered in his ear. Skylar's face was total excitement as Jonathon lifted her from the pony and handed her to Leila.

"She's so worth it." Adler wrapped them both in his arms. He placed his head close to Skylar's. "Happy birthday, Skylar. I love you so much." He kissed her forehead, and a tear fell down Leila's face.

Adler wiped it away. "Hey, this is a happy day. No tears."

"I know." Leila laughed and sniffled. "I am happy. We are both so lucky to have you."

"I'm the lucky one." He placed a quick kiss on her lips. "I have one more present."

She sighed. "Adler, it's already so much. You really. Need. To stop."

He smiled his crooked smile that made her heart flip and winked. "This one's important." He turned. "Mom. Dad."

Leila lifted a brow. What did Elisha and Don have to do with anything?

Don produced an envelope from his breast pocket and handed it to Adler. Elisha and Don both had weird grins on their faces, and when Leila turned to Adler, he was sweating and breathing rapidly. "Adler. What's going on? What's wrong?"

He shook his head and gazed intently into her eyes. "Leila, you and Skylar are my life. The first time I held you in my arms on the dance floor, and the first time I held Skylar at the fair, I fell in love. You both saved me and made me a better person. I love you both more than I ever thought it was possible to love anyone."

Leila's eyes went wide, and her heart thudded against her chest as his eyes filled with tears. "Adler." Her voice came out as a whisper.

He took a deep, shaky breath. "Leila, you and I are becoming one in May, but I hope we can become even more."

"What?" She had no clue what he was talking about.

"I love Skylar like she's mine. I know biologically she isn't, but I see her as my daughter, and I couldn't love her more. When we're married, I want to adopt her and make her a Warfield also. I want her to know every day that she was always loved and wanted by me." He let out a heavy breath.

Leila shook her head. He wants them both to be his. "Adler, that's so sweet." If she thought her heart was full before, it was overflowing now. She pulled him in and wrapped him in her arms, with Skylar between them.

He pulled away as tears fell from her eyes.

Skylar lifted her fingers to Leila's cheek and touched a tear and cocked her head to the side.

"Oh, baby girl." Leila laughed through the tears. "Adler wants to be your daddy. What do you think about that?"

Skylar smiled wide, showing off her two little front teeth. She leaned her head against his. "Dada." She said in her sweet baby voice.

Leila's heart melted.

Adler's face glowed as a tear slipped from his eye. "That's right, little beauty." He kissed her forehead and wrapped them both in his arms.

Notes to the Reader

Thank you for taking your time and reading You Are Enough. I hope you enjoyed reading it as much as I enjoyed writing it.

If you loved the story and characters, I would be so grateful to you if you would take the time and leave a review wherever you purchased the book. Reviews help authors and are so appreciated.

I'd also love it if you would join my mailing list to find out about new releases in the Orlinda Valley series, and other happenings in my writing career. Visit my website https://donnarmadden.com/ to join my newsletter and see all my books.

I love to hear from my readers, so please connect with me on Tik-Tok, Instagram,or Facebook—Donna R. Madden Writer, or email me at author@donnarmadden.com

This may be the end of the More Than Enough series, but you can continue reading with my next series: Orlinda Valley.

This is a fictional town, yet a culmination of many of the small towns around my home. It was mentioned briefly in *You Are Enough*. You will also see some cammeo appearances from Adler and Leila. The book club women are in this series—so Adler and Leila bring Skylar to hang out with the other grandchildren. I hope you come to Orlinda Valley.

Turn the page for a sample chapter of the first book *No One But You*.

No One But You

Sample Chapter 1

—Kora and Kai—

"What the fuck?" The familiar ride down the back country road turned into bumpy, out-of-control chaos as my car, which was perfectly fine a second ago, suddenly swerved and veered all over the road.

I slid to the shoulder, jammed my foot on the brake, and slammed the gearshift into park. "Damn country roads filled with potholes the size of craters. When are they finally going to pave these terrible pieces of shit?" I slammed my hand on the steering wheel, opened the door, flung the rhetorical question into the open field, and jumped out of the car. Someone had to inspect the tires.

As I suspected. Front passenger tire. Flat. As a pancake.

I stood with my hands on my hips and kicked the now worthless tire. "Dammit. I'm gonna be late for my hair appointment." With a strong exhale, I reached into the back seat of my SUV and grabbed my phone. I needed to let Summer know I'd be late.

My phone rang and rang, but no answer. "Dammit, Summer." I clicked the call end button and sent a text to my best friend for life, Darlene. She would be at the salon. Her son James had spent the night with his grandma, who was also my aunt, Tonya. Tonya—I don't use the aunt—spent her Saturdays bothering her best friends who own the salon, so Darlene was meeting her at Shear Perfection.

She could give Summer a message.

I was staring off over the pasture and watching cows munch the grass when the phone notified me of an incoming text.

I glanced at my phone. "What the hell?" It wasn't Darlene. It was a text informing me my last message wasn't sent. I gritted my teeth as my face heated, and it wasn't because of the humid morning we were already dealing with this late in May. It was my skyrocketing blood pressure. Who wanted to be stuck on the side of the road in Bumfuck, Egypt, and in this heat?

I stalked around the car, held my phone high, and gave it an evil eye. Still no bars. *Of course not.*

"Dammit!" I yelled at the top of my lungs. There was nothing around. Nothing. Except birds, cows, and a rabbit hopping across the field.

The cows stopped munching the grass, and the rabbit even stopped hopping to stare. "What? Am I bothering your busy day?"

"Moo," the cow responded as he chewed his cud without a care in the world, and the rabbit hopped off.

"See? I figured as much." I trudged to the rear of my black Nissan Rogue and opened the hatch to get to the spare as a memory hit me. *Shit.*

I wouldn't see a tire unless I got lucky and my father had helped me out. I lifted the floor panel slowly and squeezed my eyes tight. As soon as the panel was all the way up, I wedged my eyes open slowly, hoping I would see a tire where the spare tire should be. I stared into the abyss of the undercarriage and no such luck. It was empty.

Last December, I went out Christmas shopping and needed more storage for all the gifts I was going to purchase. I had a feeling they wouldn't all fit in the back seat and trunk. Yeah, I know it was a little overkill, but my cousin, Bryson, is married to Darlene, and they have the cutest little boy, James. I can never say no to him, so to make sure I had the space, I took the spare tire out of the car—who uses it anyway—and had more space to stash presents.

I glanced up at the cloudless blue sky and at the sun already shining hot and bright at nine in the morning and shook my head. I could hear my father discussing—as he never yelled—all the reasons why taking the spare tire out of the car was a bad idea. I could also hear him reminding me to put the tire back in the car "in case of an emergency, and you hit one of the many potholes on the county roads."

"Damn, I always knew he was able to see the future." I slammed the hatch closed and peeked at my phone again. Still no bars. This was the one dead zone between my place and downtown, and I was about ten miles away from the nearest house.

I could walk. It wouldn't be the first time I'd walked the roads to town.

The air was getting thick with humidity, and sweat had already formed at the nape of my neck. I pulled my hair up in a high ponytail, leaned in the car, and plucked the emergency scrunchy from around the gear shift.

This was an emergency.

My stringy, straight, auburn hair would get nasty quick. I twisted the ponytail into a loose bun on top of my head, leaned against the hood of the car, and sighed.

It was so damn hot—desert hot.

If this was any indication of what kind of summer we were going to have in Tennessee this year, I'd better be prepared for anything, and in this moment, I was so *not* prepared.

I left in a rush this morning, running late as usual, and didn't grab a water bottle or even a second cup of coffee. Death by dehydration suddenly became a possibility, and walking the ten miles to the nearest house was out of the question. "Where am I gonna get water?" The brown cow who had his head in the grass munching next to the electrified fence stopped pulling up grass, gave me a glance, and went back to munching.

How rude. "Fine. Don't share your water source, cow. See if I sacrifice my hunger next time I'm at a barbecue and have a choice between a burger or chicken. I promise you. I'm eating that burger."

The cow eyed me with disdain.

God, I must have really been losing my mind to be arguing with a cow. Maybe dehydration didn't take as long as I'd thought.

A loud, rumbly growl, along with the sound of gravel crunching, caught my attention. "Wonderful. Help from the calvary. No thanks to you, cow!" Yeah, I hollered at the cow. It was hot, he was rude, and I was thirsty.

I turned away from my nemesis and watched as a beat-up silver Ford pickup pulled up to the side of the road. To say the man who climbed out of the truck and strutted toward me was striking would be an understatement.

He wore a beige Carhartt button-up and a baseball cap on backward. His eyes, which were a unique silver-gray, held mine and caused my heart to do a strange fluttering thing, and they popped in contrast to his sun-tanned skin and, from what I could see sticking out from under his hat, jet-black hair.

My eyes traveled down his tall, muscular body. He wore work boots which had seen better days, and faded, paint-splattered jeans that were well-worn and perfectly tight, hugging his thighs. I stalled at the bulge right under his hips, and my mouth went dry.

Good Lord. Keep moving, eyes.

A loud moo pulled my attention away from the gift strutting toward me and back to my adversary in the field.

"Just go drink that water. You water hoarder," I spat in its direction. I don't know why, but that cow really pissed me off.

"I can't figure out why that cow would be walking away from you. He was keeping you company, and you sure don't seem grateful." His voice was deep, smooth as whiskey, and sexy as hell.

I started to pull my gaze from his, and a distinctive scar, which started by his brow and dipped below his eye, caught my attention. It was the shape of a crescent moon, roughly two inches long, and stood out clearly, suggesting it had been a part of his skin for quite a while. The scar's edges were jagged in places and added a bit of intrigue to his boy-next-door good looks. The couple days' worth of scruff on his face, which I yearned to rub my hands over, gave a rugged allure to his chiseled jawline, and he carried himself with confidence, which increased his overall irresistibility and caused a tingling throughout my body.

What the hell, Kora?

I was taken so off guard, I needed to clear my throat to make my voice work. "Yeah, well, the cow was keeping me company, but when he wouldn't share his water source to keep me from dying of dehydration, I threatened to skip the chicken and eat his cousin instead next time I was at a barbecue."

"Well, I'm sure that's what irritated him." The corner of this stranger's mouth ticked up, and a sexy-as-hell dimple appeared in his left cheek.

Just when I thought this man couldn't get any hotter, I was mistaken. I smirked to hide the blush I was sure colored my cheeks and nodded. "Yeah, well, water would have been nice, but a tire would be even better."

"I guess you hit one of those craters back there?"

"Yeah, I did. I wish this county would spend a little bit of money to fix these back roads, since most of their citizens live back here. But they're so cheap. It's much more important that city hall has a newly paved parking lot and cute rocking chairs on the front porch."

"Those rocking chairs are a perfect place for the locals to hang out and play checkers. I think it's a great addition."

Really? I glared at him through lowered lashes. "You can't be serious."

There was that dimple again.

Did the heat just tick up a notch? I puffed out a breath. "Look, this has been great, but you wouldn't by any chance have a tire in the back of that beat-up truck, would you?"

"Wow." He took a step back. A flicker of annoyance crossed his features, and his brow furrowed. "You don't even know me, and you're bashing Matilda. No one bashes Matilda."

Okay, now that was funny. It looked like poor Matilda had been bashed on multiple times. I laughed out loud. "You're right. I shouldn't be bashing your truck. I'm sorry."

"Matilda."

"Your truck is really named Matilda?"

"Got a problem with Matilda?" he asked as he stepped forward, his hand out. "I'm Kai."

My brows rose. *Nice name.* I smiled and shook his hand. "Kora." His hands were rough like he wasn't scared of hard work, which matched his clothing choice perfectly. "I haven't seen you around before. Are you new, visiting family?"

Kai shook his head and pursed his lips. "Nope. No family. Just got into town yesterday, so I guess that qualifies as new."

"So, what brings you by this way?"

"Well, a woman on the side of the road looking like she's in need of assistance." Again, I noticed his voice: deep yet soft, and totally sexy.

This guy was amazingly hot, had a unique sense of humor, and a sexy as hell dimple. *He can assist me anytime.* Again, I needed to clear my throat—probably a lack of water. "Yeah, well. The woman stuck on the side of the road appreciates your help, but I meant Orlinda Valley. What brings you here? Business, pleasure?" I turned my face up to see him better. He was tall, at least six feet four. And built. God, was he built.

He wiped his hands together like he was preparing for battle. "Let's deal with this tire. Where's your jack and spare?"

"Yeah, about that."

His brow ticked up.

"Yeah, well, at Christmas, I needed the space under there for presents and never put the tire or jack back in my car. It's sitting in my aunt's garage."

"You don't have a tire or jack in your car? Isn't that Driving 101?"

It sounded so much more ridiculous when I divulged the situation to him. *I hope he doesn't think I'm the stereotypical female. All about shopping and have no common sense. That is so not me. Well, I do like to shop.* My shoulders met my ears.

"Figures," Kai muttered and shook his head before walking to the back of his truck.

Hell no. He is not going to go there. My hands flew to my hips. "Excuse me? Did you just say *figures*?"

"What, you heard that?" Kai pulled a small tire from the back of his truck and carried it to the car. Then he went back to his truck and returned with a jack and a tire iron.

My gaze followed him back and forth as a heavy weight lodged in my gut. "I'm not deaf, you know. Explain yourself. What figures? Is it that I'm a female?" I eyed the tire. It didn't look big enough for a go cart. "Are you sure that tire will fit on my car?"

He didn't answer as he jacked up the car, loosened the bolts, took off the flat tire, and quickly replaced it with the donut he had taken from his truck. "To answer all your billions of questions—it figures that you don't have a tire. It *is* such a female thing, and yes, this will fit. It came from my sister's car. I gave her a full-size spare before she drove across the country. Oh, and you said it, sweetheart, not me."

Did he just call me sweetheart? I sucked in a big breath and took a beat to keep from saying the first thing that came to my mind. I scrunched my face. "I said what?"

"That you're a female, and that's the reason you were stuck on the side of the road." Kai stood up and brushed his hands against his pants.

Is this guy for real? "Are you always this rude to people you just meet?"

"Rude? I didn't say anything rude. Just pointed out the obvious and answered your million-and-one questions."

I could stand a lot of things, but I couldn't stand being treated like a weak female. Okay, maybe I did something stupid when I didn't listen to my father. I should have put the spare back in the car, but being needy and weak was not something I wanted people to see me as, especially not this irritating, yet hot, stranger. "You know what?" I walked over to him and stepped on the dead tire. "Keep this here. I don't need any more of your assistance. I'll deal with it myself."

Kai peered at me, then down at the flat tire, then back. "I can just toss it in the back of my truck and take it to the garage I saw in town. It's not a big deal."

My hands flew into the air and brushed him off. "Nope. Please don't. I'll *toss* this into my car. I wouldn't want to be seen as needy."

"You sure?"

What a jackass. I rolled my eyes toward the sky. "Yeah. Thanks for your help." My gaze rested on his, and I squinted in disgust. "Next time, though, keep driving."

Kai stepped back and lifted his hands in defeat.

Good. He might be a jackass, but he listens well.

I bent down and attempted to lift the tire off the ground. *Shit.* Even flat, it was heavier than it appeared. I slowly drag-carried it to the back and opened the hatch. I took a big breath, bent at my knees, heaved it into the back, and then had to take a second to catch my breath.

God, that sucked.

I slammed the hatch closed and froze as I caught a glimpse of my hands. They were black. I brushed them together. Still black. Then I brushed them on my pants, and the dirt smeared. "Shit."

"What's wrong, princess? Little grease on your hands?"

I shot Kai a glare, one that could kill.

I waited and watched.

No luck. He still stood there, breathing. "No big deal. Nothing soap won't get rid of," I answered with fake confidence. I'd be damned if I'd show weakness over grease.

"Yeah, maybe, but your shirt will need a little TLC."

I glanced down. There was a streak of black on the front. Must have been when I lifted the tire. "Shit. My favorite shirt."

"Dish detergent will get it out. Scrub it with an old toothbrush and rinse with cold water. Should be fine."

Dish soap. "I knew that." I pushed past him to the driver's side of my car, then stopped, and my shoulders drooped. *Be an adult, Kora, and don't be so bitchy.* I pulled myself up as tall as my five-foot-six frame would allow and shot my hand toward him. "Thanks, Kai. I appreciate your help."

He wrapped my hand with his, and warmth seeped into my skin. My chilly attitude melted instantly and caused me to forget where I was for a beat. I blinked repeatedly to regain my composure before I said, "I know we've started off rough and had a bumpy patch, but I hope everything's been fixed." I chuckled at my joke. It was funny.

He glared at me.

Okay then, maybe the heat that melted my attitude was all one-sided. *Let's try to break the tension between us one more time.* "There's a great place to eat in town—Jerry's Pub, if you want to catch a bite or anything."

"Thanks, but I've already been told about it and was planning on doing just that." He turned and strolled away.

My eyes were glued to his ass in those jeans. *Nice.*

He reached his truck. "It was nice meeting you. Stay clear of the potholes and get the spare back in your car. Maybe I'll see you around town."

"I sure hope so," I muttered to myself as I got into my car. I waved as I pulled away. The last thing I saw was his dimpled smile—maybe it was a smirk—and his fine-as-hell body as he climbed into his truck. "Orlinda Valley just added another hot-as-hell asshole to its population."

About the Author

Donna R. Madden lives in a small town north of Nashville with her husband of over 30 years, where they've successfully raised three amazing boys who are now out in the world doing their own thing. These days, their fur babies—Brier the dog and King Marcus Henry XXII (aka "Kitty Kitty")—rule the roost and demand all the attention.

When she's not teaching or dreaming up her next romance novel, you'll find Donna with an adult beverage in one hand, and a book in her lap (yes, she's mastered the art of multitasking). Her happy place is anywhere near water—poolside with friends, toes in the sand at the beach, or sitting by a lake or relaxing by a river with the sun in her face and a story in her hand.

Donna believes in happily-ever-afters, both in the pages of her books and in real life. She writes the kind of romance she loves to read—stories filled with heart, heat, and characters you'll want to invite over for wine and girl talk.

Drop her a line. She loves to hear from her readers: author@donnarmadden.com